SHADOW FORGED

BOOK 6 OF THE GIFTING

Shadow Forged

The Gifting Series #6

Forty-year-old Caroline is too old to start dating and too bored with her vibrator, but what other choices does she have. On the day she burns her shirt and breaks a fingernail, she meets Etterian warriors. As part of her job at E.S.A. (Earth Space Association,) she must 'entertain' the hot-as-apple-pie Chief Engineer she suspects isn't who he claims to be.

Operations Commander Malo, Head of Espionage, must act as an engineer and ambassador, hoping to invite human females to visit Etteria and save his dying race. From Princess Oriana, he has strict instructions to distrust humans. What he finds he cannot trust are his emotions and his body whenever in the presence of the human ambassador, Caroline. She does not believe in soulmates or in a forever with him. Convincing her to choose him is the greatest task ever set before him, one he cannot afford to fail.

Until she is stolen from him. He calls in favors, utilizes all his resources to find her. And *when* he does, he is never letting her off his battleship...or his bed.

ALSO BY SEVANNAH STORM

SHADOW FORGED

Plump Playwright Series
Plump Jane
Seducing Amelia
Loving FinleyKeeping Tessa
Kissing Navy
COMING SOON
Inkoded
Fire Forged
The Crucible of the Eternal

Contents

Chapter One

Etterian battleship Gladio
Comms Room
12254 Years, 8th Month

A melodic voice intruded on Malo's thoughts. "Operations Commander Malo."

Malo schooled his features, not willing to reveal emotion, specifically irritation, to a Maloidian operative such as Imarri ag Zennr. That he had her on board wasn't his decision but as a favor to Prince Citus. Citus was King Xeus's brother and the Etterian Ambassador, who owed a favor to the Maloidian Ambassador Barro. And Malo was left with the task of delivering the female operative to Argaxx, the royal city on Maloid. Yet here she was, loitering in the dark passage outside the Hollow. To take her to task for her wanderings would bring attention to his interrogations.

She had to be waiting for him, perhaps had something to say or needed to do. He pursed his lips. Was he her mission? Nothing was simple in the espionage world. Delivering an operative shouldn't be taken at face value.

"Lady Imarri, how may I be of assistance?" The fact that he hadn't gritted his teeth or ground out the words was due to his training.

He would've been content had she stayed confined to her quarters for the duration of the journey. As requested. He faced her and wished he hadn't. She was beautiful, he'd admit that, with her pale-yellow skin and beautiful black markings. Her tentacles from her 'hairline' were long and they undulated in a hypnotic rhythm. But unlike Etterians, whose hair moved in accordance with their moods, Maloidians's tentacles remained serene. On her, solid-black eyes were endearing, on a Yithian, it was menacing.

"Share the evening meal with me," she said, sashaying toward him. Her garment left little to the imagination, the blue fabric with gold detailing caught the meager light and enhanced her feminine curves.

He fought a smirk. As if he hadn't seen this done too many times to count. Although, she did it well indeed. His malehood remained unmoved as expected.

"I assume there is a wager of some sort?" He arched a brow then almost chuckled when, for a moment, surprise flitted across her face. Among the Maloidian female operatives was a wager. As Head of Operations, it was his obligation to know everything. He wasn't the Maker, but he tried his hardest to remain forewarned.

"Wager?" she blinked.

"Yes, who can bed Malo?" He drew closer to her, using his body to entice, to intimidate, to dominate. He brushed his chest across hers, ever so slightly, paying attention to her increased heartrate and the alteration in her breathing rhythm. "Tell me, Imarri," he purred, "how will you prove you have joined with me? An image of me sleeping beside you?" he whispered, feathering his lips along the petalled folds of her ear.

He slipped his arms around her and nudged her against his body. As a Maloidian, she'd appreciate the warmth emanating off him. And her subsequent shiver proved him correct. He brushed his fingers down her spine then drew circles at the base of it. To do this to a Maloidian's erogenous zone would drive them wild. Imarri was no exception. She released a deep sigh, and her scent changed from natural to floral. It was pleasant, but it wasn't one he was partial to. "Thank you for your time, milady." He dropped his arms, stepped back, and strolled away, this time wearing the smirk. Her curses reached his ears, but what could she do? Attacking him would have her dead or jettisoned.

Dismissing her, he focused on his new task which was two weeks away with Maloid in the opposite direction. Ordered to escort her, he'd returned to Yithia and sent a shuttle to collect her. That they were less than a day away from reaching Maloid, was a day too long a delay. Tomorrow he'd ensure she was escorted on one of his scimitars with a few chosen males less likely to succumb to her wiles. To join with a Maloidian operative was to owe her a favor, and owing favors was a currency operatives utilized sparingly.

He wouldn't inform her of her impending departure. To do so would allow her the time to strategize. A mischievous Maloidian female was entertaining, but not when he lacked the patience to attend to it.

Etterian battleship Gladio
Speeding away from Maloid, in stealth mode
Comms Room

MALO GLOWERED AT PRINCE Enyl. Perhaps in person and not through a vid comm, his angry countenance would affect his prince's stance, but Malo doubted that. He'd cultivated his scowl to instill fear in whomever he bestowed it upon. Said prince showed no reaction, only determination—an expression Malo knew all too well. He blamed King Xeus for this, having tasked Malo to 'guard' Enyl since infancy. For one of his skillset, the young male showed him a marked lack of respect.

"To expect anything else is stupidity." Malo's voice vibrated, revealing, for a moment, his frustration.

"You distrust everyone, Operations Commander. This is a skill we need. You know what rests on this." Enyl drew in a calming breath before continuing, "My Dar Eth is certain there is danger and deceit. I must agree with her. We do not know these humans and what they are capable of." Enyl sighed. "We must tread with caution, Malo. Or our only option is to rescue the females taken by the Yithians."

Malo glanced away from his prince. His eye color changing from dark to ice blue was a physical indication he had found his Dar Eth, his life force. The humans called it soulmate. Etterians believed it to be a rare occurrence, having slipped to the status of legend. That is, until his prince stumbled upon Oriana. Four Dar Eths had been found since then.

"My father requires a diplomatic approach. If these humans wish to become our enemy, that is on them. But should they choose an alliance, we will find more Dar Eths for our males."

Malo squashed the surge of envy that rushed through him. *To feel is to fail.* He repeated the Etterian mantra. There was no Dar Eth for one so unworthy as he. He wasn't the most honorable male. It didn't suit the skillset Etteria needed.

"What is your true issue, my battle-bond?" Enyl asked, his eyebrow arched.

Malo grunted, wishing his prince wasn't so intuitive. "I cannot say, Enyl. I am...irritated."

He hid his frustration and longing well, like his training had taught him. That Enyl had picked up on any emotion wasn't acceptable. Malo's pulse beat at the base of his jaw. And if he could feel it, then it was visible *and* audible to his males. Irritation would justify the pulse. Still, he kept his focus vague, his features expressionless, and his lips relaxed.

Despite his best efforts, emotions snuck into his interaction with his prince and operatives. Perhaps he was getting too old for what Etteria required? Perhaps the lack of war had softened his skills? Perhaps he was closer to the void than he'd expected to be at this age of forty-four years?

"This I see, yet you are not one to react without control."

He grunted at Enyl's keen eye. *Control? Yes. My energy levels fluctuate as if I prepare to battle an unknown enemy.*

"Then in what capacity?" Malo asked, his tone dull. Enyl's unwavering gaze meant this task was unavoidable. Not that he'd disobey an order from his prince. He could negotiate though, if he chose to.

"As an engineer. The humans wish to learn of our technology."

"Greedy bastards," a female muttered in the background.

A strong yet delicate arm wrapped around his prince's waist when a short, red-haired female appeared in the viewing panel.

"Just be confident, courteous, helpful but not generous with the information, and they will reveal their intentions. Your contact is Director Adam Reyes. I have known him for a while. He's trustworthy." She flashed Malo a grin. "Oh, and Malo, do enjoy this off-time." The panel went black, but the sound continued.

"I do not like it when you talk to my males that way," the prince grumbled.

"Why not? Everyone knows only you rock my boat." There came a giggle, then a throaty moan before the sound cut out.

Malo chuckled, he couldn't help himself. He did enjoy his talks with Princess Oriana and learning how humans thought was entertaining. They had devious minds, yet they retained their naivete, believing they were the center of their universe. Like *damu*, they had no control over their emotions or bodies, for that matter. And they had a blatant ignorance of anything that didn't align with their preconceived ideas. Which, in this case, was that a stronger, fiercer species existed. Etteria forced to negotiate with such a mid-grade species wasn't something he appreciated. His ancestor, the renowned Dalo, would have conquered with untold violence, never asking nor apologizing.

Etterians had altered their procedures extensively since the civil war centuries ago that had decimated their numbers.

He faced the interrogation room—a five-by-five cube in Maloidian steel—gray walls, floor, and ceiling was as depressing as it was comforting. This room was impenetrable. A steel table and two benches were bolted to the floor. Bright white light illuminated the room. Every nuance on the prisoner's face would be visible and caught on the sec-vids for later study.

The prisoner? He grimaced. A Yithian...again. Shimmering silver-gray skin, three fingered-hands, large solid-black eyes on either side of his head, with long fangs from a wide mouth, dripping venom. In a sleeveless tunic and military pants, he was an unremarkable male.

That Malo had accepted a communication with his prince—while the prisoner listened in—stated the end result for said prisoner. Malo's operative, Cylo, held a blaster to the back of the Yithian's head.

"This is the last time I ask you, Smez." He leveled his gaze on the sweating Yithian operative.

The room's temperature was set to sweltering. Yithian's couldn't abide extreme heat. The male would dehydrate with his skin cracking and bleeding, followed by asphyxiation. For an average Yithian, from dehydration to death took twenty-two minutes.

Neither Malo nor Cylo would feel the heat. Their suits regulated their internal temperature no matter the environment. "What is Yithia's interest in human females?"

"For the arena," Smez panted, filling the room with the sickly salty stench of sea and raw flesh. The skin on his arms and hands cracked. Gray blood seeped out. He moaned in agony. "The arena, I swear, Etterian." His wiggling and sweat stench thickened the heated air.

"I do not believe you, *xemi*," Malo roared and slammed his hands on the table. Smez jerked, splitting his wounds further. Malo's lip curled while studying this *xemi*, this *scum*. He had no time for such dishonorable males, no matter what species they were. "Humans are weak, tiny, and easily killed. Their deaths serve no purpose."

"Champion Ori served Yithia well," the Yithian stuttered. His lips had pulled back to reveal a dark gray tongue—thick and swollen. "Water, please," he croaked.

If Malo assessed Smez's skin, he'd approximately four minutes until death. Malo debated whether he should show mercy. He scowled at having received nothing for his time, and the prince's comm had delayed this further. With a glance at Cylo, he sprayed a fine mist over the prisoner's skin. The Yithian sighed in bliss as a few of his smaller wounds sealed themselves and a healthy shimmer returned to his skin. It wouldn't last.

"Let me understand you." Malo narrowed his eyes. "Yithia kidnaps females looking for another champion? All this expense? We know you have more females than what we have rescued. We have not seen them in the arena. Where are they, Smez?"

The Yithian's lips curled as if he smirked.

Malo didn't like the expression nor its implication. He regretted his leniency. "You do not take this seriously, *xemi*," he growled. He arched an eyebrow at Cylo. "Your turn or mine?"

"Yours, Operations Commander."

"Truth?" he grunted.

"Yes, I dealt with the Maloidian, if you recall."

Malo retrieved the Maloidian throwing dagger he'd strapped to his upper arm. The four-blade holster had been a gift from his father, months before the void had consumed him. At least he'd died in battle on Gika. And war was coming, the enemy Yithia and possibly Maloid. How many Etterian males would choose to face the emotionless void?

The Yithian stiffened at the sight of the compact blade, made of the finest Maloidian steel. It gleamed in the minimal lighting. Malo took a moment to admire it, but he knew better than to run his thumb along the edge. Besides, he'd be testing its sharpness soon enough.

"I have been most lenient with you, Smez, due to our history. I see you would prefer to take advantage of our bond. This is not wise."

"I cannot betray Yithia, Malo. They have my family." Smez's eyes pleaded as only soulless, black eyes could.

Pressing the blade to a finger, Malo whispered darkly, "I know you too well for that lie to affect me." He angled the blade to catch the light. "You only have three fingers. It would be a shame to lose one."

Smez pinched his lips, informing both Etterian operatives that he'd no intention of submitting.

Malo sliced the finger in one smooth stroke, the bone not impeding the blade. The cut was clean, like he'd carved through his kreso meat at the morning meal. The Yithian screamed, curling his remaining two fingers into his palm in reaction, for protection. His orphaned finger lay there in a pool of gray blood.

"I said I would not ask you again, Smez. What I *will* ask is which finger is next? I will allow you the illusion of choice."

"You are a bastard, Malo." Smez clutched his hands to his chest, as if that could stop an adult Etterian male.

Malo grabbed his wrist and twisted. The prisoner squeaked but couldn't prevent Malo from pinning his wrist to the table.

Smez's gaze followed the descent of the blade. "Iphara. There's a laboratory on Iphara."

Malo frowned, hovering the blade a few inches above Smez's middle finger. He didn't sheathe the dagger lest the Yithian believed the session was over. "Why a laboratory? To what purpose?" All those females cut open, like specimens? He cast a glance at a scowling Cylo.

"We seek to understand the attraction," Smez panted. "Why do Etterian males prefer human females?"

"That is illogical. This does not serve Yithia." Malo descended the blade again. Smez's fingers spasmed.

"Compatibility," the Yithia ground out. "If humans are compatible with Etterians, they may be compatible with other species."

"You wish to sell them." Malo stared at Smez in disbelief.

"As pleasure slaves." Smez's shoulders slumped in dejection.

"Where on Iphara?" Cylo demanded.

Frowning, Malo's gaze shot to his male. Cylo vibrated with anger. Such intense emotion was not to be revealed in an interrogation.

"It is in an underground chamber. Few Yithians are aware of it." At the ease Smez revealed more, Malo arched a brow. The loss of one finger affected him so? Was King Urio releasing untested operatives now?

"How many females are there?" Cylo roared and withdrew his blade.

Malo scowled. He wasn't done with the interrogation, and Cylo losing control might end Smez's life too soon.

"Seven," Smez stammered, his solid-black gaze riveted on Cylo. "They showed no warrior skills, were too weak. Nor did they resist the soldiers sent to retrieve them."

"How long have they been there?" Malo demanded. His heartbeat increased without his consent. He allowed this lapse. His concern was for seven innocent human females, lost to his warriors. Perhaps there was still time to save them.

"They were delivered four days ago," Smez mumbled, his eyes widening, his skin paling beneath the fresh wounds. A tremble dribbled the sweat off his chin. "May Calzantu forgive me."

Cylo glanced at Malo, who inclined his head. The Yithian didn't see nor feel the blade that slid between his two vertebrae at the base of his neck. It was a quick death, and not one he deserved. But neither Cylo nor Malo were in the mood to draw out a death. They needed to act on this information and rescue these females before there was irreparable damage.

"Take a scimitar, liaise with the patrolling battleships, and save those females. Once you have them, ensure the laboratory is destroyed from within. There must be no indication of our involvement," Malo commanded. "And deal with this." He indicated the lifeless body of the operative he'd known for years. What a pity. "Leave the finger," he stated as Cylo tossed the Yithian's body over his shoulder. "Have Trav deliver Uloz."

"Yes, Operations Commander." Cylo tapped his Optical Data Implant, or O.D.I, in his wrist and teleported out of the room.

The room descended into silence with Malo's only company being the severed finger. He drew in a deep breath, sighing when the air filtration system removed the stench of Smez's weaknesses. Malo preferred the silence, the shadows that lurked in the corners of the room. The low vibration of the battleship could only be heard by Etterians with their enhanced hearing. It soothed him as well, yet his irritation lingered. He hadn't lied about that. Perhaps he should have. Enyl worried about his father facing the void, he didn't need to worry about Malo, as well. Since meeting Oriana and experiencing the Ethera, Enyl's emotional range was beyond the norm. A lima kuu or great teacher might even note the Ethera returned Etterians to their at-birth state.

Operative Trav ported in with a Yithian trailing his heels behind him.

Trav seemed disgusted and irritated. Malo furrowed his brow. His males weren't required to follow the Etterian code—honor, integrity, and respect. But they had to follow *his* code at all times—impassivity, professionalism, and swift obedience to his commands. Anger may be shown but only when deemed necessary. If inflicting fear, shock, or agony was the purpose. To terrify, to cause pain, to kill, all in the name of Etteria.

"He is revealing secrets before reaching the Hollow," Trav spat.

Malo grunted, understanding his male's anger. An operative was revered for his strength, control, and above all, silence. Uloz displayed none of those characteristics—an unworthy enemy.

"Scans have indicated he swallowed the data chip."

"Remove it," Malo commanded.

He observed with disinterest as Trav stabbed Uloz in the torso and poured nano-meds into the wound to work with slow precision. Writhing on the metallic table, the Yithian screamed unceasingly. His cries fell on dimmed ears. Malo had lowered his ability to hear every minute decibel the moment the prisoner began to wail.

Under induced sleep, the nano-meds were painless. Their primary function was to remove inorganic objects. They could follow other commands. Commands and results Malo knew all too well. Trav pinned Uloz as the nano-meds traveled through the Yithian, who squirmed in agony. Malo remained unmoved. With a patience he didn't feel, he watched the nano-meds deliver the chip to the surface of the steel table.

Trav released the Yithian to collect the nano-meds into their glass vial. "I will deliver these to medical and the chip to Tias."

Alone, Malo glanced at Uloz, now curled into a ball. His hands held his innards in with his gray blood flowing past his six fingers unhindered.

"You have the data, kill me now," he hissed.

"I do not know what is on the chip. Best I have answers to my questions regardless. Who else has Yithia turned against Etteria? I want names. I want objectives. Stealing Teric's daughter was low, even for you, Uloz. You once swore to me you would never harm youngins."

"She wasn't harmed," Uloz spat. Gray blood formed on his bottom lip.

Trav must have pierced a lung. Malo would need to send him for training again. It was an easy mistake to make, stabbing an inch to high. It was also easy to avoid. Death would take Uloz soon, if he drowned in his blood.

"Harm comes in all forms—emotional, physical, mental. You know this. Why do you waste my time? Are you hoping death will claim you sooner?" Malo snorted, despite the possibility. Uloz didn't need to know this. "It will be hours of agony before your wound will bring you release. You know this as well." He tapped his O.D.I., as if to leave Uloz to die a slow and agonizing death.

"Kill me, Malo," he lisped as more blood stained his lips. "Please."

"Give me what I need, and you will have a painless death." Malo kept his back to him, with his hand raised to select the port command on his wrist. "Calzantu beckons."

"I do not know all the names."

"That many?" Malo glared at him, then pinched his brow, fighting for calm. He'd revealed his anger. He relaxed his stance and his clenched fist before leaning back against the bulkhead to appear disinterested—a practiced stance.

"The password to the data chip is—" A seizure gripped the Yithian, and his body writhed and spasmed with gray blood splattering everywhere.

"The password," Malo boomed, lunging forward to hold Uloz still. "Give me the password."

Uloz quieted for a moment, and a small smirk curled his bottom lip. Black oozed from his eyes, leaving pale-gray eye tissue behind. He was dead.

Malo banged a fist on the metal table while raising his other wrist to his lips. "Brynr, I need you in the Hollow. Now."

Malo scowled at the contorted body. What in Alodon's hell had happened? If he didn't know better, he'd say this male had a death trigger when uttering the password. The trigger had to be organic for the nano-meds to ignore it. Or a mental death trigger set off by a word? Like 'password?' He would not bias Brynr by suggesting it when he needed the medic to confirm his fears. Only a Durn could create such a death trigger, but why would a Durn work with Yithia? And there was only a few hundred alive after a plague had decimated their planet. To find a Durn in the many galaxies was almost impossible. Yet Etteria had two en route to Issneen.

Malo used the display vid to call forth the footage, hoping to find the trigger. Brynr ported in, scanned Uloz's body, only then did Malo gesture to the vid.

"What are your findings, Brynr?"

"His eyes are not black as usual. His brain must have been stunned. The bleaching of their eyes is the only external symptom. I must, therefore, conclude that the damage was inflicted from within. In all my life and those of our lima kuu, we have not encountered such a thing."

"Not even the great teachers?" Malo arched a brow in apparent surprise.

"No, though we are still taught the symptoms of death triggers." Malo played the vid.

The medic scowled. "We have two Durns en route to Etteria. Perhaps we should bring this to their attention?"

"See to it, and inform me of their findings." Malo leaned against the bulkhead, done for the day. Torture made him sick to his stomach, but he endured for Etteria. Any male that showed an affinity for it wasn't schooled under him. No one should feed the monster within.

"I will attend to this, Operations Commander." Brynr gestured to the dead Yithia.

Malo nodded and ported to his quarters. He would await Tias's findings on the memory chip, but he wasn't hopeful. The death trigger implied the password would be impenetrable. Taking such extensive methods to protect the data chip had him curious. Battle plans? He grinned, tempted to rub his palms together. If the data was nothing more than financial, he'd be furious.

Despite all this, he needed to study Etteria's latest technological advances in preparation. Acting the role of an engineer would not be easy for him. He didn't question everything, he questioned motives, and he had no affiliation for science or technology. Yet he'd be the best engineer he could be, for his males, for Etteria, and for Princess Oriana.

Chapter Two

Planet Earth
The Cheery Cherry Ice Cream Parlor
Year of 2254, August

CAROLINE, OR CARO, AS lazy Izzy called her, shoved a spoonful of chocolate ice-cream into her mouth. Her eyes closed in bliss. But what she wanted to do was roll her eyes.

"I don't know why you let him speak to you like that?" Izzy was saying, again.

She'd heard Izzy's arguments too many times to count. The issue was her boss, Chief Engineer Douche or Dee for short. That his name was Duncan made it even more tongue in cheek. He terrorized her and had her do tasks that were below her pay-grade. He'd then castigate her for her 'poor' performance. No one stepped forward to defend her, not even herself. She worked for a shitty company, that was for damn sure. Yet she loved her job as an astrophysicist, spending her days—when allowed to—immersed in formulae and H-R diagrams. Numbers didn't lie, didn't cheat, didn't steal money out of her acco unt... She grimaced at her negative thoughts.

It was time she moved on.

Caro raised her head to smile at Izzy. Moving on could wait until later since she was eating ice-cream in the middle of the day in her bestie's ice-cream parlor. Nothing should come between her and any form of organic chocolate.

"This is my last serving then I have to head back. I have deadlines to meet, T-off and all that," Caro teased. "How do you stay so thin?" She licked her spoon.

"I don't eat the ice-cream." Izzy bounced from behind the counter to slide into the booth. "My first few weeks here, I pigged out until I got sick of it."

"If I came here every day and had a chocolate ice-cream…"

"You'd gain weight." Izzy giggled. "Knowing your luck."

Caro harumphed.

"What did Dee have you do this time?" Izzy folded her arms on the table.

"A presentation for his son's career day." Caro stared at the ice cream cup, wondering if her tongue could reach the bottom.

"He's married?" Izzy squeaked.

Ew. Caro shuddered. His poor wife…ex-wife. "Nope, divorced."

"Shit. But not as shitty as him hitting on you if he was married."

Caro shrugged. "He was when he hit on me."

"Shit." Izzy squeaked again. "He's pure douche."

"I know, but how to get him to leave me alone."

Izzy giggled. "You should have taken him up on the offer and used your teeth while givin' him head."

Caro rolled her eyes but grinned despite her best efforts to remain stoic. Trust Izzy to find a way to lighten her mood. "Or thrown up on him when he dropped his trousers." Caro chuckled.

"Or threaten to tell the office how small his appendage is." Izzy wiggled her pinky.

Caro hummed. "He did do Maggie in Accounting."

"Now that's a conversation I would love to overhear. Hi, Mags, was hoping you could tell me Chief D's size in proportion to the average. Or better yet, you should start with the weather." Izzy laughed. "You don't have to know his size, just imply it's too small. He can't exactly go around showing everyone how wrong you are."

"That's true." Caro stuck her finger into the empty cup, swiped the sides, and licked off the melted chocolate. "Okay, next time he's being a Dee."

"You won't." Izzy huffed.

"No, I won't, but the thought of it... It's a delicious plan, Izzy. And maybe one day I'll find my balls stashed somewhere in my handbag and use them."

Izzy scoffed. "We can only hope."

Chapter Three

Etterian battleship Gladio

Comms Room

Two weeks later

"Xan, congratulations," Malo said, adding sincerity to his voice.

He *was* pleased that another male had found his Dar Eth. And judging by the footage he'd seen of Xan's Quinlan seizing the Yithian slave ship; this supreme commander had truly been blessed with a warrior female. Malo hadn't considered what he'd have liked in a Dar Eth. To dwell on it when it wasn't possible was foolhardy. If she was an awe-inspiring assassin that could kill him in his sleep…he'd be grateful.

"I assume you wish to speak to my Quin?" Xan growled.

"Who wishes to speak to me?" The human female who stepped into the display vid snatched Malo's breath.

She was exquisite with golden-yellow hair and two different eye colors; one was green, the other gray. Alodon's balls. He'd seen on the footage the various shapes and sizes of the human females, but nothing compared to the full-colored reality before him. Then again, he'd seen

Lady Jack in the arena footage, and she had sunlit hair with bright blue eyes. Lady Ava's image had struck a chord with many a male. Never had a creature appeared more enticing. The Yithians who'd abducted her had assumed she was an Etterian half-breed based on her black hair and green eyes. They'd attired her in gossamer fabric strips that left nothing to the imagination. Malo had pitied her Eth, Kanzo, who now had to live with the knowledge that every Etterian male and most of the galaxy had seen his Dar Eth so exposed.

"Greetings, milady," Malo said, his voice firm. "I was told to contact you regarding Joshua Guardian."

"His name is Joshua Bennett. It might be easier to find him that way. I sent him a message and told him to expect your request for assistance." While she spoke, Malo nodded as if she held all of his attention. When in fact she did, but not by her words. He marveled at how this tiny creature had taken a slave ship then killed Prince Yada. He wasn't surprised King Urio was pushing for war. He believed the Etterians had killed his son. It was better he believed so for Earth would not withstand a war with Yithia.

"And if he is reluctant to assist?" In other words, would Malo need to use coercion?

"Mention an intergalactic war, he'll assist."

Malo watched when she curled into Xan's side, as if the male lacked the wherewithal to stand on his own. Oriana did the same. It was a strange mannerism, yet it appealed to Malo on a basic level. Xan wrapped an arm around her, tugging her close to him.

"But I warn you, Malo, some of my guardians might volunteer. They take protecting Earth quite seriously."

Malo bowed his head. "Any assistance would be appreciated, milady."

"Call me Quin." She pressed a hand to Xan's chest.

Malo studied its placement for a moment. These humans were demonstrative. He wasn't certain how he'd feel to have a female take such liberties with his person. "Thank you, Quin, for taking the time to speak to me." Politeness cost him nothing.

E.S.A. (Earth Space Association) Engineering Building

CARRYING SEVENTEEN COFFEES, CARO stumbled into the steel and glass building. The staff at the Coffee Den knew her well, ensuring she had a sturdy cardboard tray on which to balance their hot and heavenly creations. The barista on duty had given her a worried look, which had more to do with Caro's appearance than her ability to carry that many cups.

The black stiletto heels weren't the best choice she could've made under the circumstances, but she'd broken her therapeutics this morning and hadn't had a chance to shop for a new pair. The heels were a gift from an ex-lover, Gary. *Holy noodle, was it six years ago? And I've never worn them, not even for what he'd intended.*

She blushed at the direction her thoughts had taken, admitting if only to herself, that she'd been tempted. But the moment she'd slipped into them with nothing else on and the waiting pair of hand cuffs on his bed, she'd run like the chicken she was. Doing *that* with him had seemed wrong somehow.

Here she was, single at thirty-nine and in killer heels—because they were killing her. She snickered. And she was running late for work, normal for her, though. Not that anyone monitored her, especially since she was always doing the coffee run. She glanced at the silver-gray pencil skirt that reached past her knees and hugged her wide hips. But her white blouse was a little too snug, since she'd had to borrow Izzy's. Caro burned her last shirt this morning while ironing it *and* reading an email from Chief Dee.

"Damned men. Think I need to drop to my knees and serve them. How fast and hard would you like it, sir?" she muttered, nudging yet another security door open. "I'm getting screwed daily and harder than a rocking chair too." She continued to grumble while balancing the seventeen coffees like a professional. "Oh, *Ms.* Masterson, don't forget the coffee," she mimicked in a fake baritone, ignoring her hair cascading around her and obscuring her vision.

Her hair tie had snapped after she'd managed to get the coffee out of her car—without spilling a drop, she might add. "Freakin' assholes. Won't even offer to help me. I'm an astrophysicist, able to do complex calculations but no, have a vagina, must get coffee. Four, please," she asked whoever had gotten into the elevator with her.

Only shoes filled her vision—brown corporate and the other pair military, by the look of them. Chunky too, as if at any moment he might have to walk the outside of a spaceship. She chuckled at her fanciful thoughts. He was probably a biker or one of those trendy uber-sexual men who thought wearing military boots with his suit gave him style. Those boots were huge though, and large feet meant only one thing.

Not that she had the courage to glance up. A tremble took hold of her hands at the thought of meeting his gaze. She gasped, fighting to steady her grip on the tray. Besides, she was a firm believer that if she removed her focus from the coffee cups, she'd spill them. A watched cup never messes—that was her new motto. *Coward.*

She narrowed her eyes, trying to remember if she'd messed up the order. Instead of beverages, she should be focusing on her application to use E.S.A.'s space telescope, and she hadn't even finished the draft due tomorrow. She had a PhD in Applied Mechanics, but did that mean anything? "Damned neanderthals," she muttered. "How deep do you want it?" An arm held the elevator open for her, and she thanked the person without glancing up. Her gaze remained fixed on the tray of coffee when she rushed forward.

"Finally, *Ms.* Masterson. It seems you can't even do this efficiently." Chief Engineer Douche held his arms out wide as if he were a god.

She peeked at him, pure hatred rising and churning within her. Intense heat gripped her chest and narrowing her vision. *He's such a dick.* Her heart pounded in her ears. She squeezed her eyes shut, willing her breathing to calm.

"That is unacceptable behavior, Duncan. I won't speak about this again. This is your final warning."

Caro squeaked and closed her eyes in mortification. Had she mumbled to herself with Director Reyes in the elevator with her? She ran through what she'd said, and her face tingled with the enormity of her circumstances. *And for him to defend me in front of everyone? Douche will make my life a living hell for this.*

"Caro, you will never get coffee again. And see me if he, in any way, makes you feel uncomfortable."

Her head shot up at his words. She gaped at Reyes, who stood to the right of her. The florescent lights caught his gray hair coiffed to the side and in that moment, he was her guardian angel in a crisp suit.

She ducked her head. Had she spoken aloud again? How did he know Douche would continue to bully her at every opportunity? Reyes took the large tray from her and placed it on a nearby credenza. The tingling on her cheeks had yet to subside.

"Now, gather around," he said to the command center in general. "I'd like to introduce you to our intergalactic visitor from the planet Etteria, Engineer Malo et Dalo."

Monkey's bananas. She gasped and faced the stranger, her mortification now at epic levels. Could a blackhole just swallow her, please? But then it would swallow the planet, so technically... She was getting side-tracked. When her gaze traveled from those military-booted feet, up his well-defined muscled calves and thighs encased in a black fabric that looked bullet-proof, up his barreled armor-encased chest and bare bronzed arms to meet his gaze, she released a throaty sigh. Here was a fine example of a man, even if he was an alien.

Sadness tugged her lips down. She'd have liked to see his eyes behind his sunglasses. His black hair was braided at the nape of his neck, falling to his boot heels. It didn't detract from his masculinity. He had a squarish face with defined edges she wished she could trail her fingers along. His jawline was angular and his forehead wide. His sharp nose was long, and his wide flat lips appeared soft enough to nibble on. His bronze skin shimmered, like it had been coated in body glitter. His bold-and-black, S-shaped eyebrows rose above his sunglasses in query at her ogling. She froze, shivers rippling over her skin. Had he watched her drool over him?

But, monkey's bananas, he's beautiful.

Her nipples pebbled—the sensation noticeable to an abstaining Caro. Her panties drenched in seconds, forcing her to clench her thighs together as a wave of need uncoiled. His nostrils flared as if he could smell her desire. She shuddered at the thought. If he could, she was in a heap of trouble. Lest she embarrassed herself further, she barreled past him with a mumbled excuse, escaping into the elevator. Only once the doors closed did she release a breathless whimper.

Can I move to Etteria? She giggled as relief, excitement, and lust bubbled through her. *Wait till Izzy hears about this.*

Planet Earth
E.S.A. (Earth Space Association)
Engineering Building

MALO FOUGHT A SMILE and listened with his enhanced hearing to the human female's mutterings. His constant irritation had worsened this morning, patience and tolerance almost non-existent. Until her rasping voice and nonsensical words reached him. While he waited for security access with Director Reyes, Malo had searched the floor to locate her.

Maker. His breath hitched at the sight of her. If all human females were like this, he would, in truth, enjoy his off-time hunting his Dar-Eth. Gray-encased hips and thighs moved with determination across the smooth flooring. Her straight dark-brown hair cascaded around her face, hiding her features. Her white tunic couldn't hope to contain those bountiful breasts for long. Etterian females didn't look like ripe juicy fruit. Their females were thinner, curvier, but strong, having suffered through similar physical training.

This human female was lush, like a fresh perske. Inhaling, he drew in her unique scent, sweet and elusive. He frowned when his mouth watered—a reaction he hadn't experienced before, as if he hungered.

He had researched Earth's history and watched a few of their archaic mating vids. Judging by what she said, he understood when she 'offered' to serve these males. The idea of her doing that to him, her mouth anywhere on his body, made his blood rush. It wasn't a reaction he expected when no reaction was preferable.

He scowled. Etterians were non-emotional. But within minutes, she'd drawn forth smiles and frowns. Perhaps it was something in the environment? He made a note to analyze it again later. When they entered the elevator with her, she continued to mutter. Director Reyes had smiled, though Malo was certain the elderly male couldn't hear her words.

And being in such proximity with her spicy, fruity scent, had brought Malo's temperature up a few degrees. He adjusted his armor to compensate. It was designed to regulate his temperature, to keep it at a constant, no matter the environment he was in, but it was malfunctioning. He followed her, drowning in her scent, wishing he could trap it within his lungs. His fingers twitched with the longing to run his hands over her backside, to trace the indent of her waist, and to bury his fingers in her hair.

He blinked in a daze at the disparaging words said by a human male. The way he'd insulted her tainted Malo's vision red. Unexpected anger welled within him, strong and demanding. Had he been wearing his shoulder daggers, the human male would have died.

The haze in Malo's vision froze his movements. Such intense emotion only occurred amid a battle or while performing a hazardous task. Yet it demanded he react, drove him to lose his control.

Until she faced him. Her chin tilted up caught his attention, calmed his anger. Her hair spun around her like the tail of a celestial body, riveting to behold. He *felt* her gaze traveling up the length of him to his jaw as if her hands caressed him. When she stared at his viz-wear, a white-hot pleasurable torment lanced through him. His fingers fisted when his knees weakened, threatening to drop him to a knee. He struggled to control his breathing, enduring vision after vision of her spread before him.

His malehood buried deep within her softness. Her cheeks a pale pink. Her lips parted in ecstasy. Her plump and ripe breasts beneath his hands. Her channel wrapped around him—hot, tight, so good. He *felt* her silky skin against his, *tasted* the salty-sweet flavor of her nipples, and *scented* her rich, intoxicating arousal. All this clamped his teeth down hard on his bottom lip to still the groan that threatened to shred his throat. He welcomed the self-inflicted pain, praying to the Maker that it would help him retain his dignity.

To test his control further with her standing before him, the scent of her arousal hit him. He thrust out a hand to stop his descent. He squeezed his stinging eyes shut and missed her leaving. For a moment, he imagined her scented warmth brushed past him.

With a patience he envied, Director Reyes waited for Malo to indicate he was ready. He knew not how long it had taken him to resist hunting her down, to throw her over his shoulder as Dalo would've done. *Maker.* He fought the shudder that threatened to course through his body. Fought the elation that rose within him.

He had found his Dar Eth, his salvation. The heat centering at his arousal had him adjusting his armor's temperature control again. He was desperate for some assistance. *Alodon's hell.* Why was this not documented? Why were males not informed of the Ethera's effects? Though how he could've anticipated them, he didn't know. Encountering her had been unexpected. It wasn't something he could've prepared for. And if there was one thing he excelled in, it was preparation. He hated improvisation on a task when planning and prudence would ensure the best outcome.

She had shifted his focus, making him the worst warrior for this task Prince Enyl had set before him. Malo would inform his prince at the first opportunity. He gritted his teeth and went through the motions of meeting the human staff. With each human male, his patience thinned, and by the time he'd met the male who'd chastised her, his tolerance had evaporated.

"Disrespect my female again and you will beg for death." He'd whispered it in Etterian, not wanting to jeopardize this task but needing to vent his fury. With a glower, he closed the distance between him and the male... Duncan. "I have the poison in mind for one so unworthy as you."

The male's eyes widened, and the sour tang of fear filled the air.

Grunting, Malo faced Director Reyes. "Enough," he commanded in Earth English.

"My office?" The older male's eyes twinkled before he gestured to the elevator.

Malo didn't appreciate the male's amusement, not when unsatisfied vengeance consumed his thoughts. He strode there, desperate for a moment's peace. The farther they traveled away from Duncan, the more his anger calmed. On the top level, Reyes escorted Malo into a glass-walled office. He approached the windows to admire the white fluffy clouds floating across the pale blue sky. His sharp gaze focused on the white vapor as it morphed and molded itself according to the wind's influence. It was entrancing. His stance was that of a warrior—widespread legs, hands clasped behind his back while he kept himself immobile, attempting to regain his sanity. Neither males knew how close Malo had come to killing Duncan.

"She's beautiful, isn't she?" Director Reyes asked.

At the unexpected subject, Malo faced the male, who had closed off the glass for privacy. Malo removed his viz-wear, meeting Director Reyes's gaze with unwavering directness.

The human male studied Malo in return. "I understand it's a surprise when you first meet your Dar Eth?"

Malo remained silent, raising a brow in query. If he knew about the Ethera, then Princess Oriana did trust him. "How do you know—?"

"Ori was most informative about Etteria's need for women." Director Reyes pointed to a chair, but Malo ignored him. "Judging by how well you hid your reaction, you are wiry, perhaps an unusual trait for an engineer?"

His gaze hardened at Director Reyes's implication. "All Etterians are trained in accordance with our lore as dictated by our lima kuu or great teachers."

"Even engineers, I suppose." The male's tone indicated he didn't believe him.

Malo shrugged, unable to control what Director Reyes believed without his virak of poisons.

"Let's be honest with each other, Malo. I despise duplicity. We need technology that will clean our seas and skies, heal the sick and dying, feed the hungry. I don't care what the powers-that-be want. This is what I need you to put on the table."

Malo blinked—the best response Director Reyes was going to get.

"Since we have Fusion Pulse, what else could they ask for? In exchange, we can set up some sort of registry, offering all men and women the chance for a space life on one of Etteria's many habitable planets...or as a Dar Eth."

Malo folded his arms across his chest. "This is acceptable."

"I'm not an idiot, Malo. Does Prince Enyl not trust us?"

"Princess Oriana suggested caution. My prince listens to her since she is his Dar Eth *and* a human," Malo said, not knowing the full extent of Director Reyes's relationship with Oriana. Her ethnicity shouldn't remain secret for long. It was wiser to inform the male of said fact.

"Ah, now I see," Director Reyes chuckled. "The little minx didn't mention she's married to the prince. It is wise to be cautious. Some men seek power above life. I want resolution to problems that have plagued this planet for centuries."

"I will convey your request to my prince. Why did Princess Oriana contact you and not your commanders?" Malo loomed. It was a skill that took years to master. Without moving, he made his presence known—a subtle squaring of his shoulders, leaning his head forward, bringing his arms to the front as if prepared to battle, and shifting his feet as if to pounce. While he made these movements, his skin would reflect the light and highlight his tensed muscles. "Do you have the authority to negotiate with Etteria? If you have wasted my time, Director Reyes..."

"I doubt meeting your Dar Eth is a waste of your time." The male grinned.

It wasn't a reaction Malo valued. It showed a marked lack of fear and respect. Had he lost the ability to loom? His brow furrowed. He sharpened his hearing to listen to Director Reyes's heartbeat and found it steady. *Alodon's balls, I am losing my skills.*

"I knew her uncles." Director Reyes folded his arms across his chest. "Do you have the authority as an engineer?"

"Yes," Malo snapped.

Director Reyes unfolded his arms and smiled. "Ori believes I will be more receptive to your...needs."

Malo gritted his teeth. Princess Oriana could have forewarned him. Not having all the information lowered the task's chance of success. "And are you? I would prefer not to distrust you, Director Reyes. Distrust would be an unpleasant experience for you."

"Aha. I knew it. You are no more an engineer than I'm a scientist." The elderly male was far too pleased for Malo's liking. Yet while he watched him now energized by this confirmation, he realized that Director Reyes would indeed be an ally. There was kindness around his mouth and wisdom in his eyes.

"I will not reveal my official title, Director Reyes. However, what I conveyed regarding our lima kuu is correct. We train our males in all aspects of Etterian life. If negotiations are not successful, the king will send more males. They are better and more powerful than I. The full might of Etteria has not been revealed to humans."

"I'm well aware of the might of Etteria." Director Reyes spread across the table a few images of the battleship *Gladio* and others, including Yithian slave ships. "This is why I have been given the authority to deal, Malo." He tapped the images. "E.S.A. monitors, manages, and approves all space travel. We have noted an increase in traffic. Unrecognizable ships and massive battleships make us nervous."

"These are not ours." Malo swiped aside images of the Yithians' presence. "The size of our ships should prove we can defend as well as annihilate. Hence the urgency to negotiate. Along with access to your females, we require one other thing." Malo splayed his fingers on the desk, keeping his gaze focused on the male. "A submarine."

"A sub? Why ever would you need—?" Director Reyes spluttered but halted at the look Malo leveled upon him.

"If I may continue," he said. "An intergalactic war is imminent with Earth at the center of it."

"War?" Director Reyes sank into his chair, his face pale.

Malo nodded, pleased that his character assessment was accurate. At least he hadn't lost that skill, yet.

"Yithians are kidnapping females from your blue planet." He tapped the images of their ships. "We have rescued these females. It is due to one of these altercations that we now find ourselves having to defend Earth *and* Etteria. Do not be alarmed, Director Reyes. Etteria is more than capable of doing so. The issue lies with Yithia. They hide themselves underwater, and our weaponry does not penetrate deep enough nor with accuracy to make any impact."

Director Reyes gathered the closest image of a Yithian slave ship and studied it. "A sub is a vague request. We have many types. I will need specifics."

"Of this I am aware," Malo said, having read through the information King Xeus and Adviser Cales had commed him. "A sub and a crew, with stealth and accurate *torpedoes*. Our males would not fit in your underwater ships which is why the request. We need time to construct and test submarines large enough for our dimensions. I have been tasked to speak to Joshua Bennett, who is currently testing navigation systems in your Pacific Ocean."

"Let me see what I can do, Malo." Director Reyes tidied his desk and stacked the images in front of him.

"This would be appreciated."

"I need to take this to the powers-that-be. Though E.S.A. manages space, the women you need requires more than my approval. I think discussions are done...for now." The male's smile was genuine when he pressed a button on a white device. "Lisa, please get me Caro."

At the sound of her name, Malo's fingers twitched. He clamped down the movement, not willing to reveal how she affected him nor reveal a weakness.

"You need a guide for the duration of your stay, of course."

"Thank you," Malo said with a politeness he didn't feel. That Director Reyes had thought to summon her pleased him. He didn't have to search the building for her. Not that he doubted he'd have found her. Yet had he needed to search for her, he'd have disrupted the operational staff and undermined the purpose of his presence.

"The ancient Greeks called love 'madness of the gods.'"

"Love?" Malo frowned. The word didn't exist in his world. He understood the concept but hadn't experienced such an emotion which their annals purported to be volatile, overpowering, and painful.

"Yes. It is an uncontrollable craving to touch and taste her, to inhale the essence that is her, and protect her with your every breath." The haunting pain that crossed Director Reyes's eyes caught Malo unawares. The sadness held an intensity he wouldn't have recognized had the male not mentioned it. It seemed as if Director Reyes had experienced this *love*. They were so emotional, this species.

"You have lost such a *love*?" Malo's tone was as gentle as he could make it.

"Yes, and if you feel such as this for Caro..."

"Etterians do not feel." Malo kept his voice devoid of emotion to prove it. *To feel is to fail.*

"Yes, until your Dar Eth *makes* you feel." Director Reyes chuckled. "And you, my son, are feeling."

Malo scowled, wondering how the male could see his inner turmoil? Perhaps the male wasn't who he said he was? As Malo masqueraded as an engineer, perhaps Reyes masqueraded as a director?

He pursed his lips. How had the male known about the Ethera? How much had Princess Oriana revealed? "I assume this was in the introductory profile. Under pairings?"

To which Director Reyes smiled. "Nothing was documented, Malo, just a discussion between old friends." The male settled back in his chair, placed his elbows on the armrests, and steepled his fingers.

Chapter Four

Caro rushed across the reception area to her car to collect her tablet and handbag. She was still flustered by the time she returned. It was understandable having met the sexiest man who had ever traversed the universe. And that included Earth.

A darkness gathered around him, some sort of shadow that warned observers to remain back, to not approach. An aura of lethality too, as if he could kill with his bare hands and without hesitation. He wore a black fabric that was a mixture of leather and meshing. It molded to his hard edges, leaving nothing to the imagination. Something about him made her body hum. The current state of her...*desire* had her clenching her thighs again—hard enough to do while walking. It was waddle or suffer.

"Granny's nipples." She fanned her heated cheeks. "Gimme a piece of that hot apple pie." Not that he'd spare her the time of day. She couldn't attract a human man, never mind one from another planet. Besides, he was here for a reason, and that didn't include her.

Then her traitorous mind went there.

She imagined he was here to find her. The idea was so sweet and so impossible, she chuckled. *Quit being an idiot.* But her mind refused to drop it. *What if he does everything with that same intensity that oozes off him? It would be the best sex ever, and he'd ruin me for all human men. Once I go alien, I can never go back?* She giggled, a hundred per cent ready to take the plunge. One small 'sacrifice' for mankind, one giant bang for Caro?

Two men in the same black mesh as Malo's stood in the corner of the reception, their stances military with their gazes vigilant. Thick black braids fell down their backs. Similar bulges in their cargo pants altered their profiles. They had to be part of Malo's unit. Releasing a breath on a whoosh, she scampered over to security to slide her bags across to them. Squaring her shoulders to gather her courage, she approached the alien men.

"Hello, you must be with Malo?" She tried to ignore her many colleagues ogling the alien candy.

The men glanced at her from their six-feet-something heights and frowned. That wasn't what she'd expected. Though, how else would they react? She rolled her bottom lip under the top, snuck glances at the whispering audience, and faced the men again. Them looming over her didn't help calm her erratic heartbeat.

She supposed, with their height, broad shoulders, military armor, and scowling visages, instilling fear in observers was a common occurrence for them. They were handsome, though one of them was so tall and wide that being near him made her seem childlike. She would never have classified herself as petite, but next to them, she was delicate and feminine. *Damn. So that's what that feels like?* Petiteness had an addictive quality.

The shorter one smiled at her, revealing two dimples. He had a face with a wider forehead and cheeks that narrowed at the jaw, giving him a sculpted look. He was so beautiful, he could have been on the cover of any digi-mag. His nose was perky, his lips wide and full, and his round eyes peered at her from under slashing eyebrows. At his boyish smirk, the female audience gasped as one.

The tall one had defined edges, a square jawline, and a higher forehead. He had a refined nose, thin lips, and almond eyes with a dent in his cheek indicating the possibility of one dimple. He was like a huge teddy bear, ready to protect, and by the sheer size of him, he could carry her to safety without breaking a sweat. What was odd was that they both had blue eyes. Was that normal or a coincidence?

"Ronin et Brenin, at your service, milady," the charming one said with a cultured accent.

"Garix et Orix, at your service, milady," the teddy bear rumbled in his raspy deep voice.

"I'm Caroline Masterson, but you can call me Caro. You two are drawing attention, I hope our curiosity doesn't bother you."

Offending these men would be oh-so-bad for Earth. She could read the headlines now. *Three alien men mauled by sex-starved women.* She winced at the imagery her mind conjured, because right at the center of it, leading the charge, was Caro herself. Sex-starved? Perhaps she was. Prior to this morning and her subsequent drooling over Mr.-Sex-On-A-Stick Malo, she hadn't thought about it.

"Would you like a beverage or something to eat while you wait for Malo?" Perhaps mentioning *his* name might get his men to trust her? She gestured to a side door. *We keep our sex torture chambers in the lower levels. Please follow me.* She smothered a giggle. "The canteen is through there. My treat."

"I have not tried Earthian food, though the buzz does indicate it is passionate," Garix said in an accent as breathtaking as Ronin's. They shared a cadence to the way they pronounced certain vowels.

Caro pasted on a smile, hoping it came across as sweet, polite, and not rabid. "We like our food to taste good, whether it is healthy for you or not."

The staff in the canteen fell silent. She ignored them and pointed out different meals and beverages, describing their flavors. In the end, she'd carried pizza, burgers, fries, iced coffee, and soda to a trestle table. When she sank onto the bench for the fifth time, her eyes grew wide at the amount of food they'd consumed within a minutes. She chastised herself for her reaction since they were so bulky. Massive men required copious amounts of food. That was a logical assessment, and yet logic for her had taken a sick day.

As soon as one dish was finished, the fascinated canteen staff would replace it.

"Are you not eating, Lady Caro?" Ronin asked between mouthfuls of his second pizza.

Garix wolfed down his third burger.

She blinked, torn between asking him where he put it and digging deeper into Ronin's use of 'lady.' "No, thank you, I've had breakfast. If I'm hungry, I'll eat a late lunch."

"Two meals per day? And that sustains your curves?" Garix shoved his fries across to her.

She grinned but it faded when his gaze traveled over her straining breasts. For the second time today, she cursed at herself for burning her shirt. Izzy was petite, so of course anything Caro wore of hers would be too tight. She was lucky the buttons had held on for as long as they had.

"If I eat more, my curves get bigger." She brought her elbows onto the table, clasping her hands together to conceal her 'curves' from their admiring gazes. And they did admire. These were men starved for breasts.

"Truth?" Ronin gasped, a slice of pizza halfway to his mouth.

"You get softer?" Garix asked after downing his fourth iced coffee.

She chuckled. They were like teenagers. "What's your fascination with my curves?"

Garix trailed a finger across her wrist. "We do not have softness in any aspect of our lives, and it is thus cherished."

She blinked. Where had they been for the past three hundred years? The diet industry wouldn't have been so lucrative. "Earth has many soft women," she said, sounding like a digi-ad. *Wait, if you order now, you will receive one free woman with guaranteed curves.*

"We are aware of this," Garix said moments before he shoved a chocolate brownie in his mouth. "This is my favorite," he mumbled.

"Are you sure, Garix? You've only had one of those but three burgers and many iced coffees." She swept out an arm at the array of empty plates.

He grinned. *Ah, there's his dimple.* "Your food *is* passionate, Lady Caro."

Her phone buzzed, and she squeezed her eyes shut at the memory of stuffing it into her cleavage when she'd carried the coffees. She turned her back to the men and yanked it out.

"Hello?" she breathed into the handset.

"Caro, Director Reyes is asking for you."

"Oh?" Caro sliced a glance at the overladen table. Why would Reyes need to see her? Was it something to do with Chief D? She closed her eyes as another possibility came to mind. Was it to do with the alien man and the way she'd bolted? She shivered. "Um, thanks, Lisa. I'm on my way." She faced Garix and Ronin. "I've been summoned to the director's office. May I leave you two here?"

Their bright smiles contrasted with their earlier scowls. When she scurried into the lobby and summoned an elevator, she laughed. *Apparently, the way to an alien's heart is through his stomach. Who would have thought?*

As she stepped onto the director's floor, Duncan leaped in front of her. He's sickly-sweet cologne tickled her nose. A sneeze didn't follow, thankfully. She blinked and tried to dart around him. He lunged to the side, blocking her again.

"What do you want?" She folded her arms across her chest.

"Why did Reyes summon you?"

She huffed. "I don't know yet."

"Well, Lisa tells me you're to entertain these...aliens. What is Reyes thinking?" Duncan threw his hands into the air. "I don't trust them, Caro."

Her? Entertain? Visions rose of her shimmying on stage with credits tugging her panties down on one side, her jiggling reflected in Malo's sunglasses? Maybe even a lap dance? Her skin tingled, and she barely hid a gasp. *Yes, please, hot mama.*

A caress running along her arm snapped her back to the man standing before her. "Don't fall for his looks, Caro. Don't let him fuck you either. He's an alien, and we don't know their agenda."

Let Malo fuck her? Oh, yummy. She smirked. "So, you find him attractive?"

Duncan's ruddy cheeks darkened. "That's...not what I meant." He glanced behind him, maybe to check if anyone was watching or eavesdropping. "He... When he met me, he muttered something in a strange language, but death rolled off him, Caro. Like he wanted to kill me." Duncan ran a hand over his face, his fingers trembling. "I don't think he's an engineer. I get the feeling he's some sort of assassin."

She swallowed a giggle. "Assassin?" Tapping her chin, she pretended to give his words some thought. "You may be right. He *does* look amazing in black."

"This isn't funny, for pity's sake." Duncan gripped her shoulders as if to shake her. "He studied you like a specimen, Caro."

She gurgled—yet another swallowed laugh. "Me? Aw, Chief, are you worried the aliens will probe me?" She broke away from him to pat his forearm. "I didn't know you cared."

Well, what could she say? If Malo wanted to do anything to her, he could go right ahead, all permission granted. She doubted D-for-Douche would appreciate her enthusiasm or a lecture on the purpose of desire and how it scattered her wits? He'd lock her up in an asylum for sure.

"And how do you propose I thwart a probing?" She wiggled her eyebrows. "What if he's interested in *you*? Maybe the words he spoke were some kind of mating ritual?"

Duncan paled and staggered back. "What? No, no, he wanted to kill me." He shook his head, mussing his perfectly coiffed hair. "Something about him became more...menacing...deadly."

"Maybe he's like a praying mantis and will eat you after, y'know, doing the deed?" She pinched her lips, but that didn't stop the laughter from bubbling up, so she glanced down, trying to hide a grin.

"I'm serious, Caro. Stay away from him...them." Duncan stormed off, fists at his side, then glanced over his shoulder at her. "Don't say I didn't warn you."

As she hurried to Reyes's office, she muddled over Dee's strange behavior...and warning. If Malo was an assassin, then so was Garix and Ronin in their black uniform. She snorted, trying to imagine Garix sneaking. So what, maybe all of the aliens were assassins? There hadn't been markers or designations on their uniforms to indicate rank.

She bobbed her head at Lisa and paused outside the glass door, her gaze snagging on the man staring out of the window. Everything about him screamed discipline—something she greatly admired in others. She gathered her wits about her and knocked.

Chapter Five

"Ah, Caroline. Please come in. I'd like you to meet Engineer Malo et Dalo."

She strolled in, gray shimmering across her thighs, her white tunic stark against the paleness of her skin, her dark hair swaying with each movement she made, and in an instant, Malo couldn't breathe. The spicy, rich, intoxicating scent of her engulfed him. His admiring gaze caught on her gaping tunic, showing a crisp white undergarment. His attention lingered there until she spoke.

"A pleasure to meet you." She offered her hand, which he accepted as Princess Oriana had instructed him to.

But at her touch, he shivered, his hand tingled as if it had lost the ability to feel. And the way she said 'pleasure,' she'd purred the word across his senses. He struggled not to react and to rein in his elusive control.

"Caro, m'dear, I need you to show Malo a bit of Earth, wine and dine him." Director Reyes handed her a rectangle card and a key. She accepted them, but her gaze didn't leave Reyes's. "You will need to represent E.S.A. on my behalf."

Caro gave Malo a sweet smile. "Please follow me, Mr. Et Dalo."

As if Enyl had punched him in the chest, Malo stared at her as she left the room.

"With your every breath," Director Reyes said.

Malo bolted after her. He managed to stay a few steps behind her to watch her hips sway. No matter how he chastised himself, he refused to increase his pace. Despite his internal admonishments, he couldn't help himself. Her backside looked so soft, so perfect for his large hands.

"What would you like to do? Anything in particular, Mr. Et Dalo?" She pressed a button on the elevator and held the door open for him.

What I would suggest has something to do with you naked beneath me and moaning. He throttled his need before buttoning her shirt, slipping each button through the loop with excruciating deliberateness. Accidentally, he brushed the underside of a breast with his knuckles. Not that he regretted the elusive touch, not when her shiver delighted him.

She gasped, and a pretty pink color, similar to Etterian skies, splashed across her cheeks. She whispered her thanks before glancing ahead. He smothered a rumble of delight, her response to him wonderful to behold.

"Call me Malo." He offered a smile. "Whatever you like to do. I am a visitor, after all."

She ran a gaze down his body, and her lips twitched. He liked that he made her uneasy. "You could pass as a human, just taller...and bronze."

She left the elevator as soon as the doors opened, he suspected to hide her reaction to him. Her hand fluttered to her cheek. Perhaps she was embarrassed that he affected her so. Her dilated pupils were a clear sign she liked what she saw. Her breathing had become erratic, and her heart pounded, loud enough for him to discern it without focusing his hearing. Her scent had deepened, calling forth more control than he had tested in a while.

"And handsome too," she rasped. "You probably have to fight women off no matter their species."

His blood heated at her compliment, for her words spoken were her thoughts, though he doubted she realized how she revealed herself to him. She requested her bags. He lunged forward to assist, but she waved him aside, giving a small smile as consolation. This told him she did things on her own.

That she had no male in her life pleased him. He hadn't scented another male on her. There were scents of another female, validated by the tunic Caro wore—too small for her. Not that he'd complain, longing to unfasten and remove it from her body instead of having to dress her. He grabbed her bags, regardless of her dismissal. Her fingers brushing his hand sent a sharp sensation traveling up his arm. His fingers twitched in response. He scowled, not liking how easily she passed his defenses.

Remembering her complement, he blurted, "I am not a preferred male on Etteria."

Her eyes widened. Dipping her chin, she leaped ahead and opened a door to a large room that held a variety of intriguing aromas. Her surprise soothed him while revealing that she found him suitable. She preferred him, his Dar Eth. He grinned at Ronin and Garix seated at a table, empty plates strewn around them. In mid-chew, both males blinked at him...at his eyes, now the ice blue of an Eth.

"You have made yourself at home," he snapped. They jumped up, then fell into relaxed positions when they realized he teased them. "Come," he commanded. He faced Caro, gesturing for her to lead the way. She did, her hips swaying enticingly. *Maker. I will follow her anywhere.*

She led them down the stairs into an underground ground-vehicle storage area where she opened the back compartment of a black vehicle. He placed her bags inside then waited. She opened a door for him. He studied the seat for a moment before taking it. She did the same for Ronin and Garix but stretched over them to strap them in.

"Here on Earth, you'd be considered perfect," she said, sliding into the vehicle as well.

The fabric over her thighs pulled tight and up, exposing her knees, hitching his breath. *Even her knees appear soft.* Heat flooded his veins, making his arousal throb. He scowled. He hadn't stimulated it, and he'd attended to the chore this morning, finding his release swiftly. His malehood had continued to harden since meeting her. It showed no signs of subsiding. He dragged his gaze away, trying to focus on anything that wasn't her.

"Welcome," a robotic yet feminine voice came through the curved console.

"Manual drive, S.A.D.I," Caro commanded the voice.

"Authorization please," the vehicle intoned.

Caro gripped and released the wheel. "Alpha Victor Charlie Mike one-five-zero-two-two-nine."

"Authorization and voice recognition confirmed. Have a safe journey, Caroline Masterson."

"You named your ground-vehicle?" Ronin asked from the backseat.

Caro twisted to glance at him, her brow furrowed.

"S.A.D.I," Malo said.

A smile warmed her features like the minus sun spreading its fingers across their red oceans.

"Oh, no, new ground-vehicles or cars have automated driving as standard. S.A.D.I. is a Standard Automated Driving Intelligence. Older cars can't have it installed if they are incompatible with the software." Caro pressed a button, and the engine roared to life. The vibration was...pleasant. "We've come a long way with solar cars and automated driving. In some cities, there is air traffic for those who can afford fusion pulse in their personal vehicles." She leaned across and strapped Malo in, her brown hair brushing his arm, her spicy scent engulfing him. "We had to go to electric and solar somewhere in 2064 when we ran out of oil. The switch made such a difference to our air quality, though there are still huge air-filtration stations situated in each domed city." Once she'd strapped herself in, she reversed the vehicle...car smoothly and directed it out of the storage area.

As Malo watched her knees flex, visions of thrusting into her seized his mind. He was fighting for supremacy and losing. Desperate for something to focus on, he struggled to remember what they'd been speaking about prior to leaving E.S.A.

"With Etterian males, you'd be considered perfect too," he said.

"Me?" she squeaked.

He acknowledged her surprise and the remarkable ease with which she handled the vehicle despite her emotional response. Her disbelief informed him of her opinion of herself as if she were unattractive. *Alodon's balls, I will prove her desirability to her.*

"Are your women like me?"

"No. Our females are hard and muscled. They mate with the best warriors for a predetermined period. If no female offspring are born during that period, they select another male. There are far more males than females. Is it the same on earth?"

"Holy noodle, no. We're lucky to find a decent man."

"What do you mean by decent, Lady Caro?" Ronin asked from the back.

She chuckled, the sound warming Malo in ways he hadn't anticipated. Everything about her seemed to undermine his training. "Not that all men are like this, but the good ones are taken. What most women want is a man who doesn't steal, sleep around, or abuse her, alcohol, or drugs."

"Abuse? Sleep around?" Garix growled.

Malo scowled. That a male would do so to the gift that was his female...was dishonorable.

She flicked her gaze at the mirror running the top of the window, her eyes twinkling. Her reaction implied she was uncomfortable discussing this subject. "Oh, um, sleeping around is...having sex with other women when you're a couple...together for an undetermined period. Women like to be married for life. Men, not so much."

"We cannot end a period once the agreement has been signed," Malo said, wishing he could brush her hair to the side. He wanted to see her face and touch her hair. Double the temptation, double the barrage on his control.

"Like a contract?" She peeked at him before she pulled into a painted area.

"Yes."

She switched off the engine and faced him. "That's sad. On Earth, there's roughly one man for each woman."

"There is a female for every male?" He'd known there were billions of humans, but still, one for each male? That didn't leave many for Etteria.

She laughed while circling the vehicle to open the doors, unstrapping them in the process. The way she leaned over Malo was a temptation he almost succumbed to. He wanted to tug her against his body, to grasp a backside cheek and test if it was as pliant as he'd envisioned.

"Yes, in a way. There are men for men and women for women too."

He fell into step beside her, loving her footwear on her dainty feet. There was something sensual about them. They raised her heels, forcing her to walk on her toes. Yet her calves were magnificent in them. When she noticed him staring, he gazed into her eyes until her heartbeat scattered. Only then did he glance away. They were near blue oceans, the salty tang on the air, and something...fruity.

"Our oceans are red, but your blue is as beautiful." He glanced at Ronin and Garix peering out at the horizon. Ships bobbed. People played in the waves. *Damu...* So many. Malo's chest swelled. This could be Etteria's future if the negotiations went well.

"I imagine all oceans are spectacular. All that pent-up energy simmering under the surface. Breath-taking," she sighed.

He shivered at the emotion in her voice, the awe darkening the blue of her eyes.

She steered him into a little structure. "Izzy." She greeted a young female with the same intensity he was certain she brought to every aspect of her life. It was something he wanted to experience, her passion and life force.

"Hot damn, girlfriend." The young female bounced around the counter. "Who did you bring with you?"

"Malo, please meet my best friend and roommate, Izabelle."

"Who just happens to work at an ice-cream parlor." Izzy giggled, her smile wide and uninhibited.

Malo returned her joy, unable to help himself. Where Caro was passion, this female was a fiery explosion. He wished her Eth strength. "Greetings, Lady Izabelle."

Pink stained her cheeks, almost hiding the spots across her nose. These females were too easy to please, it seemed. He drew in a deep breath, confirming that Caro wore Izzy's tunic.

"Garix and Ronin, this is my friend, Izzy." Caro introduced them as soon as they stepped into the stall.

"Greetings, Lady Izzy," they chimed in unison.

Her gray gaze traveled the length of them. Malo observed this interaction avidly. They knew so little about the Ethera. He had expected, no...hoped Izzy was another Dar Eth. Yet Garix and Ronin remained on their feet.

"Why the visit, Caro? Has it been a difficult day already?" Izzy wandered over to the multi-colored tubs.

Malo frowned at Caro. She came here when she was having 'bad' days? The need to draw her into a hug, to shield her from life's woes almost overwhelmed him. He grunted. He was supposed to react so. She was his to protect, to cherish—an obligation he looked forward to. He inhaled, taking in the various aromas. His focused settled on Caro's figure, and he grumbled. Her scent was the most delectable.

"I want a scoop of everything." She flashed the rectangle at Izzy, who squealed.

What was the meaning of this device? He suspected it was their form of currency. Since Earth was a mid-grade planet, the Global Council hadn't invited them to join the amalgamation of planets and therefore, Earth needn't conform to the intergalactic currency of tokens.

"Let's start with the sorbet." Caro took Malo by the hand, and that she'd done so without second thought, had him clasping her fingers.

She led him to a padded seat and gestured for him to sit. He did so but refused to relinquish her hand, urging her down beside him. No matter what he did, what he thought, he couldn't command his hand to release her. She gasped but didn't pull away. The weight and warmth of her thigh pressed to his calmed his erratic thoughts yet sent heat coursing to the ends of his body.

"You don't mind if we share? I couldn't eat them by myself."

He nodded and accepted the offered spoon. Izzy slid a tray of various colored cups onto the table for the four of them. Garix and Ronin dived in without restraint.

"Try everything, but don't feel you have to finish it." Caro scooped a spoonful out of a cup and popped it into her mouth.

Malo stopped breathing when her pink tongue darted out to lick her lips. Her subsequent moan of pleasure kept him riveted. When her blue eyes fluttered open, she took his spoon to offer him a taste. He opened his mouth and waited for her to feed him. She gaped, her fingers trembling where they gripped the spoon, and her gaze rose to meet his. Something intense crossed the gap between them. His body pulsed, his focus narrowed on her. She slipped the dollop of purple into his mouth, then with a delicate touch, rubbed her thumb across his bottom lip. The cold tart flavor exploded across his tongue. His eyebrows shot up. He mumbled in delight.

"It is cold," he said around the mouthful.

She giggled and removed her touch to choose another cup for him. Tray after tray arrived, flavor after flavor, and even though he diligently opened his mouth, what he wanted to taste was her. He admired her face, trailing over her eyebrows, her exquisite blue eyes, down her tiny nose to her plump lips. What would she do if he kissed her? He was ashamed to say he lost track of how many flavors she spooned into his mouth. All he could state was that the sustenance was cold. He couldn't recall the strange flavors even under torture. But he knew how many spots dusted across her nose and cheekbones. He could describe the perfect shape of her lips, the enticing color of her tongue.

The ache in his stomach brought him back to reality. "I cannot anymore."

"You cannot? I now believe the three burgers were not wise." Garix rubbed his stomach. Ronin had abandoned his spoon, as well, his eyes squeezed shut in agony.

"Just one more? The death by chocolate. I was saving it till last." When she jumped up, he allowed her hand to drag out of his. She grabbed the cup from Izzy and smiled at Malo. "Let's go for a walk. It will help you feel better."

"Stay," Malo muttered.

Garix and Ronin obeyed. She shrugged when they didn't rise and handed Malo the cup before swiping the card. Looping her arm around his, she led him down a sandy path. She knew not that he'd let her lead him anywhere. To be with her was a treasured gift. The single sun hid behind a bank of clouds, but she didn't seem to notice.

He watched her with absolute fascination when she drew in a deep breath, lifted her face to the sky, closed her eyes, and exhaled.

She combined words in a strange melancholic birdsong with the same breathlessness with which she spoke. His resistance crumbled. He dipped his head to brush his lips across hers. The descent had been slow, to allow his mind to capture each moment. Her eyelids fluttered. She met his gaze. Her eyes widened. But she hadn't jerked away. Her fingers tightened where they clasped his forearm. Her breathing became ragged, her heart pounding. The instant his lips touched hers, his world unraveled and reformed. The connection tugging at his heart was new and breathtaking. He marveled at the lushness of her mouth, at its expected coolness, at the sweetness of her breath. *Maker, one touch of her lips is not enough.*

"What was that for?" she whispered.

"For this experience, thank you."

"My pleasure," she said.

His eyelids stuttered closed at her purr. He savored being in her presence and the affect she had on him. Opening his eyes, he nudged her, encouraging her to resume walking. The location wasn't suitable for everything he wanted, no, needed to do to her, with her and once wouldn't be sufficient. After a while of contented silence, he had to admit, his stomach didn't cramp anymore.

"Not much to show you other than monuments, museums, and restaurants. The good stuff is illegal." She pursed her lips. "Want to see a movie?"

Movie? His O.D.I. hurried to update him. Not that he spared much thought on the results. She'd tossed the empty cup in a black drum and now licked a finger.

His gaze unblinking, unwavering, he watched with the same intensity he studied an opponent. He snatched her hand and sucked her pre-licked finger into his mouth. A groan escaped him at her flavor. That he'd shocked her, he had no doubt. She was showing all the signs of arousal again, so he addressed her suggestion, hoping to distract her from his audacity.

"Movie?" he asked while twirling his tongue around her fingertip then grazing his teeth across her skin. Her shudder summoned his smirk. Her nipples pebbling wiped away any amusement. He was playing with fire.

"Yes," she rasped. "Maybe have a good laugh at how our storytellers foretold space travel." She sighed when he released her hand.

"An entertainment vid?" He had browsed through their extensive information database of Earth but hadn't bothered with entertainment; had, in fact, considered it unimportant.

"Yes, we'll drag Izzy with, if you don't mind, that is? She's my best friend and rarely goes out."

He nodded. "If it pleases you."

Her glorious smile raised his temperature. *Maker. I will give her anything she asks for if she looks at me like this.* He wouldn't reveal to her that she had become a weakness. He sighed in response to that revelation. Weaknesses were to remain a minimum. Now that he had a Dar Eth, he couldn't continue as the operations commander. It would place her in constant danger. No regret or sadness rose at the years studying to be the best operative. Giving up his skillset for her wasn't a hardship. He hadn't considered how much finding his Dar Eth would mean to him.

"Thank you." She looped her arm through the crook of his.

"Humans are a passionate species," he said, losing himself in her sparkling eyes.

"Yes, unfortunately. It gets us into all sorts of trouble." She led him to his males. Her hand rested on his forearm, so he cupped his other hand over hers. She peeked at him before glancing out to sea, the sunset throwing vivid colors across the sapphire surface.

"Your planet is beautiful." Not that he glanced at the ocean. His focus remained fixed on her. *She* made her planet magnificent.

"It is," she said, ushering him into the stall.

"No way," Izzy said from the table where she sat with Ronin and Garix. "You can't be wanting more?"

"Oh, holy noodle, no. I thought you and I could take our guests to see that star movie you like so much. There's a banned showing this week."

"With buttered popcorn? Soda?" Izzy climbed onto her knees. Her eyes widened with each question. "And maybe dancing afterward? Since we're doing illegal things tonight, might as well do everything."

"Dancing? I don't know, babe." Caro met Malo's gaze before dipping her chin.

Her expression implied hesitation as if there was something terrible about this *dancing*. What his O.D.I. revealed was a gyration of one's body. Seemed harmless enough.

"No alcohol, not even wine." Caro pointed a finger at Izzy.

"Deal. We can't have your inner porn star making an appearance," Izzy said.

Inner porn star? Malo frowned, making a mental note to explore the reference later. The images his O.D.I. showed him were of the mating vid he'd seen as part of his research. They couldn't be applied to his Dar Eth.

"Just gimme a sec, and I'll close up shop." Izzy bounced up and dashed around the stall.

"Is she always this energetic?" Ronin asked.

Caro's answering chuckle stroked across Malo's sensitive nerves.

"Yes, sometimes I'm tired just watching her." While they waited, Caro asked his males what their favorite flavor was, and a heated discussion broke out between Garix and Ronin.

Contented, Malo sat next to her and observed her in silence, listening to her voice, drinking in her scent. He laced his fingers with hers, squeezing her hand. She stiffened. Pink stained her cheeks and traveled down her throat. He nodded, liking that nothing Garix or Ronin said flustered her, yet the moment he touched her, she reacted gloriously.

"Okay, I'm ready," Izzy said, now out of her pink knee-length tunic and leggings into blue leggings and a white tunic. Her hair cascaded around her in wild disarray—the abundance of it surprising on a female so tiny. She ushered them out of the building to lock up.

Caro opened the ground-vehicle's doors again and waited for them to climb in. Izzy clambered across the back to sit in the middle, allowing space for Ronin and Garix to join her. Caro grinned when she closed the doors behind them before opening the door for Malo.

"It's like having children," she teased, gesturing to the three in the back.

The O.D.I's images aligned with Etteria's *damu*. He drew her into the circle of his arms to brush his fingers along her jaw and embed them in her hair below her ear. Mesmerized by the curve of her lips, he stared at her upturned face. Because he couldn't help himself, he brushed a kiss over her mouth. Her lips parted as if she begged him to taste her…thoroughly.

"Do you want children, Caro?" Malo asked, drowning in her dark blue eyes. They revealed her joy of life, the dark flecks against her blue irises striking.

"Yes," she rasped. "Do you?"

"Very much so." He rubbed another kiss across her lips, wishing he didn't have to slide into the vehicle. Her lips were lush, sweet, and warm and tempted him to linger.

"Granny's nipples," she whispered when she hurried around the vehicle.

Judging the potency of her scent, he'd aroused her again. As she sank into the driver's seat, she didn't know he could hear and scent her. He'd inform her later of his Etterian traits, anticipating—with eagerness—the pink that would spread across her cheeks.

"You better hurry, babe, the show begins in less than an hour," Izzy leaned forward, her face inches from Malo's shoulder.

"Strap everyone in," Caro said, then buckled Malo in, her fingers brushing his hip.

"Shit. I was kidding. There's plenty of time." Izzy's voice rose in alarm, but she fastened Ronin and Garix's seatbelts before yanking hers on.

Malo glanced between Izzy's paleness and the excitement on Caro's face. *What is this?* He twisted in his seat to admire Caro's profile, and his body warmed at the joy on her features. *Alodon's breath, does she have to entice me so? Is everything she does designed to arouse me?*

The answer to that was *Yes, yes, oh, Maker.*

With decisive, confident twists of the wheel in her steady hands, she maneuvered the vehicle with a power and accuracy that robbed him of his breath, set his heart pounding, and had him harder than the Fuyra rock Etteria exported. She didn't glance at him once, yet he hadn't been able to remove his gaze from her. He was riveted by her skill. Ronin and Garix laughed in exhilaration while Izzy yelped in fear, but his Dar Eth remained focused. To say he was impressed was an understatement. To say he was aroused was a minimalist description of the aching need within him. It had taken ahold of his malehood and his heart with a ferocity he didn't understand.

By the time they pulled into a painted area outside a nondescript brown building, the vehicle tinkled and the engine hissed as if it was breathless.

"Alodon's balls," Garix boomed then laughed.

Ronin chuckled. "I enjoyed that." He'd draped an arm around a trembling Izzy. The sour stench of her fear saturated the vehicle, but they'd chosen to endure it in light of this surprising experience.

"My pleasure," Caro said with a husky laugh before sliding out of the car and rushing around to Malo's door.

Pleasure, she'd purred that word again, and after what he'd just enjoyed, his control was at its lowest. A deep guttural groan ripped from his throat without his permission. He wanted to escape the torment but couldn't bear the thought of leaving her even for a moment. Her masterful control of the ground-vehicle had called forth something primitive within him, something he couldn't fight, didn't want to resist.

When he stepped out, he yanked her against him, trapped her within his arms, and crashed his lips over hers, thrusting his tongue in to taste her. His temperature rose, his breathing altered into gasps, and his heart pounded in his ears, muting all other sounds. Except those originating from her—whimpers and throaty purrs.

"Remind me to train you to pilot," he said in a voice so hoarse it bordered on animalistic, even to his ears. Drawing in ragged breaths, he rested his forehead against hers.

"Fly? I'm scared of heights," she said.

He stared at her pink and swollen lips, fighting the urge to kiss her again. "You cannot fall in space, Caro, there is no gravity."

Despite her laughter, he recognized that surprised and confused expression in her eyes. She mistrusted the sincerity of his interest. He sighed. With the good emotions—joy, pleasure, excitement, and contentment, came the bad ones—doubt, fear, rage, and jealousy. And his beautiful Dar Eth doubted her attractiveness.

"You weren't frightened by my driving?" she asked in a small voice.

He frowned. "Etterian males do not fear. And you had excellent control of the vehicle." Dipping, he rubbed his cheek across hers. "It was exhilarating."

"She should have control. She's taken advanced driving courses," Izzy said from inside the vehicle. She leaned across Ronin's lap to pull the door's handle. She did the same for Garix before unbuckling them all. "Still, it *scared* the *shit* out of me." She clambered out of the car but leaned against it as if her knees were weak.

"Fear makes you pale?" Garix brushed a finger across Izzy's cheek.

Caro squeaked and broke out of Malo's tight embrace to hug her friend. "I'm so sorry, babe. I forgot."

Izzy nodded with her lips pressed together. "I'll take a taxi home, if you don't mind."

Caro shoved the rectangle device carrying their currency at her friend and gestured to the black door.

Izzy pushed off the vehicle and entered the building with a slight bounce to her steps.

"Her parents died in a car accident. Only she and her sister survived," Caro said to them. "I was thoughtless to drive so..." She shook her head and walked through the door.

Malo wished he could convey how much the experience had meant to him. How she could never save Izzy from fear, sorrow, pain, and to do so would only harm her friend. This was something Caro would have to discover on her own. When they strolled into the dimly lit foyer carpeted in red, Izzy stood in a line at the food stall. The aromas were incredible—rich, salty, and sweet.

"More food?" Garix moaned.

"If you can't eat it, I will." Izzy grinned while rocking on her heels.

"Like I said, children," Caro said to Malo, who had settled close to her.

He rested his hand on her hip to announce to all she was his. She peeked at him, but she hadn't pulled away from his kisses, confirming she *was* his. Only not soon enough for his liking. And from the many visions he'd endured, becoming his was inevitable. It was the path he chose that he struggled with. He could rush their first joining and nurture her affection afterward. Or he could draw on patience he didn't have, encourage affection now, then when she was ready, join with her, finalizing their pairing. Instinct had him leaning toward the latter, though his arousal urged the quicker path.

"It's a good thing we aren't here to meet men." Izzy giggled, thrusting a container of white odd-shaped sustenance at Caro, who grasped it automatically.

"I'll share with Malo." She gave him the container to accept the beverages.

He popped a few of the white things in his mouth and grumbled at the salty, rich flavor. He slipped one into Caro's mouth and stole a kiss, tasting her through the food. He rumbled his approval, his gaze drowning in hers. Her enticing scent rose, her arousal calling him to his salvation or doom. If he was with her, whichever end mattered not. He admired her face, imprinting it on his memory. No matter what happened, he would cherish this day.

Chapter Six

Caro snuck glances at Malo, excitement bubbling inside her. He kept kissing and touching her. It was a little fast for her, after all, she wasn't Earth's high-priced call girl sent to spread her legs for visiting aliens. Yet something about him made her body hum with desire. He was gorgeous and took what he wanted—all good things. Never had she met a man with more self-assurance. He smelled so good; he tasted even better which bolstered his appeal. This was a...seduction. Parts of her squealed like a teenager. To be so admired...

And he stared at her, extensively.

He was doing it again, resting his hand on her hip, claiming her in a caveman sort of way. She scanned the crowd. No use staking his claim if no one cared. But they were indeed the center of attention. She should have expected this. *Honest-to-goodness, sexy-as-apple-pie aliens? What isn't to like?*

Garix's height would draw anyone's curiosity, despite his intimidating military attire and giant boots. Ronin had easy charm spilling from his twin dimples. And Malo, granny's nipples, he might as well have been made of chocolate, he was that delicious. They were well-mannered, not once hitting on Izzy or commenting on women in a disparaging way.

Caro wasn't saying they didn't notice their surroundings. The way Malo analyzed everything had her questioning whether he was an engineer. If they reversed roles, she'd have asked him a million questions by now, nor did he behave as a scholar would. He assessed his surroundings, and she had no doubt, he knew the exits. He had probably catalogued the people around them, as well. Even when he stared at her like now or when he kissed her, he remained vigilant. It was as if he expected an attack. *What sort of life does this man lead? Does he ever just let go?* She almost snorted. No way would he lose control.

With a sigh, she led him and Ronin to their seats. Close behind, Izzy was feeding Garix tiny chocolates despite the alien's announcement he couldn't eat another thing. She shoved a box of popcorn into Ronin's hands and placed his soda into the holder. After ushering Garix into a seat, as well, she did the same thing with his popcorn and soda that he'd clasped with ease. The jumbo box looked miniscule in his huge hands.

Caro sank into a seat next to Malo, lowering their sodas into their holders before reaching across his lap to grab a few kernels. He angled closer, shifting the box to the middle. She smiled in thanks but refused to glance his way, expecting to catch him staring at her. His interest made her dizzy and warm. This had to be the craziest day of her life.

"I'm so excited. It's been so long since we did this, babe. Tonight, I doubt I'll be able to sleep," Izzy said while popping chocolates into Ronin's unsuspecting mouth.

Sleep? Holy noodles. Caro faced Malo. "Where are you and your men sleeping tonight?"

She hadn't thought to reserve him a suite at their nicest hotel. If he'd nowhere to sleep, she'd need to organize it now. She'd prefer not to go from hotel to hotel, trailing three aliens like an ingratitude of children. As it was, people stared. She shot a glance at the three. They could be star athletes or digi-mag models. With a chuckle, she imagined the stampeding sex-starved women tossing Izzy and herself out of the way. Well, at least in this image, she wasn't leading the charge anymore.

"We can port to my battleship," he said, squeezing her hand.

Butterflies unfurled in her belly, sending tendrils of warmth outward. She'd forgotten he still held her hand, like he'd no intention of releasing it.

My? As in he owned it? "Your what?" she squeaked.

The arrogant man chuckled. "How do you think I traveled here?"

"I hadn't thought about it, to be honest." She winced at her stupidity.

Of course, he has a spaceship, he's a freakin' alien. Renewed heat dipped her chin to her chest at remembering his comment on gravity. *Holy noodle*, that *had* been silly of her.

He wanted to teach her to be a pilot? That would take time which meant he planned on knowing her for longer than these few days. Or had it been a line? She could imagine him as a charmer if the need was there.

"Why not stay with us? We'll use the blow-up mattress. Ronin can get my bed. Malo can have yours, and the three-seater should handle Garix," Izzy said then stuffed her mouth from her box of popcorn.

"Izzy's right," Caro said, wishing her smile didn't feel as if it was about to explode past the borders of her ears. "If you don't mind it not being luxury accommodation?"

"I am an Etterian, Caro," Malo said as if that explained his ability to sleep anywhere. "I thank you and accept your offer." His breath fanned her ear, sparking an ebb and flow of shivers.

As the movie began, she couldn't focus. The popcorn and soda were forgotten while she visualized Malo sleeping in *her* bed. Just sleeping. Nothing more carnal than that. She didn't have the imagination nor the experience to visualize him in all his magnificence. And she had no doubt he was just that—glorious, perfectly sculpted.

The story made no sense. The dialogue was a jumble of words she couldn't process. Her body thrummed on high alert with Malo seated next to her; it was ludicrous. Out of the corner of her eye, she admired his folded legs, the fabric mesh of his pants pulled taut over his knees and carved thighs. It was a heart-pounding sight. He still held her hand, brushing his thumb over hers, freezing and mesmerizing her. And when a few words on the huge screen snared her attention, he'd lean across and kiss her temple, scattering her thoughts again. She was wound so tight. He had be aware of the tension gripping her, the bastard. She needed to escape, to breathe. But no matter how much she sucked in air, it wasn't enough. Spots circled her vision, and her body flushed then chilled. Panic set in next. She tugged her hand free and rose, realizing she managed to do both because he hadn't expected either. He leaped to his feet too, faster than she had.

"Stay. I need to—" Words lodged in her throat, unable to voice what engulfed her body, and how he made her feel. She bolted, heading to the ladies room.

She burst through the swinging door, stumbling to the basin to wet her hands and press them to her flushed cheeks. Almost not recognizing her wild hair, wide eyes, dilated pupils, and pouting lips, she stared at her reflection. *Granny's nipples, is this what I look like when I'm aroused?* A fresh wave of lust slammed into her, warming her skin. With a fascination that bordered on hysteria, she watched it disappear into her cleavage.

"Breathe," she said when she realized she was panting. He's a sexy man, yes, but still a man. She shouldn't be so overwhelmed. None of her previous lovers had inspired desire if this was what it truly felt like. Glancing to check her buttons hadn't popped free, she whimpered at her pebbled nipples. Slapping her palms over her breasts, she willed her aching nipples to soften. First opportunity she could find, she'd take care of the steady drum of need between her legs. She couldn't go around stabbing people with her dagger-like nipples.

"Caro?" Malo pushed open the door. He dominated the doorway, filling it from frame to frame.

Caught fondling her breasts, she dropped her hands. "Malo, you can't be in here. It's for women only."

"Are you unwell?" he asked, his voice thick with concern even though he ignored her words. As per usual, his gaze shifted around the room to assess its exits and threats.

"I'm fine, thank you for asking. I need to use..." Heat scorched her cheeks again. *Monkey's bananas.*

"The waste receptacle?" he teased her, his eyes softening in a way that drenched her panties. She clenched her thighs together, trying to resist another wave of lust.

"Yes," she gasped. "I'll join you soon." She waddled over and chased him out of the room before enclosing herself in the cubicle farthest from the door. "Holy noodle," she muttered while using the toilet, "overprotective much?"

She'd had one of those boyfriends where she couldn't be on the street side of a walkway; it was too dangerous. More baby potatoes weren't allowed until she finished her peas. No, thank you. It had taken her months to get out of that relationship. She sighed, hurrying to wash her hands. To be fair, Malo hadn't known why she'd left so abruptly. It made sense to assume she was ill. And of course, he was waiting for her outside, his posture once more military, his manner threatening. Any woman wanting to use the ladies must have returned to the movie theater unrelieved.

"Malo?" His gaze was already on her when she approached him, so she hadn't needed to call his name to gain his attention. "Don't you have dealings with women? Because there are so few of them?"

"My interaction has been minimal," he said, once again lacing his fingers through hers, using the handhold to draw her closer than was proper.

Proper? She snorted. There was nothing decent about her thoughts nor with her desperate plan to relieve the desire burning through her body. He moved then, pulling her behind him. His destination was a bench against a wall shrouded in darkness. *Darkness isn't a good idea with the way I want to ravage him.*

"You're not enjoying the movie?" she asked when he pushed her to sit on the bench then joined her.

"You are far more interesting." His statement—said so matter-of-factly—wasn't meant to compliment her.

The steady way he gazed into her eyes screamed the truth in his voice and words. He *believed* she was more interesting. *Are all these aliens this intense?*

"How…how long are you visiting?" She glanced around the foyer, trying to keep her gaze off him. His chest flexed when he leaned back, drawing her attention despite her best efforts.

"As long as it takes," he answered cryptically.

"So you're on earth for something specific?" She twisted on the bench to face him.

"Yes, our requirements have been communicated."

So vague. Why? Why hide what they were after unless Douche was right? "Did your planet only send you?" She winced, having not meant to imply he wasn't enough.

A low growl escaped him, and he stiffened. "Do you believe me incapable?"

"Of course not, Malo. I just meant, it's huge pressure placed on your shoulders."

When he squeezed her hand, as if to apologize for misunderstanding her, she almost slumped with relief. She didn't like angering or offending him, not to mention having to explain to the powers-that-be how she'd pissed off the new aliens. She supposed misunderstandings would happen. They were not only from distinct cultures but were diverse species and from different solar systems.

"I will not fail Etteria," he said with conviction. "I have not failed."

"Etteria? Is that your homeworld?" At his nod, she grinned. She'd dreamed of other planets, imagined and studied them. To know what he's seen, on which planets he'd walked… Excitement rushed through her, stealing her ability to breathe. "Tell me about Etteria. You said your oceans are red?"

He stared at her for a long time, not speaking but allowing his gaze to travel her face. She shifted on the bench, sparks skittering across her skin. *Did I say something wrong? Is he deciding whether he can share this information with me?*

Squeezing his knee, she tried to convey it was okay. "I promise not to tell anyone if its classified. Or don't reveal in which solar system your planet is." Registering the dense muscle beneath her fingers froze her. She snatched her hand back. *Granny's nipples, my fingers tingle, for tart's sake.*

"I do wish to share my world with you, Caro," he said in his sexy baritone. "I do not know where to begin, how to describe it."

He dragged her onto his lap as if she weighed nothing. Then with exquisite tenderness, he wrapped his arms around her. His cologne, the strength in his embrace, the warmth seeping off him, all combined to melt her against his chest with the crown of her head brushing his jaw. She shouldn't succumb to his will so easily, yet she'd never been cradled like this...cherished.

"It has pink skies, two suns, red oceans with gray beaches, and our favored white flowers we call hahyt blossoms. They grow wild and are beautiful, an emblem of home."

"It sounds spectacular." She rubbed her cheek across his armored chest, unable to resist. The leather absorbed the heat from his body, and the velvet texture of his skin she touched was an aphrodisiac on its own. *I probably look like a cat. Maybe I should purr for effect?* She smothered a giggle.

"All the buildings are constructed in our white Fuyra rock. It is the hardest rock in the universe and only Maloidian steel can cut it."

So, white buildings against a pink sky and gray sand? "Are you going home after Earth?"

"Yes, I hope to. I have lived on a battleship for most of my life."

She fell silent, trying to imagine a life with only his fellow engineers for company. "Why can't you go home?" She leaned back to meet his gaze, then wished she hadn't. Time hadn't diminished the effect of his handsome face. She curled her fingers, fighting the trembling need to touch his cheek, trace the line of his jaw, test the texture of his bottom lip.

"I cannot share this with you yet, *ensa*." His focus shifted to her mouth. His nostrils flared a second before he lowered his head to pluck at her bottom lip with his. It was a strange thing for him to do, but the effect of his lips teasing hers flooded her body with a welcome warmth. "Let me taste you, Caro," he rasped.

She obeyed while her mind unraveled his words. *Taste?*

He dipped his tongue into her mouth. The heat and force of it snatched her breath. He groaned—the sounded rumbled through her—spurring something deep and needy. She clasped his neck and parted her lips wider, demanding more of him. She inhaled through her nose, desperate for air but not willing to release him. He had no right to taste so good, to be such a divine kisser. *Holy noodle, are they given lessons?* She thrust her tongue into his mouth, meeting his onslaught with her own. He shuddered and broke away to press a wet kiss to her neck.

"Hot damn," Izzy said.

The urge to ignore her swept through Caro. "Go away, Izzy, please." She tilted her head to meet his mouth for another deep kiss that curled her toes. Her skirt pulled tight, hindering her movements. She wanted to straddle his thighs, to crush her breasts against his chest, to use her hands and slowly peel away each item of his uniform. He drew away first but held her, giving them time to calm their breathing.

"You two done now?"

Caro gritted her teeth. "So help me, Izabelle Reeves, when I get my hands on you—"

"In those heels, you couldn't catch a dead skunk."

Caro released a sigh, burying her face in the curve of Malo's neck, drawing on his strength, breathing in his mind-blowing cologne of sunbaked soil and lemon.

"Has she gone yet?" she whispered.

"No." He chuckled.

She leaned back to smile at him. A silent and deadly Malo was gorgeous but a chuckling one—revealing those two dimples—was sin incarnate.

"We have to get ready for the club." Izzy stamped her foot.

"Argh," Caro groaned. "The club? Do we have to?"

"You promised," Izzy said. "I can take a taxi with Ronin and Garix. You two can follow...whenever." Her stomping footsteps faded.

"She had pain in her eyes," Malo said in that calm manner of his.

Caro winced at having hurt her best friend's feelings. Sometimes, she wished she could do what she wanted which was to kiss Malo until the Earth stopped spinning or it exploded, whatever came first.

"I'll apologize." She rested her temple on his chin. "I'm sorry you have to go with." She climbed off his lap and tugged her skirt into place. Closing her eyes, she savored the memory of him cupping her bare thigh. His touch hadn't registered at the time.

"What is wrong with this club?" he asked, once again grabbing her hand.

"You'll see. I don't want to influence your opinion."

On the walk to the car, his silence tumbled her thoughts. Did he regret the kiss? Was her lack of consideration for Izzy's feelings repugnant? She rolled her lip, trying to smother the lump in her throat. She adored Izzy, but sometimes... Caro slumped. Love didn't care for sometimes. It was all or nothing, good and bad.

Malo opened his door this time and slid in, strapping himself in, as well.

She blinked before darting around to climb in. "There's time if you have something else you need to do. Y'know, ambassador business."

"I need to comm my prince." He tucked her hair behind her ear.

The contented sigh he released had her wondering. She snuck glances at him while reversing the car.

"You are beautiful, *ensa*." His intensity and belief was resolute. She didn't...couldn't say anything. What would have been the appropriate response? *You too? Thank you? No, I'm not?*

"You are close to the prince?" she asked a few minutes later.

"Yes, he is young enough to be my son. King Xeus entrusted me with Enyl's protection. It is a chore and a blessing."

He had to be more than an engineer. By his words, he revealed he was. Protection of an heir didn't fall to anybody. Malo had to have the skills... *Assassin.* Chief Dee's word echoed through her mind. And after spending a day with Malo, with not a single question asked about Earth's technology, antiquities, history, future plans, and his ability to vibe lethal had to mean he lied to her. Then that meant Ronin and Garix were assassins too, right?

She pulled the car into the first available parking spot and switched it off. Grabbing his arm before he climbed out, she pinned a look on him.

"So, not an engineer then." She arched a brow. "And don't try to lie to me, Malo. You don't have the characteristics of one."

"In my culture, it is dishonorable to lie, unless you are me." He gave her a breathtaking smile. "You are intelligent, my *ensa*. This pleases me."

Compliments? Mm. She was warmed and wary. "So why the lie then?"

"Princess Oriana does not trust humans. Only Director Reyes and you know I am not who I say I am."

"Reyes's an honorable man. You can trust him," Caro said. *And me.*

"I have assessed his character as so." Malo opened his door and climbed out.

She blinked. Still, he hadn't revealed who or what he was. Was Malo his true name? Was Izzy safe with Garix? Sweet-cheeked Ronin?

Malo waited on the walkway outside her apartment. He held out his hand. "And Malo et Dalo is my name, *ensa*." He grinned. "Your exquisite face is expressive."

Caro snorted but slid her hand in his. It was wiser to capitulate since he'd claim her hand anyway. Besides, she loved holding his hand. It was so old school as if they were courting. She huffed at the thought. *Courting? Holy noodle. To be his wife? To wake up to him every day? Sheer heaven.*

Then again, that could be the lust talking. The fact that she wanted to pin him to a bed and ravage him until he bellowed her name when he orgasmed? That had no effect whatsoever on her wanting to marry him. People married for less. And if it didn't work out, cross-species and all that, she'd divorce him. Simple.

She frowned, unable to imagine Malo letting his wife leave him. He was too much of an alpha male to give up on a marriage. She shrugged. Why was she thinking these thoughts? He wouldn't marry her, enough said. And dammit, why was she torturing herself? She was almost forty, her childbearing ability was lapsing even as she trailed him. It sounded like Etteria needed women, and probably ones to bear their children. Caro was almost out of the running. Perhaps she should tell him before he became invested in her or worse...she fell for him. That was going to be an interesting conversation.

Chapter Seven

Silence descended in the elevator to Caro's apartment. Malo clasped her hand, enjoying running his thumb across her skin when it elicited gasps from her. He smothered a grin and distracted himself from claiming her by studying the square box carrying them levels up. It had a musty smell that didn't detract from Caro's appealing scent.

He leaned in, brushing his nose across her temple. His hearts fluttered. This was insanity having so much temptation before him. The air grew thick, his arousal throbbed, and every muscle in his body tightened, as if he would pounce. He grimaced. Like a predator.

Thankfully, Izzy had escorted Ronin and Garix up first.

Leaving Caro and Malo alone.

At that realization, he spun and pinned her to the thin wall. Resting a palm on either side of her ears, he leaned in but was careful not to press his body to hers. Therein lay his doom. She squeaked, raised her hands to his chest and her wide gaze to meet his.

Words lodged in his throat. What she meant to him swelled, rose, overflowed until only warmth engulfed his chest. He studied this beautiful creature, wishing he knew how to convey what she invoked within him.

"Um," she glanced to the side, "we're here."

He pressed his forehead to hers for a moment, allowed himself to share her breath, before he pulled away. Never would he reveal how much effort it took to do so.

She gathered his hand. It served as a consolation, for now. Along the passage, they strolled until she paused in front of a gaping door. Ronin and Garix were chuckling about their sore stomachs. Izzy held open a white box with cool air pouring out of it.

Their home was the size of Malo's quarters. Large chairs dominated the space in bold red. Under them was a multi-colored thick rug. A display vid was mounted to a wall. The counter to the side held odd gadgets he wasn't curious about. Two doors led off to the right, and a wall of windows to the rear showed the domed city beyond. A door led onto an enclosed balcony.

Caro *swung* the front door shut behind him. He frowned. How odd when theirs slid into the wall.

"Ronin, Garix, scout this building. I want a full security assessment." Malo raised Caro's hand to his lips, pressed a kiss to her knuckles then strode to the balcony. Enyl needed to know Malo's circumstances had changed.

"What did they think of the movie?" Caro asked Izzy. He paused to listen before he commed the prince. Izzy unfurled a rectangle while Caro wheeled in some sort of machine.

"They laughed from start to finish. I didn't have the heart to tell them it wasn't a comedy," Izzy said after she'd pulled out pillows and a blanket from a nearby closet.

"Did they find Earth's early space conceptions to be childish?" Caro's chuckle warmed his heart. "I suppose in hindsight it could be seen as such. Discovering Fusion Pulse has changed that aspect of our lives."

"Of *your* life, not mine," Izzy harumphed. What discussion followed was drowned by the strange machine Caro had plugged into the rectangle. It inflated into a...bed. The buzzing didn't bother him, and he approved of their thoughtfulness. Most Etterian females would have demanded the best room and bed. He ventured deeper onto the balcony.

"My prince," he spoke into his wrist and grinned when his hands trembled. *Yes, Caro is a weakness, but a cherished one.*

"You have updates?" Prince Enyl's voice came through clearly, the delay minimal, proving all comm relays were operational.

Malo grunted at that wayward thought. "Yes, I have spoken with Director Reyes, and he assures me he will assist regarding the submarines. He will contact Joshua Guardian, as well." Malo glanced at the city around him, the dirty air cooling his heated skin through the open windows. "He has defined what Earth needs and insists I align with this. I have agreed since it is as per Princess Oriana's stipulations."

"You have done well, Malo." Enyl's praise was unexpected, and it shot warmth through Malo's chest. Prior to finding Caro, he wouldn't have acknowledged his reaction.

"I have done better, which is why I request reassignment," he said. "I have found my Dar Eth. My priority is no longer Etteria."

"This is wonderful news. Oriana will be most pleased." The sincerity in Enyl's voice was what Malo had hoped for. The weight that had rested on his shoulders for most of his life disintegrated without fanfare. "My father has dispatched Cales and Citus to assist you. He'd prefer to have his most trusted males attending to this."

"Excellent. The Ethera's timing is perfect." Malo grinned. "I am grateful that there will be no further delay. I will await their arrival."

"In addition, Brenin has been tasked with the submarines." His clipped words revealed Enyl's disapproval. "He is an engineer so there is merit to this decision."

"Perhaps Brenin requires an active mind to not cause mischief?" Malo teased. It was occurring more and more, this smiling. Years and years of training were unraveling before him. He scowled at that thought, not liking its implications. To lose his training because a female touched him as Oriana did Enyl? A grin burst through. He would sacrifice more for Caro.

"We can but hope. I have forewarned you. It is now in your hands." The prince chuckled. "My father has also found his Dar Eth."

Malo stilled. Another burden sloughed off his shoulders. Xeus's mood of late had worried him and Enyl. "Finding your Dar Eth is the reason we are negotiating, Enyl." Movement at the door to the balcony drew his attention and held it. *Maker.* "What...are you wearing?" he asked. His voice was coarse with unknown emotions roiling within him. His vision focused with all clarity on Caro. He refused to blink while he drank in the sight of her.

"Malo? I am in my armor, as usual," Enyl said.

"What?" Malo grimaced. Had he just asked his prince what he was wearing? He scowled. As operations commander, he never revealed his emotions. "My apologies, Enyl. Please, excuse me." He ended the call on his prince, yet another violation of protocol.

"Sorry to interrupt, Malo, but do you want to go to dinner, as well?" Caro nibbled on her *red* bottom lip, snagging his gaze before it returned to what she was wearing.

"No," he growled then cleared his throat. "I am not hungry." *For food.*

"Did you hear that, Izzy?" Caro raised her head to project her voice, exposing the curve of her throat to his avid perusal.

"Yup, thanks," Izzy sang.

"What language was that, Malo?" Caro faced him.

He wished she'd clothe herself. Whatever she wore defined her shape, so clear and irresistible. "Galactic. What are you wearing, Caro?"

She glanced at the black garment that hugged her curves like a ceremonial dress yet ended above her knees. Her feet were once more in raised footwear that tightened her calve muscles. Her arms were bare and pale against the black cloth. She'd lifted her hair off her shoulders and piled it high on her head with escaping strands falling around her face.

And her lips. He groaned at his malehood hardening. They were an unnatural red, calling his attention to the shape and plumpness of her mouth. Disarmed by her attire, he didn't know where to focus on the offering before him.

"It's a dress since we're going to a club." Her tentative smile drew his heated gaze.

She spun to leave him, and at the sight of her exposed back, his breath caught. His body broke out in a sweat, and he had to throw out a hand to support his weak knees. He drew in quick breaths. Shudders ripped through him, running along his hard length. He stumbled after her then drew to a halt.

Izzy came out of a room in a dark blue dress that made her skin appear translucent. She showed more of her breasts but less of her back and her footwear was a bright red.

"This is normal attire?" he asked, drawing in deep, silent breaths. He didn't need Caro to know how delectable he found her, nor that he ached to rip the dress off her body with a desperation that bordered on lethal.

"Ready?" Izzy question snapped Malo to the moment.

He'd been staring at Caro's lips, mesmerized. "You...cannot wear this." He approached her, his throbbing arousal almost hindering his ability to walk.

"Why? Does it look bad?"

Faced with her insecurities, her belief that she was unattractive, he was met with a decision. He could command her to change, and she would. But she'd believe it was because of her appearance and not for his sanity. Or he could endure seeing her as such and ensure she felt beautiful.

"Do I need new garments?" He was an Etterian male, a warrior in his own right. He could endure, for her. And a change of garments would delay their departure for at least a little while longer.

"No, the military uniform is a good look on you," she rasped while opening the front door, attempting to hide her appreciation from him.

He almost grinned, pleased that she liked his appearance. It wasn't something Etterian males placed much value on. A male's appearance was uncontrollable. His worth lay in his training.

"Alodon's balls," Ronin growled at the sight of them.

"I'll take that as a compliment," Izzy teased. "Believe it or not, this is conservative for where we're going."

"Females should not reveal themselves so," Garix muttered in Etterian. "I do not wish to kill this night." He too took the time to admire the curves on display. Both males glanced at Malo expectantly. What did they expect him to say or do?

"How would you like me to force them to change?" he asked in Etterian.

"I have never seen anything more beautiful." Ronin fell into step behind the two females with his gaze fixed on their swaying backsides.

"If any male dares to touch them..." Garix threatened an intergalactic incident.

Malo might instigate it himself. "Assessment?"

"The building is secure. Inquisitive neighbors, though." Garix pointed to a door behind them.

"Irritating," Ronin mumbled.

"Malo?" Caro frowned. She stepped to the side of the passage to let Garix pass. "Is something wrong?"

"It is your garments, *ensa*. Etterian males are not prepared to see such beauty nor your shapes so on display." Ronin grumbled at the half-truth Malo had concocted.

How else was he supposed to phrase it? That their garments enticed Etterian males to act on an emotional level? To succumb to a physical need? An Etterian male losing control was *never* a good thing.

"Taxi?" Izzy asked from upfront.

"Two please," Caro said, glancing down to hide her pink cheeks.

"You *are* beautiful, Caro," Malo said, and her blush spread.

It was as he'd assessed. He would continue to compliment her until she believed it. Grabbing her shoulders, he turned her to face the elevator door, then gave her a nudge. She strode ahead on her footwear, mesmerizing him with her ability to walk. He held back a moment to adjust his arousal and choose the lowest setting of his armor in the hopes of cooling his ardor. He doubted it was possible, but he could hope. As soon as the first ground-vehicle pulled up, Caro opened the door and gestured to Malo to slide in.

"You two go ahead. We'll catch the next one and meet you there," Izzy said, flagging down another taxi.

Caro joined Malo. After informing S.A.D.I. of their destination, she leaned back against the seat. She crossed her legs at the knees, the sight of her foot so close to him made him lose focus for a second.

"What can I expect?" he asked, his gaze riveted on the red color of her toenails. It was too bright to be natural but, Maker, if the sight of them didn't make his malehood twitch.

"Loud, smelly, vibrations." Excitement strained her voice. "If you need to say something to me, you have to yell it into my ear."

"And you like going to this place?" Malo blinked at her. *Loud, smelly? It sounded like the Yithian Arena.* If so, he could see the appeal.

"You will see." She patted his knee.

He flipped his hand to grab hers, lacing his fingers through hers.

She stared at their entwined hands and raised her gaze to meet his. "Is it my softness?"

He traced her skin with his thumb. She was lush, silky, sweet, tempting... No, it was many things.

"That makes you want to hold my hand? Garix and Ronin explained how your men are attracted to softness."

"Holding your hand is the least of what I want to do to you," Malo said, his gaze unwavering; his attention riveted on the play of color across her cheeks.

"There'll be women there..." *More attractive than her.* Her tacit words lingered. She believed them, and perhaps there were such females.

Never for me.

"You misunderstand me, Caro." He poured all his need for her in the gaze he leveled on her. "Etterian males, well, excluding the youngins, do not seek meaningless fulfillment. We mate with one female. It is for life."

"And humans are compatible with Etterians?" She nibbled on her bottom lip with her tiny white teeth, snagging his focus.

"Yes," he rasped, his breathing affected by her scent, touch, and bright-red lips. "There have been several Dar Eths found. You would call them soulmates." *I cannot tell her yet that she is mine. I am uncertain how she will react.* He grimaced. *I cannot lose her.*

"Soulmates?" She jerked back then chuckled. "You can't be serious?"

"I understand your disbelief, *ensa*, and in this I might have agreed. Some things are best experienced to be believed."

She patted his hand clasping hers. What that was meant to portray he didn't know. As soon as the taxi stopped, she paid S.A.D.I. before climbing out of the vehicle.

"Now we wait for Izzy." She crossed the road, opened a nondescript door, and sashayed down a narrow flight of stairs into a dank, dark underground warehouse. Then she fell into place at the end of a lengthy line of humans. A miasma of floral and fruit scents hit him, along with old urine. He grimaced.

His eyes widened at the unclothed females in the line with them. Some tunics revealed their nipples. They might as well have been wearing nothing. But none of what was on display affected him as much as the black dress Caro wore. He fixed his gaze on Caro to memorize the glow of her skin under the insipid light, the curve of her back as it disappeared into the black fabric hugging her backside, and her tiny feet in those remarkable footwear.

He kissed her neck, just where it met her shoulder. She gasped and shivered with tiny bumps forming on her skin.

"What is that scent, Caro?" He buried his face in the curve of her neck to inhale.

"My perfume."

"It is not as captivating as your natural scent," he said. "We have the ability to smell over great distances."

"I suspected as much," she said.

He raised his gaze to meet hers, reading acceptance in her eyes. Like a hunter, his vision narrowed, his senses focused. He wanted to—

"There you two are." Izzy rushed toward them. She took Caro's free hand and ushered her to the front of the line. "I found her, Max," she said to the bulky human male who guarded the door.

"Oh, sweet Caro." The human ran his gaze over the length of her. "Always a pleasure to see you, babe."

Malo tightened his hand around Caro's, the need to damage this male overwhelming. She pressed her back against his chest. Her touch calmed him. He released her to snake his arm around her waist, holding her closer, staking his claim so to speak. *Mine*, he ached to roar.

"Bodyguard?" Max gestured to Malo.

"No, though he might as well be. He guards my body quite nicely." Her suggestion took a path to Malo's balls.

He crushed her to him, letting her feel his arousal against her backside. Her breath hitched. She trembled, his Dar Eth. "*Those* are *his* bodyguards." She gestured to Ronin and Garix.

"Come now, Max. Caro's entertaining them for E.S.A." Izzy rubbed against the human male, who wrapped his arm across her shoulders in a too casual manner.

Garix rumbled in warning.

"To feel is to fail," Malo snapped under his breath. If his males lost control, it might trigger a primal response in him. "And be on your guard."

His males drew to attention, their training coming to bear.

The human male was saying, "—Babe and only because you're my favorite."

Izzy snorted and thumped him on the arm with her strange bag. "Damn right." She gave him a peck on his cheek, grabbed a glaring Garix and a stunned Ronin, and led them into the club.

As soon as the door opened, the stale air filled with a *thump-thump* that vibrated the walls. Malo lowered his hearing volume but still winced when he forced himself to follow Caro inside.

Chapter Eight

THE SOUND HIT HIM first, then the stench of sweat, perfume, and sex followed by vibrations. His first instinct was that he hated this place. The three of them stood on the top step and stared down two floors to the ground floor where bodies writhed like half-dead Gikas. Eyes, bare limbs, light glinting off unknown objects peered from the shifting shadows. Izzy ushered them to a table on the first floor that overlooked the ground floor. Padded chairs circled the table, but not on the side in front of the metal railing.

Izzy guided Garix into a chair then waved over a passing server, whose breasts might as well have been bare. Ronin gaped, scowled, then clenched his fingers around the railing. Malo was thankful he'd found his Dar Eth or he might have been as horrified and furious. With Caro here, he didn't see the other females. They ceased to exist.

"I ordered three beers for the boys and sodas for us," Izzy yelled.

Caro settled into a chair and tapped the one beside her. When Malo sat, she pressed against him to speak, brushing her lips across his ear. "You want to dance?"

His hearts fluttered, and he leaned to the side to focus on her mouth. He had no idea how to writhe like a half-dead anything and had no intention of trying either.

In response, he whispered, "I would prefer to observe."

Looping an arm around her waist, he drew her closer for what he longed to do. He nibbled on her earlobe, slipping his tongue into her the shell of her ear before kissing her neck. When her heartbeat fluttered against his lips, he pulled back.

Izzy jumped up and down. Her wild hair bounced around her face.

Despite her hooded gaze on his face, Caro rose to her feet. He took up sentry at the railing to stare at the floor of twitching and jerking bodies.

"Alodon's balls," Garix boomed. "I would have killed that Max-male."

Ronin scowled when another semi-clothed female sashayed past. Malo studied the bottom floor, searching for his Dar Eth. A female thrust an ice-cold glass bottle into his hand. He glanced at Garix and Ronin in query, but they watched the same female place two red canisters on the table. She winked at Ronin. Malo chuckled at his gaping males. Perhaps he should amend their training protocol to include such temptation?

He raised the bottle to his nose and sniffed. Izzy had ordered it, so it had to be good. He took a sip and rumbled his approval at the beverage's sharp bitterness. The alcohol tingled his tongue before it's affects fizzled. His focus shifted to the floor until he found Caro. The sight that met him had him gripping the bottle almost to breaking point.

She swirled her hips. Her splayed legs raised the dress to mid-thigh. From this height, he had a line of sight down the front, revealing soft curves meant only for his eyes. She moved like she was in the throes of fulfillment with her arms above her head. Her eyes were closed, her head thrown back, and her mouth parted as if she was breathless.

His malehood hardened to its full length, anticipating her tight sheath. With a growl, he lifted the bottle to his mouth to take a gulp, hoping to calm himself. He wanted to storm down and toss her over his shoulder, perhaps have her move like that just for him.

"Imagine if Etterians did that." With the same skill as a six-eyed Algri, Garix darted his gaze between random females. "There would be carnage."

"They are enjoying it, though." Ronin drained his beer before glancing at Malo. "If you need to port Caro, we will ensure Izzy is secure."

Malo grunted. With the way he was struggling, porting was fast becoming a viable option. The loudness changed as well as the vibrations, and both their females stopped writhing. Malo kept his gaze down, not wanting Caro to know he watched her every move. They were at the table in minutes, all laughter and excitement. The joy on her face was breathtaking.

"It's been ages since I've danced," she said, assumed a chair and opened the closest canister. She took a decent sip then smiled at Malo. "Do you want to try dancing?" she asked, eager to share this with him.

He grumbled at her. What he'd prefer to share with her was something a little more...horizontal.

"Caro, tell me, why does the female rub her backside against a male?" Garix pointed.

Izzy's brows rose. She giggled.

Ronin frowned. "Is it an act of mating?"

"Sort of. It's a way to show they're interested," Caro said.

"Interested?" Malo scowled. *Interested in what?* Even though he had a suspicion he knew what she meant, he needed her to verify it.

"In sex," Izzy said before sipping from her canister.

Fury pelted Malo's mind. He roared, "You brought me to a human mating ritual?" He clenched his fingers into fists and rose to throw her over his shoulder.

Caro's mouth parted forming an 'oh.' Her eyes had formed massive circles. He sighed, realizing she hadn't thought this experience would be offensive to him. He couldn't remain angry with her, after all, she knew less about him than he did about her. At least he had the data annals and Princess Oriana as guides. In addition, Caro hadn't truly wished to attend, had done so out of obligation, for Izzy. His gaze fell on the smaller female and frowned. *Why did Izzy want to endure this? What is her motivation behind this need?*

"Would you like to get some air?" Caro spoke into his ear to which he grunted

He followed her, giving his males a pointed look. If he didn't return, they were to see to Izzy. They tapped fists to their chests in confirmation, but by their tortured expressions, Malo didn't foresee them staying any longer than he planned to.

He scented the cleaner air before Caro pushed on the door, and the thumping quietened once the door closed behind them. A scan showed the narrow balcony empty. The view of the domed city and a cool breeze did little to calm him. When she gestured to a nearby bench, he ignored her. She winced and opened her mouth, no doubt to apologize, but he didn't give her a chance. No words could ease the agony he was in. He yanked her into his arms and crashed his lips over hers, swallowing her gasp.

MALO'S TONGUE DELVED IN, demanding, commanding, stripping Caro of her thoughts and inhibitions. With his arms wrapped around her, he lifted then crushed her against his chest, her feet dangling a foot off the floor. He didn't break contact, continued to ravage her mouth and senses. She sighed, melting into his hard edges with one thought remaining.

How can an alien kiss so well?

"Caro, *ensa*. I do not need you to inflame my need for you when I have such fragile control of it." His voice was guttural and smothered when he buried his face in the curve of her neck. Him rubbing his lips over her erratic pulse started a tumble and eruption of butterflies in her core.

"I...I'm sorry, Malo, this is normal...," she stammered, a little lost at the intensity in his voice. *His control is fragile? His need for me?* Her heart leaped into her throat. Granny's nipples, he was potent, yet for a man to need her so much that she rattled him...

"If a human male had touched you, he would have died this night."

She gaped at his lethal promise. Her anger kindled and burst into a blaze at his domineering manner. *Did he say he'd kill a man?*

"Put me down," she snapped, and he obeyed. Air cooled her cheeks, but it was too little too late. "You can't just decide I'm yours, Malo." She gripped her hip and waved a finger at him. That alone made his lips curl into a sweet smile. She shouldn't be waving her finger in the face of an alien. All right, he had a right to laugh at her. "What am I, the first human woman you've met? I don't sleep around with my kind, what makes you think I'll sleep with you?"

"I plan to do more than sleep, Caro." He chuckled, his arrogance breathtaking. His huge *two*-dimpled smile—despite usually exploding butterflies in her core—now infuriated her.

She stomped her foot. "See. There you go planning on doing things without my input."

"You do not want to be with me?" he teased, grasping her waist to tug her closer.

She let him. *Of course, I did. He's Malo.* "Not when you're so highhanded," she harrumphed, realizing by his smirk, he found her attitude adorable.

"Caro, my *ensa*, I scent your arousal." He drew in a deep breath, flaring his nostrils. "I have never scented anything so intoxicating."

Mortification was swift to strike. Her body had betrayed her, yet part of her was amazed at his preternatural senses. He'd said he could smell across great distances, but she hadn't known he could identify her desire. Ice replaced heat tingling down her spine when she realized he'd been *smelling* her since they met.

"Damned alien," she muttered but allowed him to pin her against him again. She raised her hands to splay over his chest despite his laughter.

"I did not know humans had mating rituals." He stroked her bare arm, his fingers too close to the swell of her breast. She ached, throbbed, tingled, desperate for his touch.

"What?" she said a little distracted. "We don't."

He stiffened. "Then what were your humans doing inside?"

She groaned. Coming here had been a bad idea. When on a dance floor, her inner slut resurrected all the dance trends and turned them into sex-cyborg advertisements. Men who'd ignored her at the bar would then hit on her. All the time and without fail. Izzy teased her about her *moves*.

What could she tell Malo in a way he'd understand? "Most are looking for sex." She gritted her teeth, waiting for him to lose his shit. This was so going to get her fired.

His expression darkened, and his lips clenched together. Those lingering shadows thickened, reminding her she knew nothing about him or his species. "Are you seeking meaningless...?" His voice had hardened, become guttural and a little scary.

"No, I like to dance. Just dance. To lose myself to the beat pounding through me." She grabbed his arm, trying to convey her sincerity.

"You will not incite another male. You dance only for me," he said.

Huh? She blinked. It took a moment for his roared words to make sense. *Like he owns me? Commands my every move? What am I, his possession?* "What I was doing wasn't provocative," she hissed then did the stupidest thing. She plastered her body to his, to grind all over him in a seductive swirl. His breath hitched. Only then did she step back despite a deep yearning to melt into him. "That's inciting."

He vibrated with restrained power like a predator preparing to pounce. A chill in the air coated them. A stillness settled as if the city's vermin—animal and human—knew to remain hidden and silent against such a threat. Her acquiescence came too late. His fists clenched at his sides, his gaze intensifying with heat and shadow. He took a step toward her. She shuffled back, her feet carrying her away from his threatening scowl. Flinging out her hands as if to keep him back did nothing. Only when her backside hit the brick wall, did she realize she was in trouble.

He grabbed her wrists with one hand and lifted them above her head, forcing her to arch. He did so with little effort. Her breasts thrust at him like an offering. He glided his free hand down from her shoulder, over the side of a breast, and under it to cup it, testing its weight in his large hand. She gasped at his touch, and when he flicked a thumb over a taut nipple, a moan ripped from her. He toyed with her nipple with a gentleness that had her squirming. He pinched and tugged on it, flicked it until she writhed before him. His ragged breathing didn't deter him, despite the lust that hardened his features. He slid his hand down her bare back to disappear into the dress.

He shuddered. His reaction vibrated against her skin. She squeezed her eyes shut at what he'd discovered. She couldn't wear anything but a G-string with this dress dropping so low in the back.

His hands had encountered bare skin. He grabbed her backside, digging his fingers in convulsively, confirming her assumption. His coarse palms sent a fiery dart of need into the depths of her.

"Caro...your undergarments are...," he growled into her neck.

"It's there, just small," she said.

His hot breath on her skin made her shiver. "Give them to me," he said.

"What?" she rasped. Had she heard him correctly? Lust must have clouded her mind, distorted his words.

"Give me your undergarment, Caro," he gritted out.

"Why? I'll be naked under—"

"Fitting punishment for dressing so provocatively." He dug his fingers into her butt cheeks, massaging until bolts of liquid desire consumed her and weakened her knees.

She struggled to think past the need bombarding her. "That makes no sense, and if you're not understanding me, the answer's no."

At her defiance, he stroked across her backside, searching until he found the thinnest of bands. With a sharp yank, it tore. She struggled between disbelief and anger. *How dare he?* She drew in a deep breath to chastise him.

But before a reprimand could leave her mouth, he drew back and slipped his hand up the front of her dress, caressing her bare thigh, to run a finger along her seam. His touched burned her through the thin fabric of the G-string hanging on by a thread. She whimpered as a shiver of pleasure rippled outward. All thoughts of a reprimand skittered out of her mind.

MALO GROWLED WHEN WET heat drenched his fingertip. As if madness drove him, he dipped under the thin fabric, brushing across the silky hair to slip into her folds.

"You are ready for me, Caro." His voice was no longer his to regulate. When he touched her hard nub, she arched, and the most exquisite sound emanated from the back of her throat—a throaty purr.

"Malo," she moaned, beading sweat on his temple with the effort it took not to lift her garment to taste her.

"We need to leave. Now," he growled. "If we stay, I *will* claim you against this wall no matter who sees. And if we go home, I will take you on your bed..." He shuddered.

"All right." When she straightened her garment, he gave her undergarment one tug, yanking it free.

She gasped, but by then, he'd crumpled and shoved it into a pocket. He laced his fingers through hers and ushered her through the door to where Garix and Ronin waited.

"Keep Izzy secure," he commanded in Etterian, then dragged Caro past them and out the main door. As soon as they stepped outside, he shot Max such a glare, the male didn't say a word. "Where to, Caro?" He prayed to the Maker that she chose her bed.

She gestured to the corner where the aroma of coffee tantalized Malo's nose. "Coffee?"

At her choice, he wanted to roar his frustration. He stilled, studied her upturned face and the rise and fall of her breasts. If she lay naked before him, his 'eagerness' might harm her. Trying her Earthian beverage would calm him, and perhaps, this night, he would regain his control enough to find himself between her thighs.

With a firm grip on her elbow, he escorted her there, his stride long, angry until her breathlessness penetrated his fury. He slowed his steps, having forgotten she wore the ridiculous footwear that made him think lustful thoughts. Why they did so, he didn't know. There were many things he didn't know—a circumstance he abhorred. When he approached the glass door, it opened. He paused to allow two human males to pass. Instead, one drew to a halt to stare at Caro. The urge to hit him ripped through Malo, calling forth a frown at his volatile emotions and marked lack of control.

"Caro?"

So, this human male knew his *ensa*? Malo glanced at her then smiled at her lip curling with derision. She knew the male but detested him.

"Gary." And the way she spat his name revealed exactly how deep her opinion went. "How...how are you?"

His *ensa* followed human protocol even though she inched toward the coffee stall.

"I'm well but look at you. You're gorgeous."

When the male ogled his *ensa*, Malo's anger rose, fresh, bold, and potent.

The male smirked. "Nice shoes."

"Thank you. It was great seeing you." She tried to move past him.

He grabbed her hand to stop her, glancing between her and Malo in the process. "Lose the soldier, babe, and come home with me."

She froze, spun on a heel and faced the male. "Are you insane?"

She shook off his hand but tightened her hold on Malo's. She pulled him with her, tucking his hand between her breasts and forcing him to hug her from behind. He looped an arm around her, drawing her snug against him.

"Look at him, Gary. How on God's soil could you tempt me away from him? If I remember correctly, you overestimated your skills anyway." With this, she turned as if to enter the stall, not taking the time to admire the angry flush that mottled the male's face.

"She speaks for you, big boy?" he asked Malo, his sneer most unpleasant.

"I can kill you with impunity. Since my Caro is with me, I will not." Malo called forth his skills, making himself appear taller, bigger, stronger...lethal. "However, I could break a few bones if you insist?" And the expression he chose was one of eagerness which merged into a hopeful smirk. He wanted this silly male to test him, test his words.

"She's all yours. She isn't worth it anyway."

Malo punched him, relishing the snap of the male's nose breaking with a satisfaction that was exhilarating. And for someone as puny as this human, the smallest amount of pain Malo could inflict would feel like torture.

"It is you who does not deserve her." His voice was low, menacing when he glanced between Gary and the male with him. Said male held up his hands in what Malo assumed was a passive gesture. He nodded before following Caro, urging her stiff body into the warm and coffee-scented stall.

"Did you just...defend my honor?" she asked a few minutes later with a cup of coffee in her hands. He'd ordered it for her when she'd gaped at the waitress, her eyes glazed with her lips curling yet not breaking into a full smile.

"And it felt good." Malo grinned—the joy easy to convey.

Her eyes widened. "It did?"

"He taught you that you are not worthy, not desirable."

"He did?" she squeaked, but her gaze lowering proved Malo's assessment true.

"Caro," he whispered then captured her chin for a gentle pinch, forcing her to meet his gaze. "He is not an honorable male. Do not take his unkind and thoughtless words to heart. You are the most beautiful female I know." Malo grinned. "Had you not been here, I would have done worse to him."

"What?" She giggled. "I wouldn't have stopped you. It felt good watching you punch his egotistical ass."

"I see my *ensa* is a little bloodthirsty," Malo teased then lifted his cup to his lips and admired her flushed face over the rim. "I approve." He savored the heated beverage's bitterness. She'd sweetened and whitened hers.

"So, why are you here? On Earth?" she asked, and her expression said she expected an honest answer. He was proud of her frankness, but not when she was using the question to divert the conversation away from Gary.

"If I told you, you would disbelieve my word and mock my belief."

She winced as if he'd slapped her, then nodded as if she agreed with his assessment. "Would you tell me if I promise not to judge?"

He chuckled. "Caro, *ensa*, you cannot hide your reactions from me. I see you, the Caroline you hide."

She gasped and sat back, her alarm clear. "You want me anyway?"

"I will always want you. Nothing you say or do will ever change that."

"Malo." She breathed his name, her alarm rising. Her posture tensed, and she wrapped her arms around her waist.

"What concerns you, Caro? The truth? Me? How I make you feel or talk of forever?"

"Can I say all of those?" She flashed him a cheeky grin, hitching his breath.

Yes, this is my Caro—sweet, charming, teasing.

"Do you not understand, *ensa*?" he whispered, the urgency no less intense. "I have found you, and nothing else matters. I have spent my life believing Etteria is everything. It is not. You are."

She stiffened. Yet he couldn't regret his words. He hadn't told her that without her, he'd die a lonely death. To allow that to occur to an Etterian male was unforgivable. It need not be his fate. For regardless of her choice, he'd forever be hers. No other female existed for him. He *would* succumb to the dark void. Memories of her would be insufficient to save him. Added to the longing and the loneliness would be the loss of her. Without her constant presence, the scent, feel, and taste of her, the void's influence would rapidly conquer his soul.

He'd stared at her for a while. Yet her eyes reflected a turmoil that pulled at his hearts.

"I'm scared, Malo," she said in her sweet voice. He smiled, proud of the courage she displayed. "Humans don't commit easily, not after only knowing each other for a day." When she raised the cup to her lips, her fingers trembled. "Can I have time to think about it?"

He couldn't smother the grimace, despite his legendary skills. She could have a day. *Maker*. A thousand, but it mattered not when he needed her. The bastard he was would kidnap her, regardless of her decision. He couldn't leave her behind.

Her gaze traveled his face as she used that mind of hers. He could only imagine what internal debate she was having.

Then she asked the correct question "What happens if I say no?"

The grin that spread across his lips warmed like a supernova and was beyond his control. He was so pleased with her, his intelligent Caro. "Do you truly wish to know, my *ensa*? It is not pleasant."

Her tempting mouth parted.

Good. She understands. He released a deep sigh of relief. There were a few more things he had to tell her, but his possible death had been one of his critical points.

She needed to know that the Ethera would cause her to become addicted to him. They hadn't known what the Ethera would do to humans, but the few who had become Dar Eths had admitted to forming an addiction to their Eths. It was something he was looking forward to since his addiction to her was complete.

When he left Earth, she had to travel with him. Unless she remained, then he would also. Separation was impossible. He wouldn't stand for it.

They'd been united by Etterian law the moment the Ethera burned through him. Humans called it marriage, yet it wasn't the same thing. A union between a Dar Eth and an Eth couldn't be abolished, not even by the king.

Caro was his wife.

"You die?" she asked, drawing him back to her, to the warmth of the coffee stall, to the cup in his hands.

Here was not the place to have this discussion. He wanted her alone, focused solely on him.

"Come, let us return to your home. I grow weary." He rose from the table.

Her eyes widened. "But, Malo...?"

"The details are best revealed when we have both rested." He flicked his fingers expectantly.

She pushed off the table with a sigh then hurried to pay for their coffees. When she returned to his side, he grasped her hand and led her out of the stall.

Chapter Nine

On the ride to the apartment, despite the tension thrumming between them, his Caro couldn't smother her yawns. He'd wanted to claim her, to appease the Ethera, and now, he had to wait, to put her needs first. Her falling asleep on his shoulder in the car had validated his decision.

She'd ignored his urgings to go to the air-bed, instead, she'd remade her bed with fresh linen and in a color he wasn't used to seeing—purple. He frowned at the lost opportunity—her scent would've permeated her pillow and bedding. Yet she'd insisted it was done so... Protocol. Then she'd grabbed a white garment and rushed out of the room with a sweet farewell.

He sat on her bed, bouncing to test it. Scowling at the dismal end to the evening, he removed his boots and chest armor. But hesitated at his pants. They irritated his hyper-sensitive skin, but without sleeping pants, he would be naked with one less barrier between him and Caro. He chose to keep it on, for sanity's sake. When he lay back on her bed, tucking his hand behind his head, her scent engulfed him. He beamed while drawing in deep inhales. Warmth unfurled in his chest, sweet and intoxicating.

Her home was quiet after she'd cleansed, with only her sighs when she drifted off to sleep.

His males and Izzy hadn't returned yet, not that it concerned Malo. He trusted them. They were good Etterian warriors. Even Ronin had improved under Malo's guidance, and it had been but a few months. After a year, Ronin would be a different male, with the right to be called an elite warrior.

Sleep was elusive. Energy pulsed through Malo, twitching his limbs. With his Dar Eth on the balcony, it was to be expected.

With a grunt, he swung his legs off the side of the bed and went in search of her. She sprawled on the air-filled bed. She was as clear as if she was in sunlight. He planned to observe her only, to allow the gratitude, pleasure, affection, and yearning to flow through him unrestrained. Instead, he kneeled next to her strange bed and stroked her exposed ankle. Even her skin there was soft.

She'd covered herself with a blanket that scented of Izzy. Her dark hair spread across the white pillow. And in the moonlight painting her pale skin silver, he memorized her face. She appeared so innocent and trusting.

He slid a hand up her calve, marveling at her silky skin. A quick stroke of her knee preceded a caress along her thigh. He nudged the blanket aside, venturing his hand higher.

She sighed in her sleep. Her scent darkened. He parted his lips to release a breathless moan. She couldn't awaken and find him touching her. It might jeopardize their tremulous relationship. Yet he couldn't bring himself to remove his hand. Her skin was so warm. *Maker.* How was a male supposed to resist such temptation?

Footsteps snapped his gaze up. He paused to listen. This planet was in a constant state of activity and sound. He'd lowered his sensitivity to sleep. Due to the proximity, Izzy's small steps in her red footwear reached him. He glanced to where his fingers rested on Caro's thigh. He lifted it to hover an inch above her skin. Flexing his fingers, he fought the compulsion before he removed his hand completely.

He rose to his feet and strode toward the front door. It opened with Garix entering first to verify the room was secure.

"Operations Commander," Garix said, striding farther into the room.

Izzy snuck in behind him, more subdued than Malo had ever seen her.

"Hi, Malo, is she sleeping?" she asked while kicking off her footwear. She didn't wait for his response but disappeared into her room. "Just let me change, Ronin, then my bed's all yours."

"We didn't stay long after you left," Ronin said to Malo when Izzy closed her bedroom door.

"I never wish to attend such a place again. It was horrifying." Garix opened the cold box's door. He pulled out a stick of meat which he ripped open and consumed as if it were a protein bar.

"Agreed." Ronin grabbed a fruit off the counter and bit off half of it.

"What is planned for tomorrow?" Garix asked, sinking into the red padded bench.

"We will return to Caro's work. I hope to meet with Joshua Guardian."

"Good. I wish to return to the *Gladio* soonest," Ronin said.

"You do not like Earth?" Garix asked around a mouthful of meat.

"It is filled with temptation. We should train our warriors here and not on Gikaet. If they can survive an evening at a club, then they are warrior enough for any challenge." Ronin chose another fruit. Something yellow which he bit into then spat out with a grimace.

"You were tempted?" Malo frowned. He hadn't been, not now when he'd found his Dar Eth. "Port to the *Gladio*, and send Trav as your replacement."

Ronin tossed the mangled fruit. "Tomorrow, Operations Commander, if I may. I am exhausted, and Izzy's bed does look inviting."

Malo grunted. "What did you do after you left?"

"We had coffee at the stall across the street," Garix muttered.

"And encountered your handywork." Ronin washed his hands, then faced Malo. "A male complained to a law enforcement officer about a soldier who punched him in the face for no apparent reason."

"Oh, the reason was apparent, I assure you." Malo grinned, pleased to relive that event. "I enjoyed punching him."

"He insulted Caro?" Ronin arched a brow.

"Apparent reason to me," Garix said around his meat bar.

Malo forced his legs to carry him to Caro's bedroom. He'd have preferred to scoop her in his arms and take her with him, to curl his body around hers, to share his warmth with her. When he closed the strange door, he stared at it for a moment. It swung in or out, taking unnecessary space, unlike their efficient doors sliding out of sight when not needed. This swinging had to be a hazard of some sort.

Sighing, he lowered himself onto her bed and folded an arm behind his head. Wondering how he'd survive the night, he stared at the white ceiling, willing his eyes to close and sleep to claim him. He needed her. Tugging the pillow from beneath him, he smashed it to his face, drawing in a deep breath. It was an insufficient substitute. With a bright grin, he dug into his discarded chest armor and removed her undergarment. He hooked his fingers around the thin straps and stretched the tiny piece of black fabric. It was silky, but not like her skin. He held it to his nose and inhaled. Her scent clung to the fabric—potent, rich, and bewitching. With a low groan followed by the desperate and demanding throb of his arousal, he draped the undergarment over his mouth and nose.

Yes, better.

MALO AWOKE WITH A start in a softer-than-usual environment, pale yellow sunlight pouring through a window. His feet hung off a dark purple bed, and when he inhaled, he grinned, remembering. He was in *her* bed, *her* scent overcame him, and he reveled in it. *Caroline. My Dar Eth. My complete opposite. She is kind, sweet, considerate, and mine.* He stretched, before flopping onto her bed to bury his face in her pillow. *Alodon's hell. I am behaving like an idiot.* But the permanent grin wouldn't go away. Tapping either side of him, he searched for her undergarment, found it, and swapped it with the pillow. He held the delicate black fabric to his nose for a deep inhale. Her scent had faded a little. A knock made him sit up and shift his backside to the edge of the bed. He almost laughed at his reaction as if Remi, their base commander on Gikaet, had caught him sniffing Caro's undergarment.

"Malo? Are you awake yet?" Caro's voice was the best first thing to hear in the mornings.

"Yes, *ensa*. I am awake." *And so is my malehood.* He grunted. Time to take care of the chore.

"May I come in? You have all my clothes. Oh, and I brought you coffee."

"You may enter." He smiled while shoving her undergarment into his pants pocket. She'd brought a peace offering as if to barter for entry? The silly female...woman had no idea how precious she was.

The door opened, and she stood in the doorway. The sight of her he vowed to remember until the end of his days. Her brown hair cascaded around her in wild abandonment, sleep had flushed her face, and her large tunic stopped at mid-thigh. Her gorgeous legs were bare and breathtaking, even more beautiful than last night. He stared at her tiny feet when she came closer, her toenails a bright red. When he dragged his gaze upward, his focus snagged on her tiny pink tongue pressed against her red top lip while she concentrated on not spilling a drop.

"I made it black. It's always easier to add milk and sugar than to remove it." After placing the cup on the bedside table, she peeked at him, but her gaze strayed to his bare chest. "Sorry." She dipped her chin. "I'm not used to seeing a man so..." She dashed to her closet and grabbed garments at random. With her arms full, she buried her face in the bundle and mumbled, "If you need help with the shower, um..."

"Caro." He chuckled and stopped her from escaping by taking the bundle from her and dumping it on her bed. "Come here," he whispered, holding out a hand while admiring her flushed face and alluring innocence.

"Why?" she asked, her eyes large.

"Have faith in me."

She nodded and let him tug her toward him. A sharp burst of joy warmed his chest at her immediate trust. He placed her hands on his chest, palms down. She jerked back and snatched them away. With unexpected patience, he collected her hands again and held them over his hearts.

"Be calm. It is just my chest."

When her hands remained in place, he slipped his arms around her, pulling her closer and more securely against him. He spread his fingers across her lower back. Thoughts of stroking her back, maybe peeling her tunic up at the same time tormented him. The desire to touch her bare skin was a craving almost unbearable.

"It's beautiful, Malo." She stroked his chest, indents, and angles. "Do you always burn this hot?" Her fingers traveled his contoured stomach, and he let her. Her touch was an exquisite torture, but it was a painful pleasure he'd willingly endure.

"I am a few degrees hotter than normal..." *Because of your touch, presence, and scent, my Dar Eth.* His eyes stuttered closed when she brushed over a nipple, hitching his breath.

"I liked that," he mumbled and opened his eyes to gaze upon her, willing her to see just how much.

Her fingers trembled, and she panted as if breathless. He smiled, enjoying the stutter of her heartbeat.

She appeared a little dazed, mesmerized while gazing at him. "You have beautiful eyes, Malo." She gasped. "Holy noodle, did I say that aloud?" She lowered her chin, no doubt trying to hide the beautiful pink on her cheeks.

"Sorry to interrupt, but when you guys are done doing whatever you're doing, wanna go out for breakfast? I think Ronin's finally awake, and Garix keeps mumbling," Izzy called from their seating area.

Malo couldn't help but chuckle. Garix was speaking to Ronin, just too low for Izzy to understand the words.

Caro groaned and rested her forehead on Malo's chest, unwittingly snuggling closer. He tightened his arms around her, wishing he could press her curves to his angles in such a way that no weapon nor toxin could separate them.

"I'm sorry about Izzy." Her warm breath across his skin made him shiver and hardened his nipples in unabashed arousal.

"I heard that," Izzy snapped.

Laughing, he tipped Caro backward, catching her with a splayed hand between her shoulder blades. He slashed his mouth across her parted lips, delving in to taste her. "I cannot stop kissing you," he growled into her mouth.

"I don't mind, to be honest. Even when you're angry with me..." She squeezed his shoulders where she clung to him.

Last night, he'd pinned her to a wall and could've claimed her there. To do that to a female as a youngin may be acceptable, but not to his Dar Eth. She required, no, deserved better control from him.

"Now, show me how to work your cleanser," he said, steadying her on her feet before giving her a gentle push.

She entered her cleansing room and paused. When he hovered behind her, he realized why she frowned. There was no way he'd fit. He doubted he'd even get through the cleanser's door.

"Um, Malo? Perhaps you need to shower on your battleship?" She gestured to the size of him. It was unnecessary, he knew his dimensions.

"Garix, Ronin, cleanse on the *Gladio*," he said.

"Acknowledged, Operations Commander," Garix said.

"Afax," Malo spoke to his wrist.

"Yes, Engineer Malo," Pilot Afax said.

Malo managed to smother a smile. Afax was always on point even when Caro couldn't possibly understand him either.

"Two to port to my quarters." Malo looped an arm around Caro's waist.

He claimed her mouth, thinking to distract her from her first porting. Yet the kiss *wasn't* just for that reason. He craved the taste of her. Groaning, he cupped her cheeks and lost himself in her whimpers and swirling tongue. This, with her, was his heaven.

"Welcome to my battleship, *Gladio*," he said into her mouth before nibbling on her bottom lip.

She blinked her dark blue eyes, a little dazed from his kiss. He liked her so.

"Welcome to your...what?" She dragged her gaze away from his then squeaked. She threw her arms around his waist in a death grip as if gravity would drag her down to Earth.

He shuddered at her pressed so against him, her softness engulfing him. "This is my quarters." He gestured to the gray room, ignoring the rough quality of his voice. It was beyond his control. "I invite you to use *my* cleansing room, Caro," he said, trying not to imagine her pinned to the white bulkhead while water poured off them with his face buried in her feminine folds. *Alodon's balls.* Too late.

He removed her arms to lace his fingers through hers, then ushered her to the cleansing room. The door glided opened when he neared.

"It's huge." Still clasping his hand, she ventured into a room the size of her bedroom. Compared to her cleansing room, there was a bowl and waste receptacle, and his cleanser didn't have glass panels.

"Standing here will activate the water at a temperature three degrees warmer than your core. The soap is in the water. It cleanses your body, hair, and mouth. It has no taste and scent. When done, leave and the water will deactivate. Press the blue button to dry and the gray button for a wrap."

"What'll you be doing while I shower? You won't leave me, will you?" Her eyes were large.

"I will wait here in this comfy. I too wish to cleanse." He smiled at her with a tenderness that amazed him.

As Head of Operations, smiling in a gentle manner wasn't one of his skills. He'd never had a reason to learn it, but under the right circumstances, it came naturally. Allowing the door to close between them, he retreated to settle into a comfy like he'd vowed. Because he was a bastard, he commanded the bulkhead, "Opacity, half-mirror."

The gray tinted, revealing Caro whipping off her tunic. Fire coursed through his body. She was naked beneath it. The heart-shaped curve of her backside, the indent of her waist, the flare of her hips down to her smooth thighs and calves to her tiny feet... *Maker.* Then she stepped under the cleanser, giving him a profile of her.

And involuntary groan escaped him. His enhanced vision focused on the curve of her breasts where the water rivulets caressed her nipples. He adjusted his military pants around his arousal, not that it eased the throbbing.

"Opacity, normal," he said, cursing his stupidity.

He shouldn't have done that. It was a violation of her trust. That was the least of his concerns. Though he was supposed to be honorable as an Etterian male, honor had been drilled out of him. It wasn't honorable to deceive, to torture, but it was a needed skill when war was on the horizon. And even though Etteria had been peaceful for a few hundred years, that didn't mean they couldn't prepare for war. They were a warrior race, of course they planned for it.

What made him angry was that he tempted himself needlessly. He wouldn't be claiming her soon. She had to come to him willing and needing him as much as he yearned for her. The kisses and touches he'd stolen within the last day had been risky. She might think he was rushing her, his one goal to have her beneath him. He'd tried to convey that Etterians weren't built for meaningless fulfillments, had hoped she'd understood when he'd said they mated for life.

The air-dryer activated. He gripped the arms of his comfy, fighting the urge to command the bulkheads again. Squeezing his eyes shut, he focused his breathing, ordered himself to calm, to gain control. He'd never once imagined the true test of his strength would be a tiny, beautiful creature from a mid-grade planet.

"All yours." Her fingers trailed over the grooved edges of the door's frame, the touch almost seductive in his current state.

"Thank you." The words tore through his vocal cords.

"Malo?" she asked, a delicate frown forming on her brow.

He did appreciate that her concern was for him, he just couldn't bare her touching him at that moment. When she closed the distance between them, he bolted.

Chapter Ten

"I am well, Caro. Only..." Malo dodged past and closed the door on Caro.

What was that all about? She shrugged and sank into a comfy then lunged out of it. A squeal lodged in her throat when it had cupped her backside like a horny old man.

Not willing to chance it again, she meandered around his quarters, finding nothing of a personal nature. Did he have a family? Friends? A wife or lover? She didn't like the last two but doubted he had either. She couldn't see him kissing her if he had a soulmate.

Soulmate? Her heart leaped at that thought. Sure, only one person as the other half of her soul? She didn't believe in that nonsense for one important reason. What if it was true? Then no man she married would be good enough. After every argument, insult, or neglect, she'd always wonder if she'd chosen the right man. There were so many scenarios of what-if-she-had-a-soulmate. It was insane to put that kind of pressure on a relationship or marriage. But Malo believed it.

Perhaps it was different for aliens? Humans tended to be fickle. They'd dismiss any tangible evidence as a hoax or coincidence.

Then how could she ignore how much she liked him and that her affection for him had grown so fast? After one day, she was ready to hump his leg. She was a bad human representative. He must think all human *females* would do him. Guilt burned her cheeks. Sure, she dreamed of doing him. Hoped to. She brushed her fingers over strange glass surfaces in his 'kitchen.'

The bathroom door opened, and Malo stepped out in a matching wrap. A deep V exposed glorious abs, bulging pecs, and sinfully delicious bronzed skin. *Yes. All females would do him. Hot jam and buttered toast, he's the sexiest man I've ever met.* She could be forgiven for succumbing to the temptation that was all of...him.

"Now what?" she rasped then cleared her throat.

"If I had my way, you would be beneath me, and I would be buried in your softness," he growled.

She gasped at his bluntness, despite the heat on her cheeks spreading. If he could be bold, so could she, right? "What if I said...yes, please?" She raised her gaze to meet his while fanning herself.

"Caro, no meaningless fulfillment. If you give yourself to me, you *are* mine." His voice was steady and firm, but his body was taut, his hands curled into fists.

"Holy noodle, Malo, what does that even mean?" She threw her hands into the air. "Am I like your concubine to travel the stars with you until you discard me on some penal planet? Does that mean I'm yours for now, for forever, or for a set period?"

"It means forever, as my life force and the mother of my *damu*," he said, his gaze unflinching.

Damu? As in children? She gaped. Sure, she'd thought of marrying him but when confronted with the reality... She shivered and folded her arms around her waist. "After one day?"

"As all Etterians do, I knew the moment I saw you," he said.

She stilled. His words were a revelation. *He knew when he met me?* When he glanced at the distance between them, she realized he wished he could cross it. Yet he hesitated to do so. His wariness confused her. *Does he want me or not?* She studied him, his eyes, the fleeting expressions. He did want her. He'd *told* her numerous times. Yet he didn't want to rush her. *What does it matter if he calls me soulmate and I call him husband? Was it simply a terminology difference?*

"Come, *ensa*, let us return to your Izzy."

"But Malo...you need clothes." Her gaze roamed over the length of him.

He groaned then stomped toward her as if she'd asked him to eat his Brussel sprouts. When he drew to a halt beside her, he gripped the counter with enough force to dent the surface. He punched in commands on the glass, and his military uniform appeared. With a cry, she brushed the glass. She almost laughed at her reaction. A science so fantastical, it appeared as magic?

"What's this? What happened?" She stabbed at the glass surface like he had. The screen flickered with strange hieroglyphics. His language? Her mind reeled. Teleporting? Replicators? Holy noodles, she was inside an ancient movie. Faced with his weirdness, his strength, potency, handsomeness glossed over that he wasn't of earth. But this? She brushed her fingers over his bare forearm, marveling at his smooth and shimmering skin.

He captured her fingers and held them to his lips. His breath burned her, sending tingles to her elbow. "Caro," he whispered. "There is much in my world I will need to teach you."

He took the bundle and disappeared into the bathroom.

She pressed more buttons, no doubt accidentally ordering an explosive device. That thought froze her fingers, and she snapped them back. Best to wait until he explained.

Within minutes, he strode toward her, once again in his full military armor. She sighed, refusing to blink. He was gorgeous, but not as sinful had he been naked and leaning over her. But like he said, she needed to be sure she wanted him for...forever. *Granny's nipples, to decide on forever after one day together? He'd known when I stood there drooling over him? How insane is that? Wait till I tell Izzy. She'll pee herself.*

He looped an arm around her, pulling her against his hard body. His ice blue gaze met hers with a level of intensity that snatched her breath. He didn't blink or glance away when he spoke into his wrist.

"Holy shit," Izzy squealed. "You can't go around evaporating, then bam, coming back. Give a girl a warning, please."

A shiver rippled down Caro's spine. Teleportation was far beyond Earth's technology and here she'd twice been molecularly dismantled and rebuilt. Caro forced a chuckle and disappeared into her room to don her usual office attire—pencil skirt meets shirt. Today was the dark blue skirt with a pale pink button-up shirt. She dressed as fast as she could, her knee twitching and her thoughts on Malo in the kitchen. Everything within her compelled her to join him, to languor in his presence. Her heart fluttered and sparked another wave of butterflies lower in her core.

Holy noodle, am I thinking forever as a definite possibility? Or is this just lust? Love can't blossom this quickly, can it?

While glancing at herself in the mirror on the back of her bedroom door, she tugged on her stilettoes—wincing when her toes complained. She grabbed the brush off the chest of draws and ran it through her hair. Another glance at her reflection summoned a muttered curse. Her red lips were like sirens luring sailors to their doom. *Monkey's bananas, I can't even lure a dead cat with a leash attached.* She grabbed the citrus oil and scrubbed the lipstick off. *Noodles, the citrus and my perfume clash. Is there time for another shower?*

"Izzy, sweetheart, could you come here for a sec?" Caro called, desperate to talk to her friend. She needed guidance, ASAP.

"What is it?" Izzy opened the door a crack to peek at her.

"I need your help." Caro gestured with her head to the bathroom.

Izzy entered the room, closed the door behind her then tip-toed into the bathroom. Caro snapped the door shut, then ran the basin's taps at maximum.

"I need to talk to you," she whispered.

Izzy smirked. "I can see that."

"They have excellent hearing." Caro ushered Izzy onto the closed toilet, only to pace in the tight confines. "Firstly, they believe in soulmates. They call them Dar Eths."

"What?" Izzy squeaked. "For real for real?" She giggled, clasping her hands together. "That's awesome."

"Yes and no," Caro said.

Izzy gaped. "Malo's yours?"

"According to him." Inevitability settled on Caro's soul.

Izzy's eyes widened and she mumbled, "Hot jam and buttered toast."

"He's given me time to think about it."

"What? Why? What's there to think about?" Izzy stilled. "Are you insane? You snatch that man up this instant, Caro. He's the best thing that's ever happened to you."

Caro waved her hands, trying to get Izzy to calm and lower her voice. "It's not that easy." She snuck glances at the door, half expecting Malo to appear.

"Babe, I know you're scared, I see that, but to not grasp this opportunity for happily-ever-after? Then you take one for the team. You do this for all women on this planet who would snap him up on his offer in a heartbeat."

Lose him to someone else? No, he'd said one female ever. "I would love forever with him, Izzy." *There*. She'd admitted it.

"Do you think I could have a soulmate?" Izzy raised her big gray eyes, hope shining through.

Caro grinned. "You want one?"

"Hell, yes. To be loved forever, to be treated as if I matter?" Izzy tilted her head to the side on a sigh.

"Malo said he knew the moment he met me. Since Garix and Ronin remain protective and haven't tried to kiss you, I would say neither of them is your soulmate."

"Right, so I just have to find my alien." Izzy rolled her eyes. "Not daunting at all."

Warmth, exploding butterflies, delicious aches, and intense need swelled within Caro. "I can't believe I'm considering this."

"If you don't do this, Caro, I'll be so furious with you. Even Simmy will be disappointed."

"Simmy would not." Simone was Izzy's older sister. She'd lost her sight at an early age. That Izzy had caused the accident was something her friend had yet to forgive herself for.

"Then think of your aunt." Izzy leaped to her feet to wag a finger in Caro's face. "She didn't raise a fool, Caroline Masterson."

"That's a low blow." Caro flinched as pain throbbed in her chest. Some days she was fine, other days she missed Aunt Lucinda, her wise council, and dry sense of humor.

"Not at all, babe. Your aunt would have dragged you onto the spaceship by your ears." Izzy winced. "She was stronger than she looked." She rubbed her ear. "Caro, I've seen how Malo stares at you. He's smitten."

"Smitten?" Caro chuckled at the word choice even though her heart lodged in her throat with hope and delight.

"He sniffs you, for tart's sake. He's always touching and kissing you. And he punched Gary in the face. What more do you need?"

Caro jerked back. "You know about Gary?"

"He was crying like a baby when we went for coffee. He tried to get the police to arrest Garix and Ronin, pointing at their uniform and making demands."

Caro grinned and relived that moment. *Yes, Malo defended my honor.*

"Now, hurry up." Izzy switched off the water then left the bathroom and bedroom.

Caro sank onto the closed toilet seat. Izzy was right. The more she thought about it, the more it was a no-brainer. She wasn't afraid of change but to risk her heart. Malo had been nothing but honorable, polite, and too damn sexy for words, so she couldn't see him toying with her. He cared—it was obvious how much he did.

"Caro, are you ready?" Izzy asked not a minute later. "I'm starving."

"I'm here," Caro sighed and pushed to her feet, marching with determination to the kitchen, hoping she didn't perspire at any time during the day. At least her underarm was odorless. "I'm running out of shoes," she said to Izzy. "Where's Garix?"

"He went to *cleanse*." Izzy bit into an apple, leaned across, grabbed another and tossed it at Ronin. "He waited for you two to return before evaporating. Said something about ensuring I'm protected." She paused, pressing the apple to her chin. "I almost died. There was bacteria on the counter. Oh, heavens, thank you, my heroes." She threw her hand over her temple in a melodramatic pose, her sigh overdone as per usual.

Caro snorted at her friend's theatrics.

"You mock our need to protect you, Izzy," Malo said, his frown thunderous to behold.

"We're in our apartment, Malo. There are no wild animals, no attackers, just a pain-in-my-ass neighbor." Izzy peered at him then her lips twitched into a sweet smile. "I'm sorry if I've offended."

"We may be *too* overprotective, but your safety matters to us," he said in a gentle tone.

"It matters even more to Garix. He is large for an Etterian male. Your size calls forth his protective instincts," Ronin said, while munching on another apple.

"Thank you for explaining. I'll try to be more understanding," Izzy said to them. "But if he doesn't get his ass here soon, I'll need to be rushed to the hospital. My stomach's swallowing me whole."

"She's joking, just Izzy being Izzy." Caro waved her hands at Ronin and Malo, who looked like they were about to call for medical assistance. "And you, can it. You ate enough yesterday, so much so there should be two of you."

"Garix and Ronin ate more than their share." Izzy pouted. "I had to suck the butter from my fingers to avoid starvation."

Caro arched a brow. "You would've licked your fingers anyway. Now get us two taxis, and allow Malo and Ronin a little peace." As soon as Izzy bounced out of the apartment, slamming the door behind her, Caro faced the room. "She's my friend, and I love her. My life would be pretty dull without her."

"She says outrageous things." Ronin grinned, revealing both his dimples. "Although, she *is* refreshingly joyful, Caro."

"You won't feel like that when she bounces on you to wake you."

"She did so this morning. This was why Garix was vocal." Ronin chuckled while he washed his hands in the kitchen sink.

Caro handed him a clean kitchen towel, lest he shake his fingers dry or use his military cargo pants. Garix appeared in the middle of the lounge. Ronin explained where Izzy had disappeared to before the bigger man asked. But as soon as Garix heard where, he bolted for the door. His thunderous steps echoed along the passage.

"What is that scent?" Malo grasped Caro's hips to hold her against him, not that she tried to resist. It was futile. "It is sweet, tart, surprisingly pleasant."

"I'm not wearing perfume." She fought to keep her breathing steady and failed.

He sniffed her neck then face and finally her lips when he brushed his mouth over hers. Drawing back, he rubbed his lips together on a hum.

She raised a hand to her chest, hoping to calm the warm fuzziness. "It's citrus oil. I use it to remove my lipstick."

"Lipstick?" His eyelids fluttered, as if he battered his eyelashes. "That captivating red substance on your lips? It was *mesmerizing*."

"What just happened? Why did your eyes twitch?"

"My O.D.I. or Optical Data Implant explained a word I did not know." He tapped his wrist twice, activating the holographic buttons then touched his temple. "It is connected to my neural system and transmits data into my brain."

"That's incredible." She grasped his wrist to study the hieroglyphic symbols—like the replicator—hovering an inch above his arm. Unable to stop herself, she stroked his skin under her thumb. It was like velvet and so warm.

"Caro, where are the black lines around your eyes and the color on your eyelids?" By his wide-eyed expression, he hadn't realized it wasn't a permanent feature on a human.

"I didn't put cosmetics on this morning. We apply it to feel nice and look pretty." She stilled under his steady gaze, his ice blue eyes filling with an intensity that invoked something strong within her, something unfamiliar yet potent, and addictive.

"You do not need this...*cosmetics*." He brushed her hair behind an ear, his fingers unerringly tracing the shell of her ear and down the line of her neck.

How he knew to do that, she didn't know, but it swirled heat in her belly, uncoiling into a throbbing mess a little lower. She clenched her thighs together, praying she didn't scent aroused...again.

"You are truly beautiful this morning, *ensa*."

Her heart ceased to beat when his gaze traveled down her throat with a focus that bordered on obsession. The way his lips parted told her he would press an open-mouthed kiss to her skin if he could. And she'd let him. He had to know that. She had no resistance with him, no willpower. He made all her inhibitions crumble.

"Guys, the taxis won't wait forever, y'know," Izzy said from the door. Garix hovered behind her.

Ronin approached her with eagerness, but Malo held Caro back, wrapping his fingers around her wrist with a tender yet firm grip. She glanced at him, not expecting him to brush his lips across hers, to pluck at her bottom lip until she parted her mouth. He gathered her against him, one arm around her waist, and his mouth on hers, slipping his tongue in, groaning at the same time. It echoed her sentiments. When she met his onslaught with an exploratory forage, he rumbled before stepping back. He grasped her hips, strong enough for her to feel his hands shaking.

"I do not know why I keep doing this to myself," he said in a hoarse and sexy voice. He didn't glance away but gazed at her with hooded eyes. No wonder she had tambourines going off in her core. It had a right to throw a party.

"You're a sadist and masochist, Malo," she said.

"Caroline," Izzy screamed from down the passage.

Caro chuckled and grabbed Malo's hand, her bag, then slammed the apartment door behind them.

"About damned time," Izzy huffed. She ushered Garix and Ronin into a taxi before climbing between them.

"Why do we not take the ground-vehicle...car?" Malo asked when they slid into the other taxi.

"I asked Izzy to organize the taxis to distract her. After breakfast, we'll return to Director Reyes. He'll want to know if you enjoyed your time on Earth."

"And what would you prefer I tell him?" Malo teased then laced his fingers through hers before resting her hand on his thigh. The heat of him permeated his armor, making her shiver. The weather wasn't cold, yet there was something enticing in his warmth and cologne.

"The truth." She smiled.

"The truth, *ensa*?" He leveled his ice blue eyes on her upturned face. "Do you believe your superiors would accept my evil plans to abduct you?"

Mm. She tapped her chin as if giving his question serious thought. *Abduct me, hold me captive, pin me to your bed, and promise to never leave me.*

"Planning on restraining me? Blindfolding me and tying me to your..." Her tongue tied when she imagined what that must be like. Under his seductive gaze and mouth, with the heat pouring off him and the strength in his embrace?

He cupped her cheek, brushing his thumb across her bottom lip, then chuckled. "If you ever misbehave, I might do so."

"Promise?" she rasped.

He laughed. "A vow I will easily make, *minus susa*."

Chapter Eleven

Breakfast was an amazing experience. Thank the Lord for E.S.A.'s account. They had ordered so much food that the table groaned under the weight. Even Malo had indulged. It had felt good to see them so well-fed. Izzy attempted to keep pace but had lagged after her first stack of pancakes. Caro laughed at their reactions to the variety of foods and to the many children who approached the men for their autographs. The awe on Malo's face when a little girl wrapped her tiny arms around one of his legs, was priceless. Caro would cherish that memory for a long time. She was, at last, able to herd them out of the diner, hurrying to the busy road to summon two taxis.

"Izzy, you entertain Garix and Ronin while Malo meets with Director Reyes. Is that all right with you?" Caro asked Malo, not wanting to make decisions on his behalf.

"That would be acceptable," Malo said then grumbled at his men. They nodded as if they spoke 'grumble.'

She made a mental note to ask Malo about it. After giving Izzy the card, she climbed into the taxi. That Malo held the door open for her was unexpected and sweet. She shuffled across the seat, tugging her skirt down. Women shouldn't slide, not in tight pencil skirts.

She leaned forward to inform S.A.D.I. of her destination.

Perhaps she should take Malo shoe shopping? She smirked. That would be mean of her. *Holy noodles.* The image of Malo holding and staring at a delicate shoe in his hand, rose to mind. He would be damn sexy even shoe shopping with her.

"Why are you laughing?" He settled next to her.

She met his gaze and sighed at his clear interest. He'd given her time to decide. As it was, she was leaning toward forever. What did she stand to lose? A freedom she often resented? Loneliness that ate at her soul? More boyfriends who would hurt her and fail to compare to this perfect specimen of a man?

"I need new shoes." She jiggled her stilettoed foot at him. "I thought to take you shopping with me but that would be mean. Men don't shop with women."

"I would do anything with you, *ensa*." He glanced outside, then rested his gaze on her again, as if he hadn't just made her swoon.

"Men don't shop." She splayed her fingers over his warm, black-uniformed chest. *Monkey's bananas, he feels wonderful.*

"I am not a man, Caro. I am your soulmate who will share everything with you if you let me. Just being with you gives me infinite joy."

Granny's nipples, he's perfect. What man spoke like this and meant it? And yet he managed to not sound cliché.

"To watch you try on footwear like these would be time well spent." His gaze lingered on her shoe.

"Oh, you like these?" She angled her foot from side-to-side, trying to imagine what he saw. They gave her height, made her calves look amazing, but they hurt like hell.

"I like them on you." He dipped his head to steal a kiss. "With nothing else on would be perfect."

She gasped. Yes, with Malo, she'd dress in whatever way he wanted. Fiddling with the edge of his uniform, she couldn't resist testing the texture of his skin. "Let me take you to a lingerie store then we shall see if you'd prefer I wear nothing."

His eyelids stuttered and fluttered opened. He leveled a smoldering gaze on her. The effect was breathtaking with his ice blue eyes against bronze skin. "You have stalls selling these...garments?" His voice was guttural and had a mainline to her ovaries.

Shit. She winced. *Sorry, Aunt Lucinda.* Caro wasn't equipped to handle this much sex appeal.

"I'll try them on for you. You can decide which ones to get."

He shuddered. "We will order through the replicator. You can wear them in the privacy of our quarters." He lifted his finger to trace a path from the pulse in her neck to her collarbone.

She shivered, relishing his touch. "Or that."

"Footwear too." He dropped a hand over her bare knee to glide down her calve.

She squirmed in her seat, trying to keep her panties dry. "Sounds good." At her whisper, his head shot up to meet her gaze.

His hand remained on her calve, and a pulse beat hard at the base of his jaw. "Why are you agreeing with me?"

"Because I like forever with you, Malo."

His eyes flew wide then he crushed her to him for a thorough plunder. He placed his hands behind her waist and up her back, pulling her impossibly close. She melted in his arms, in her shoes, and in her imaginary stockings since she hadn't worn any. He had to have been a pirate in a former life because when she said plunder, she meant ravage, debauch, and all other delicious descriptions that slipped into her mind at that point. Every part of her body tingled, her nipples were hard, but who could blame her. Did she mention he was an amazing kisser? Well, he was. He was so good her ears rang...incessantly.

Holy noodles, that's my phone. She shoved his chest until he leaned back then snatched the phone from her bag.

"Caroline, hello," she rasped which was sure to sound like a sex-cyborg, if they could speak, that is.

Her gaze remained on his face, taking in the heated intensity in his eyes, the way his top teeth dimpled his bottom lip, the warmth of his hand where it rested on her thigh. He showed patience and impatience at the same time. How he managed that, she didn't know.

"Caro? Come in a taxi," Reyes yelled above the din in the background. "Someone has leaked that a new alien species has made contact. We're trying to find the breach. The news-vids have every conceivable technology at the gate. If they spot the E.S.A. car, they will go berserk. I'll have security at the glass doors waiting for you."

She arched an eyebrow at Malo, querying whether he'd heard. He nodded while he toyed with a closed pink button on her blouse.

"Yes, Director. We're on our way." She hung up, dropped the phone in the bag, and leaned forward, as far as Malo would let her, to warn S.A.D.I. When she settled against the seat, Malo yanked her onto his lap, pinning her against his chest like he'd done at the theater.

"There are a few things you need to know, but believe this, Caro, my *ensa*, your decision cannot be reversed. I cannot allow it. It will be the death of me."

"I'm listening, Malo." She cupped his cheek, an intimate gesture to be sure but one she couldn't resist.

"You will become addicted to me..." His fingers spasmed where they grasped her backside.

"This craving for you to hold me, touch and kiss me? Then it's too late. I'm a Malo-addict," she said.

The glorious two-dimple smile he bestowed on her was awe-inspiring.

"I am pleased to hear this. I too am addicted to you."

She blinked, unsure how to respond to that nugget. "Good," she managed.

"You will live with me, wherever. I would prefer to return to Etteria, but I go where you go."

Leave Earth and Izzy? A leaden blanket settled over her. How could she say goodbye to Izzy? This would devastate her. "Malo, you say that like it's easy to up and move. To never do programming again? All my research? My databases?" She chewed on her lip, wondering if Izzy and Simone would be willing to relocate...to another planet?

"This can be done anywhere, perhaps traveling past the stars you are calculating or sharing information with Etteria's cartographers and astronomers."

Her eyes flew wide, tears threatening to spill. He'd gifted her with something precious. And it was, to her. She kissed him hard, breaking away to sniff while stroking him from temple to jaw. "Malo, I didn't think of it that way. There is so much I could learn, so much you could teach me."

He acted as if it were a given. Didn't he understand? His people could deny her this knowledge, and she wouldn't have a say. That he'd allow this, would support her in this... Her breath hitched. The emotions swelling in her heart were hot, sweet, and intense, threatening to overwhelm her. There had to be a catch.

"They are our lima kuu, our great teachers."

She stilled. "Okay, out with it, you're giving me the dessert before the broccoli."

When his eyes twitched, she smiled.

"It is a good analogy," he acknowledged before releasing a deep sigh. "When I met you, I experienced the Ethera. It is what converts my eye color from dark blue to this." He gestured to his beautiful eyes. "It is an outward sign that I have found my Dar Eth, that I am your Eth. It also means, by Etterian law, we are what humans call...husband and wife."

"What?" She studied his face as the full meaning of his words hit her like a cream pie. She was married? Shock must have set in. No emotion rose as if she was numb.

While she poked her heart for a reaction, she admired his features and the expressions crossing his eyes. He'd stiffened, his fingers digging into her as if dreading her response, was expecting her to lose her toys or worse, turn away from him, reject him. That she held him so in the palm of her hand, that she could hurt him so easily, that he trusted her to have mercy breached the shock. Warmth exploded outward, sending shivers and tingles through her. This was...happiness.

"I'm your wife? For real?"

Marriage was a serious commitment, and it had happened without her say so, without any fanfare. Not that that was bad either. Besides, if she was truthful with herself, she didn't care that she was married already. She got Malo, he was hers, and whatever sacrifice she needed to make to keep him, she'd make it with pleasure.

"I never could understand the bended-knee proposal so no loss there." She gave him a tremulous smile.

"Your males propose on bended knee?" He grinned, raising his fingers to embed in her hair. His smile was breathtaking, one that should grace this month's issue of a men's digi-mag. "Our males drop to a knee when experiencing the Ethera, so in a way…proposing."

"It's powerful enough to bring you to your knees?" She frowned, having not once seen him kneel for her.

"I managed not to with Director Reyes watching me," he said as if he could read her thoughts. "It was a difficult compulsion to resist, Caro." He ran his finger along her jaw to tilt her face up to his. Then with excruciating slowness, he lowered his lips to feather across hers. "I still fight the urge. My knee *wants* to bend for you. When I met you, you in that black garment, in your footwear…" He pulled back, set her onto the seat, then kneeled in the narrow confines of the taxi, which was no easy feat for such a large man. "Will you be my Dar Eth, Caro?"

Stranger than his proposal and the sudden tear streaming down her cheek, was the taxi rocking from side-to-side. She whipped her gaze at the crowds surrounding the car. The taxi had drawn up to the front security gates at the E.S.A. Engineering building.

Malo had returned to his seat so fast, she hadn't seen him move. He shielded her with his body. No one had ever done that for her. Shoved into the corner, she could do nothing but peer out of the car window.

As much as she liked being pinned by him, the crowds were mostly desperate-looking women holding up placards, some flashed their breasts like that would work. She peeked at Malo, but his concerned gaze rested upon her. Now that was impressive. Come to think of it, he hadn't ogled the scantily dressed women at the club either.

The other contingent of the crowd were enraged men and women demanding the Etterians leave their planet. "No more galaxy whores," they chanted.

She frowned. That didn't make sense. Sure, Etterians making contact is newsworthy, but why would they tie it to sex? And of course, they were so narrowminded. These new aliens were perfect. Her giggle arched Malo's brow. "If I had a chance, I'd be flashing my breasts at you and begging you to kidnap me."

He smirked. "I would have noticed, my Caro. To make you mine, I would have stolen you."

"Yes, I'll be yours." She wiggled, trying to kiss him but had to settle for his bare shoulder where his armor ended.

He shivered and flashed her a heated look. "We will celebrate later."

She grinned. "Yes, please."

The taxi drew up at the front entrance. She paid then grabbed her bag and Malo's hand. He ensured she reached inside the building without further ado, ushering her along as fast as she could run. But as soon as the doors closed behind him, he lifted her to his chest and kissed her in full view of the reception, now packed with spectators. She squeaked, squirmed, then melted into his embrace and under his masterful lips. The crowds faded. Her senses filled with him, his cologne and firm hands.

"My wife," he whispered between kisses along her jaw then back to her lips.

The audience broke into applause. She ducked her head, letting the fall of her hair shield her. He lowered her to the tiled floor and amid well-wishers, led her to the elevator.

"What is this feeling?" He rubbed his chest.

Not that she could answer. As soon as the door closed, he was kissing her again. He released her swollen and tingling lips the moment their level was announced.

"If you keep kissing me like that, I won't be able to string two thoughts together," she rasped while following him on trembling knees.

"Remember my name. That is all that matters to me."

"Is that all? Wouldn't you want me to remember that you rock my world?" she teased.

He drew to a halt. "Boat." He hauled her against his body and buried his face in her hair, breathing her in.

Holy noodles, Izzy was right. He does sniff me.

"No, world. A boat is too small. You rock my *world*, Malo." She peered at him, trying to convey her sincerity. He did, without a doubt. By his words, touches, protectiveness, and sensual potency. She was overwhelmed to the best degree.

"When you speak to me so, *ensa*, I feel something here." He patted his chest, right where a human heart would be, like he'd done in the elevator. "Warm, powerful, and breathtaking."

"Never felt it before?" she frowned. If he didn't know what it was, neither did she.

"To feel is to fail, wife. For an Etterian male," he said.

Monkey's bananas. Was he serious? They try not to feel anything?

"But I will need your guidance, *ensa*."

"It will be my pleasure," she said.

His eyes stuttered closed, and his lips curved in a seductive curl. *Alodon's nipples, he was sexy.* Her eyes widened at her thoughts, and she giggled.

When he opened his eyes, there was warmth in his gaze. "And your humor this time?"

"I have these sayings I inherited from my aunt, to help me not to curse. I usually say stuff like 'holy noodles' or 'granny's nipples' but this time I thought 'Alodon's nipples.' I think you're influencing me, Malo."

"Alodon's nipples." He chuckled and released her, except her hand. "I like that, *ensa*."

"I like *you*, my Eth."

He drew to another halt and wavered. "If you keep speaking to me so, we will not make it to Director Reyes or a bed worthy of what I plan to do to you."

Do to her? Her breath rushed out in a whoosh as desire warmed her core. This time there was no stopping the dreaded thigh-drench. Then again, she didn't need to hide it from him anymore. Not that she'd done such a fantastic job of that, either.

"Maker, your scent is delicious," he rumbled in that sexy way of his.

"Director then bed," she said, pulling him behind her. The quicker they saw Reyes, the quicker she could see stars, the rarer kind. "And if you hurry, I'll even let you do me with my shoes on."

"Do you?"

"Make me scream your name," she said.

His deep groan raised the hairs on the back of her neck and sparked a ripple of goosebumps. "Female, you make me so...hard."

She winked at him before striding into Reyes's office. "Director, good morning."

She didn't knock when it didn't matter anymore. Her resignation would be tendered, effective immediately. Besides, Reyes was expecting them when security notified him of their arrival.

"I'm happy you made it safely. It's been chaotic, to say the least." He circled the desk, only to sit on the edge. With twinkling eyes, he studied her and Malo's clasped hands, their proximity to one another, then nodded at Malo.

She sliced glances between the two men, wondering what that nod meant.

"You have a breach?" Malo asked, drawing her closer to him, using their joined hands as leverage.

"Yes, we're investigating various avenues. I have scheduled a press conference at two this afternoon." Reyes rested his hands on his lap. "I'd like you to be there."

"Very well, Director Reyes, and Joshua Bennett?" Malo asked.

"En route. He agreed to meet with you and will be arriving tomorrow. I'll communicate his arrival time once it's confirmed. And the submarine's approved. I explained the impending war and the necessity for our assistance. They were reluctant, but I did call in a few favors. She's smaller than you might have liked. We didn't know your cargo capacity on your battleships so opted for the most powerful and compact model we have. The crew has been selected and have agreed to travel with you to whichever planet. It has a minimal crew of eight due to the onboard AI managing most of the tasks."

"Thank you, Director Reyes. Etteria is grateful." Malo thumped his chest with a fist.

Reyes's shoulders slumped. "As to the women you seek, that will take more negotiating. Most of the council have daughters or sisters. I understand their caution. But the sight of you two should inspire many women to apply."

"Anything else?" Bouncing on her toes, Caro glanced at Malo, eager to get to the ravishing.

"Not for now." Reyes grinned.

"I hereby resign." She chuckled with glee, freer than she'd ever been. Married and about to start her honeymoon, what more could she ask for?

"I assumed as much, Caro. Sign here." Reyes slid the prepared resignation letter across his desk and placed his personalized pen on top.

She signed it, unread. "How did you know?" She gave him his pen.

"I saw Malo's reaction to you when you met, and his eyes changed color." Reyes gestured to Malo with his pen before pocketing it. "Two signs of the Ethera, I believe. Congratulations, by the way."

She smiled and settled beside Malo to loop an arm through the crook of his. "Thank you. If you don't need me...us?"

"Go, and don't be late for the conference. We'll be opening the gates to those maniacs, and once we've addressed their concerns, perhaps they might grow a brain cell." Reyes snorted. "Or get a life. Some people *need* hobbies."

"Pilot Afax, two to port to my quarters," Malo spoke into his wrist while gathering her into his arms.

A male responded in what she recognized as Galactic like she would Russian without having to understand it. Within seconds, they were in the privacy of Malo's quarters. She pushed out of his embrace and unbuttoned her blouse.

MALO'S BREATH CAUGHT AS Caro undid each tiny button with slow, methodical movements. He wanted to rip it off her now that she was alone with him.

"You're not ruining the shirt or skirt," she said in a regal and commanding tone that made him smile.

His gaze fixed on the cream skin her gaping tunic revealed. She slid it off her shoulders and draped it over the back of a comfy. Reaching to the side of her skirt, she unfastened and shimmied out of it, bending to collect it off the floor. It joined the tunic, not that he focused on the draped garments. He was fixated on the female before him.

She stood in her white undergarments and arousing footwear. Even though her fingers twitched at her sides, she didn't try to hide herself. Her top garment pushed her breasts up, so that they swelled, overflowed, begged for freedom. He freed them with a tug. She gasped, and color splashed across her cheeks. He didn't spare her pink skin more than a glance, more riveted by her large and pebbled nipples a few shades darker than her skin.

He glided his hands along her shoulders, brushing the garment remnants aside. She twitched, and her breasts bounced, stealing his breath, drying his mouth.

"Caro," he whispered in a voice he didn't recognize.

He brushed the underside of her breast, to cup it in his hand, to rub a thumb over the nipple. She shivered, and on a throaty moan, tilted her head back, revealing the vulnerable column of her neck. He narrowed his eyes, zeroing in on her expressive face while he spanned her waist with his hands, running them down to grasp her hips to gather her against him. She gripped his forearms. Her scent rose to torment him—intense, rich, mind-altering. White lust shot through him, stiffening every muscle including his malehood. His control thinned. His breathing became ragged. His mind roared commands to claim her. He grunted. He had venoms that could drive a person wild, but she did it to him with nothing but her breasts.

With a groan that surely wasn't his, he lowered his head to suck a nipple into his mouth, looping his arms around her, keeping her close, preventing her withdrawal. She purred from the back of her throat. Tiny bumps rippled over her pale skin. Her fingers kneaded his shoulders. He trailed across to her other breast, to suck and twirl the nipple into his mouth, marveling at the texture, the taste of her.

"Malo," she whimpered, her husky voice feathering over his sensitive nerves. Her heartbeat pounded in his ears, and her scent darkened.

"Mine," he ground out, raising his gaze to meet her hooded eyes. "You are beautiful and mine, Caro." He scooped her into his arms, ignoring her startled squeal. His strides to his room were swift and desperate. But the gentleness with which he lay her down on the bed was paramount to him. Nothing would harm her. He wouldn't stand for it.

"Shouldn't I finish undressing?" She gestured to the bottom garment hiding her sex from him.

With a smirk, he tugged, and the fabric tore under the precise strength of his hands. She gasped, but he ignored her, pocketing the torn garment like he was wont to do. Then he stilled, admiring the female spread before him. *Maker.*

His hands shook when he touched the release mechanism on his chest armor. It unclasped, and he shrugged it off, letting it fall where it may. He yanked off his boots and removed his pants. His gaze remained fixed on her face and eyes while she absorbed everything about him. And she did, his *ensa*. She licked her lips, her gaze heated, and the scent of her need drenched the room.

"Malo, please," she begged, holding out her hand to him. "I need you." Her whispered plea went straight to his chest again, swelling it with unknown emotions.

"I need...a little control, Caro," he said in a voice below guttural.

"Oh?" She lifted herself onto her elbows. "Take me quick and again slow."

His brow furrowed at her strange instruction. "I will not waste our one time today because I lacked control." The urge to plunge into her bombarded him, deafening him. His gaze strayed to her glistening seam. Once again, his mouth watered.

"You orgasm only once a day?" she asked, gazing at the thick and hard length of him bobbing under her admiration.

"No," he said.

She offered him a sweet smile. "Women can go more than once."

He stilled. Heat burned his ears and stung his eyes. He grinned. "Maker."

"So take me as many times as you want, Malo," she said, but this time, his Caro spread her thighs.

He shuddered when her seam blossomed, revealing dusky pink feminine folds. Without forethought, he settled between her thighs, nuzzling her curls with his nose while inhaling her scent deep into his lungs. She shivered under his touch, when he'd yet to taste her, to dip a finger into her. He did so now and spread her folds with his tongue. He groaned at her flavor, his addiction *now* complete. Using the tip and flat of his tongue, he found and teased her nub as the instructional vid had demonstrated. It hardened under his ministrations. He thrust a single finger into her channel and shuddered when the hot, wet silk of her wrapped around it. She was so tight and small, he feared he might harm her. He tested her with a second finger and sighed when her channel stretched to accommodate his intrusion.

She writhed beneath his mouth. He showed her no mercy. That she was ready for him was apparent, but he wanted, no, *needed* her to find her fulfillment before he claimed her. Her channel tightened around his fingers when he pumped them in and out. Her hips jerked, and her fingernails scraped across his scalp.

Then she exploded on a whimper, her channel clamping around his fingers, her body convulsing with her need drenching his tongue. She panted his name, her hair flying from side-to-side when she splintered beneath him. He could watch her find her fulfillment for an eternity.

"Caro?" He pushed back to hold the head of his arousal at her entrance.

She glanced up to meet his gaze and smiled.

His heart froze at the look she bestowed upon him. It invoked something hot and crushing in his chest—that same intense emotion that had plagued him from the moment she'd agreed to be his.

"Malo." She trailed her nails over his chest and across his nipples. They were hard, begging for her touch, like hers had ached for his. He pressed forward, his balls spasming under the control he exerted. Doing this slow would ensure he wouldn't harm her.

Maker. She was...soft.

As he penetrated deeper, she arched and writhed, unable to control her reactions. Her body flushed, and he was mesmerized as the pink spread from her throat to her breasts. While he withdrew to push in farther, he latched onto a nipple, sucking it into his mouth. He drowned in the taste of her skin, even though he advanced, withdrew, advanced until he buried his length within her. At the tightness wrapped around his malehood, squeezing him, calling him to sacrifice himself on the altar of her, he shuddered.

"I have never felt this way," he mumbled, holding himself off her to gaze at her.

She looped her legs around his waist, urging him on. His senses documented every move she made—the twitching of her legs, her arching back, and rising hips. Her eyes were hooded, lust-filled...needy. He withdrew and thrust into her, his balls tightening even as they slapped her skin. She moaned, clawing him to lay on top of her. But he dared not. He might crush her under his weight. His Caro wasn't content with his caution. She circled her arms around his neck and crushed her breasts against his chest. He groaned at her curves engulfing him, barraging him on all fronts.

With his fulfillment rushing toward him at a breathtaking speed, he plunged in an out with more urgency. And when he thought his Caro couldn't surprise him further, her channel rippled again. Wave after wave of contractions clamped tight around his arousal and sucked him into the sweet depths of her. Sheer pleasure ripped through him and tossed him over the edge of time. He roared when he released, unable to slow it, to prevent it. He could only endure, experience, a spectator at his fulfillment. His body was no longer his—it trembled as a fine sheen of sweat coated his skin. The side effect of a single human female. Balancing on one hand, he slid the other around her, keeping her quivering form close to him.

She was his. He was never letting her go.

Chapter Twelve

Caro peppered kisses along Malo's jaw. She couldn't stop herself. His lovemaking was better than she'd dreamed. Her body tingled, satiated, yet hunger stained the edges of her consciousness, murmuring with need. He held her to his chest, his strength phenomenal, and above all, it felt right to be there in his arms. Grinding her hips, she tested the steel length of him still buried in her. She liked his cock, liked him filling her to exploding. The sensations that licked at her channel were exquisite. She gasped, wriggled again, and moaned. He grumbled at her, but she didn't listen.

"You feel so...good, Malo," she panted before pressing an open-mouthed kiss against his throat. "I want you again," she marveled. Her gaze flew up to meet his.

She fluttered her hands over his shoulders and down his biceps, holding on, kneading, caressing, grazing with her fingernails. That he watched her with his unblinking stare and said nothing didn't matter. She was desperate for him to move.

When he withdrew, she pouted her disappointment. But he thrust into her, hard, and to the hilt. Crying out, she arched her. Tingles spread out from her nipples as they puckered. He lowered her to the bed and grabbed her wrists with one hand, holding them above her head. She didn't care, she writhed on his length, urging him on, needing this...him.

"Please," she whimpered, not above begging, not with Malo.

He plunged into her again, so hard, her body trembled at the force, at the burst of sensations tearing through her. She kicked off her shoes, clamped her legs around his hips, and held on, squeezing, urging, demanding. Friction rippled along her channel. She was so close.

Then he stopped.

She mewled, unable to form words. With a flip of her body, he had her kneeling. He looped an arm around her hips and raised her backside to meet his descending thrusts. It was too much, too intense, too incredible. She shattered, screaming his name, bucking beneath him while her body convulsed along its own trajectory. He bit down on her shoulder, roaring his release. A second orgasm tore through her. She was helpless to still the minor tremors in the aftermath yet still singular distortions. He dropped next to her, keeping her in his arms. She went willingly, resting her face against his shoulder and her hand on his ridged abdomen.

"You are mine, Caro." His voice was hoarse, she wasn't sure due to his roaring or thick with emotion. It didn't matter. He had the right of it. She was his. Case closed.

"Yes." She kissed his shoulder.

"Hungry, thirsty, cleanse?" he asked.

She shook her head, snuggling into his side, and sighing when he drew her closer.

"I'd like to stay right here if you don't mind?" She hesitated, not wanting to force him to cuddle if it wasn't something Etterians did.

"Mind? Caro, my gift, try and leave my arms and see what I will do." He sounded like he was smiling. That was rare, so she pushed herself up to glance at him. He was, and it was breathtaking. Free to do so, she raised a trembling finger to stroke a dimple.

"You're beautiful, Malo," she blurted then winced. *What man likes to be called beautiful? Granny's nipples, I'm an idiot.*

"You are the beautiful one, my Caro." He chuckled and blessed her with a sweet kiss. "Do you have things you need to collect?"

"Collect?" she said in a daze—his lips tended to do that to her. The man was lethal. Her eyes flew open when she realized what he was saying. He wanted her to move in as his wife. "Yes, a few things. And I'll have to tell Izzy." She sighed, dipping her chin to hide the sadness at a chapter of her life ending. He might misunderstand, or worse, take her sorrow to heart. "Later."

She snuggled into him again while twirling a pattern around his nipple. It pebbled under her fascinated gaze. She glided her hand down over his ridged abs to cup the head of his erect cock still coated with their combined orgasms. It bobbed and dribbled in anticipation. He released a hissed breath. She giggled and slithered on top of him, positioning her entrance at his head. When she rubbed along the length of him, her eyes fluttered closed at the sensations created. He gripped her hips, as if to hold her still. She ignored them, instead, she wiggled down and impaled herself.

"Malo," she rasped, tingles spreading from her core to her nipples.

She tugged his hands free and held them against her breasts while arching her hips to slide, up and down, her head falling back in ecstasy.

She moaned, unable to stop riding him, unable to be embarrassed, knowing he watched her every move, knowing she'd helped herself to his gorgeous hard cock.

He sat up, crushing her to him, with one hand gripping her ass and the other wrapped around her back. As he thrust upwards, meeting her descents with a need of his own, he tried to hold her still. But she was adrift in a sea of sensation too exquisite for words, breath, or thought. She screamed she knew not what, just that it tore from her throat with such force it hurt. Like she couldn't get enough of him. He roared, heat bathed her insides, her nub throbbed, begged, and ached. His ragged breathing along her shoulder made her shiver. Her world tilted, he leaned back and pinned her against his chest, keeping her near. It wasn't close enough. She doubted she'd ever satisfy the urgency within her. Addicted? Yes, she was.

"So precious to me," he whispered.

If he was going to whisper sweet nothings, she wanted to hear his words but couldn't bring herself out of the lassitude that enslaved her. She drifted off to sleep in the safety of his arms, unable to prevent her fall into satiated rest.

~*~

Malo held her against him, tightening his arms around her sleeping form. His Caro, his Dar Eth...*his*. How could a male such as he be so blessed? His mind, body, and soul were in harmony. There was nothing in the Maker's universe as precious as this female in his arms. Everything she was enticed, pleased, and completed him. He'd never known such emotions when buried in her, finding his fulfillment, or holding her.

None of his youngin interactions with females could compare to the joy he found in Caro. Still buried within her, her tight sheathe clenched around him, milking him, calling to him. Her body was made to be cherished, adored, and he'd every intention of doing so. She wouldn't regret choosing him, and that she *had* chosen him made his chest ache. He'd have stolen her, despite her wishes, no matter the cost to her, to him. Her choosing him of her own free will was infinitely sweeter. She snuggled into him, distracting him with a press of her lips to his chest.

Maker. Will I ever get enough of her?

He would let her rest for now, then they'd need to cleanse. He shuddered at the imagery that bombarded him. The last time she'd used his cleansing room, he'd wanted to spread her thighs, to taste her. At the thought, her flavor burst across his tongue in remembrance. Nothing tasted as tantalizing as his Caro. He shifted his hips, enjoying the vibrations rippling along his length. She moaned, and he rubbed a hand up and down her bare back to soothe her. He wanted her again, would always want her, of that he had no doubt. And she'd let him have her, despite her exhaustion. He saw that now, her selflessness.

"Malo?" Her movements summoned a groan from him, her channel invoking scintillating sensations. "Shouldn't we get ready for the press conference?" She arched her back, stretching her limbs while still impaled on him. He grunted. She was going to be the death of him.

He grabbed her hips in the hopes of sliding out of her, but at the pleasure that spread across her face—with her mouth parting on a throaty purr—he paused. She tempted him to claim her again. *Alodon's balls, I am stronger than this.* He withdrew from her warmth, ignoring the shaking of his hands and his ragged breathing. Her care came first.

"Yes, it is time," he said.

"I don't want to," she pouted.

She leaned upward and brushed her mouth across his. He growled and drowned in the flavor of her, following the seductive lure of her mouth. She had a bewitching control over his senses, he realized when he returned to reality to find his fingers fluttering across her breasts and his hips positioning to piston into her. *Maker.*

"Evil female," he teased, shivering when she scraped her nails over his nipples. "Temptress." He placed a kiss on her nose and pulled back, not focusing on any part of her other than her eyes. For his sanity's sake.

"Me?" she squeaked, then shook her head at him, sending her mussed hair flying. "You're an Adonis, Malo, sent to tempt all females."

His gaze focused on her swollen lips and the rise and fall of her trembling breasts. He tempted her? He grinned, pleased that she thought so.

"You'd better get off me then," she said.

He leaned farther back, allowing her space to shuffle to the edge of the bed. Once her feet touched the floor, she was up and striding to her garments. His gaze followed her swaying backside—the sight brought a heated warmth to his chest and loins. He grunted and turned to his closet for another set of armor.

"Holy noodle, Malo, did you have to snap my bra?" She dangled a strip of white from a finger.

"Is that garment necessary?" he chuckled while tugging on his pants.

He donned it—his movements swifter than usual. The need to be with her again drove him, even if it was just being in the same room. While locating his boots, he relished a smile at how he hadn't cared where they'd fallen.

She grinned. "Yup. Now make me another." She hitched a thumb at the replicator.

He snapped his boots on while admiring her standing there expectant. *Maker.* Like this, she was perfect. He crossed to her, looped an arm around her waist, and swung her into his arms. Her softness filled his hands. Her scent mixed with his tantalized. If he kissed her as he longed to do, they would miss this 'press conference.' Even though his priority had shifted to Caro, he had to continue in this role as engineer-ambassador. And if his presence calmed these overzealous humans before Prince Citus and Adviser Cales arrived, then Malo's final task would be a success.

Lowering her beside him, he tapped the replicator, switched the language to Earthian English, and captured Caro's hand. He splayed her fingers on the glass surface. "Enter your dimensions and choose a *bra.*"

She gasped and raised wide eyes to his. "Just like that?" With a squeal, she bent over the replicator and tapped the options.

He collected her footwear from his...*their* bedroom then hovered in the door frame, admiring her when she clipped on the white garment that contained her breasts. He fought the urge to rip this one too. If he had his way, she'd remain naked always.

But when she added garment after garment, he had to admit, watching her do so was mesmerizing. Her undressing was more pleasurable, but under the circumstances, he could be forgiven for finding her slow, controlled movements breathtaking. She flicked her hair to the side and ran something through her hair. Whatever it was, it made her locks smooth and shimmering.

"I'll shower later," she said to him. Her cheeks flushed while her gaze traveled over the length of him. "I kind of like the idea that a part of you is still on me and *in* me."

His gaze flew to meet hers. He growled, dropping his hand to adjust his hard length. His eyelids stuttered closed. He drew in deep breaths through his mouth. He didn't need to scent her, not now, not after what she'd said.

"Let us return to Director Reyes. I want to rush back here." He strode toward her to gather her into his arms. She rested her hands on his shoulders and wiggled her feet into her footwear.

"How do I look?" she asked a little breathlessly.

Obedient for now, he studied her face and hair. He finger-combed through her locks, while plucking at her lips with his.

"Like a female thoroughly loved," he said. "Two to port," he said to his wrist. "Director Reyes's office, Pilot Afax."

"And bam," Izzy said as they materialized. "They're back." She was sitting in a chair with Ronin next to her. Garix stared out of the window, turned to nod at Malo but said nothing.

"You two are just in time." Director Reyes sat behind his desk, relaxed yet tapping a rhythm with his fingers.

"Many people wish to speak to you, Engineer Malo," Garix informed him, though he didn't glance at Malo.

"I called in extra security." Director Reyes rose from behind the desk and headed to the door. "A few reporters are outside, but the rest are women. If you manage to charm them, Malo, they might champion your cause."

"Caro?" Malo raised their clasped hands to kiss her knuckles. "Are you ready, my Dar Eth?"

"Dar Eth? You agreed?" Izzy jumped out of the chair to hug Caro. She bounced up and down, shaking Caro, who was attempting to hold her still with one hand.

"Yes, I do listen to your advice, y'know."

"Sometimes," Izzy teased, stepping back still clasping Caro's hand. Her grin summoned Malo's smile. This little female adored his Caro and was happy for her. But Director Reyes hovered at the door to his office. Malo circled an arm around his *ensa*'s waist, ushering her out.

"I want details." Izzy trailed them, flanked by Ronin and Garix. "I know where you've been these past few hours, babe."

"Get your own Eth, Izzy." Caro chuckled when she trailed Director Reyes.

"Spoil sport," Izzy mumbled.

"What do you wish to know, *minus susa*?" Garix asked Izzy, curiosity in his voice.

"Women who don't get any live vicariously through their *friends*." Izzy huffed. "Remember that, Caro."

"Any what?" Ronin asked.

"Sex," Izzy sighed.

Caro sliced a glance at Malo, her eyes twinkling.

"You would share with Izzy our union?" He frowned.

Caro shook her head. "You're mine, Malo. I'm not sharing you."

His breath caught. How she managed to affect him so easily was something he couldn't fathom. His *ensa* made his head spin and chest ache without trying. He liked that about her despite his inability to control his responses.

"You want sex?" Garix asked Izzy.

Malo hid a chuckle. Sometimes his males were like *damu*.

"Yup." Izzy popped the 'p.' "Don't you?"

Malo's chest rumbled, but he attempted to tamp down his laughter.

"With my Dar Eth, yes," Garix said.

"So, nothing with anyone unless she's your soulmate?" Izzy asked.

"Yes."

"Holy noodles," Izzy squeaked. "But you've done it though? You're not a virgin?"

"I am not," Garix said.

"Okay, so you've done it but have now vowed celibacy?" Izzy hissed, 'ouch.' "And you, Ronin?"

"I am not a virgin," Ronin answered.

Caro's shoulders shook with silent laughter.

"So you guys get it on when you're younger, then just stop?" Izzy asked.

"Yes, we learn it brings the void closer faster," Garix said.

"The what now?" Izzy harumphed. "What's a void, Garix?"

"The darkness that will consume our souls without our Dar Eths."

Izzy gasped. "Shit. You're dying?"

"We're all dying, Izzy," Caro said as they stepped out of the elevator into the crowded reception.

Director Reyes cut through, the chattering ceasing when Malo, Garix, and Ronin followed.

"We, at least, get to have sex, babe," Izzy whispered.

Before slipping her hand into Malo's, Caro glanced over her shoulder at her friend. "But meaningless sex scars our souls too."

He liked that she sought his touch. With a squeeze, her grasped her hand to his chest, pulling her closer.

"True again," Izzy sighed.

They marched through the glass double doors and into the afternoon sunlight. The ground was a solid gray stone, white and yellow markings marred its surface, similar to other roads Caro had taken him on. Other cars filled the space, and around them, those inside the building gathered, some joining the original crowd. Peppered throughout were the security males Director Reyes had promised.

Malo arched a brow at Garix and nudged his head at Izzy. Garix took her by the arm and guided her to stand behind the screaming humans waving lettering, bras, or fists. From the rear, Garix and Ronin could monitor any and all potential threats. Releasing Caro's hand, Malo ushered her to where Reyes faced the excitement and rage.

"Thank you all for coming. I'll come right out and say it. The rumors are true. We've been contacted by another alien species. The arrival of the Algris opened our eyes to life beyond our solar system. And though they are far from humanoid, we welcomed them. I have seen footage of other species, some yellow or silver, far on the outskirts of known space. And now the Etterians, who come in peace, are offering healing planet technology we desperately need."

"In exchange for what?" someone called from the audience.

Director Reyes shielded his eyes from the sunlight and flickering camera flashes. "There are many items on the table. I'm not at liberty to discuss them until the deal has been finalized."

A few demanded he reveal the details, others waved fists while screaming their displeasure.

"Are you brainwashed?" another person asked Caro, cutting through the chaos.

Fury rose within Malo, but he hid it well. He tightened his hand around her waist.

She cupped his jaw, drew in a ragged breath, then stepped away from him. "Brainwashed to do what?" she asked, clasping her hands before her.

"As his sex slave?" The crowd waited in bated breath for her response.

Her husky laughter raised Malo's core temperature, but he didn't adjust his suit. He merely reveled in the lust and delight her joy summoned.

"Are you blind?" She glanced across the audience before gesturing to Malo. "I see a handsome alien man who likes me for me. I don't need to be brainwashed to want a piece of that. You see..." She paused, raised a trembling hand to flick hair off her face, and offered a tremulous smile. "Etterians mate for life. They commit to one woman, and all others cease to exist. Trust me when I say, it's breathtaking, their loyalty and honor."

"So you *are* brainwashed," a human male smirked.

With his enhanced hearing, he caught the leap of her heart. Pink stained her cheeks. She flicked a dismissive hand. "I'm not; my brain doesn't take to hypnosis. The only brainwashed person here is you.

You came with preconceived ideas and an unwillingness to see the truth before you."

"Is he a good kisser?" A female giggled.

"The best." Caro looped her arm through Malo's before resting her head on his shoulder. "Malo chose me, and I couldn't be happier."

"And the other two men? Are they taken?" someone asked followed by a few females agreeing with the question while others bellowed like *damu*.

Caro glanced at Garix and Ronin. "They haven't met their soulmates yet, so no, they're not taken."

"Soulmates?" another female asked.

"Yes, they know when they meet you. So those tempted to flash them, that's not how it works." Caro ran a hand down her body. "Once he sees you, he'll find you."

"So, they're here to steal our women?" A murmur rippled through the crowd. Some females cheered.

Caro frowned. "We've had plenty of opportunity to cherish each other. If by welcoming Etterians to our world means *men* and women find happiness, then I say let's give gorgeous, sexy Etterians a chance."

Malo stilled. He hadn't considered that these human males could be Eths for Etterian females. The possibility was there, of that he had no doubt, but would their females find these weaker males attractive? He studied those scowling at him. Who knew how the Ethera might work?

"Here, here," a female spectator called out.

Caro raised Malo's hand to kiss his knuckles, smiling at him. "Anyone else have questions?"

Chapter Thirteen

CARO AWOKE WITH A start. Fiery pain lanced through her right shoulder. She sucked in a shallow breath at the sharp, burning sensation that traveled to her lungs and affected her breathing. She couldn't inhale deeply, as she'd just discovered. It hurt like hell. She slowly sat up, taking note of many things at the same time. She was sitting on a cold metal floor in a cell with yellow lighting. And her shoulder was bloody, the pink of her shirt stained red.

What the hell happened? Where's Malo?

She lifted the collar of her shirt to assess the wound. The fabric had stuck to her skin. There was no way she was going to peel that off.

She was missing a shoe too, and her knees were scraped raw and bloody. The sting didn't penetrate the haze of pain from her shoulder.

The last thing she could remember was a boom, fire lancing her shoulder, and falling into Malo's arms. The wound implied she'd been shot. The lack of scorch marks on the shirt fabric meant no laser or stun weapons. Hadn't antique guns been abolished? She remembered Malo's expressions of fear, disbelief, and fury.

"Malo," she whispered as a tear slipped free.

She shivered against the cold of the cell, as if the hollow in her heart mirrored the cell's despair.

This made no sense. Why would someone shoot her? And kidnapping her gained them nothing. Earth or even E.S.A. wouldn't launch a rescue or fund a ransom. It had to be something Malo did or enemies of the Etterians. He wouldn't abandon her, would he? He'd said she was his forever. She wanted to believe it, so desperately.

A wave of pain racked her, doubling her over. She cried out. There was no one here. She could moan, complain, and wail if she damn well wanted to. But one sob later she reined it in. It hurt too much to cry, jarring her lungs. She shifted on her backside until her back rested against a metal wall. From this position, she studied the submarine-type door and its thick rubber rim and realized it was air-sealed. That wasn't a good sign. Air-sealed could mean air or liquid could flood this cell, and it wouldn't leak. She was truly at the kidnapper's mercy. If they'd stuck to Earth, she could've escaped via a window, door, or loose floor panel... She giggled. Yeah, right, her backside fitting through a floor panel?

She hastily tamped down her humor, lest it broke into full-on hysteria. Laughing would hurt like hell, and the sobbing afterward would be just as bad.

She'd heard the gunshot, had felt the blinding and breathtaking burn in her back and shoulder, then fallen into Malo's arms. In a daze, she recalled how he'd lowered her to the ground and was on a knee beside her while he spoke into this wrist. He crooned to her, words she couldn't understand. His lips had moved but with a droning sound as if she was underwater. He glanced away, his cheeks darkened, then he roared something, and leaped up.

Cold fingers had touched her wrist. She'd tilted her head to the side and stared into large black eyes against skin—shiny, pretty, like molten silver. The thing had flipped its hood back and hissed something to her. Tingles had traveled over her body, the same as when Malo had taken her to his battleship, then nothing as darkness claimed her.

The silver alien had taken her.

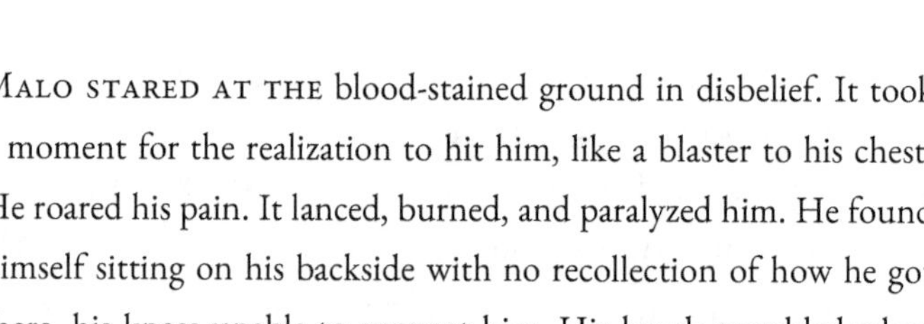

MALO STARED AT THE blood-stained ground in disbelief. It took a moment for the realization to hit him, like a blaster to his chest. He roared his pain. It lanced, burned, and paralyzed him. He found himself sitting on his backside with no recollection of how he got there, his knees unable to support him. His hands trembled when he touched where the warmth of Caro's body lingered along with droplets of her crimson blood. Like the color of her lipstick and toenails.

"Malo," Ronin bellowed in his ear.

Malo tilted his head in slow motion. Ronin rested his hand on Malo's shoulder. They ported onto the *Gladio*. He was still sitting but now on the floor of the teleportation room, the chill of the recycled air torturing his sensitive skin. Ronin hoisted Malo to his feet. Purely by instinct, Malo threw out his hand to stop his descent to the grated floor.

"Operations Commander, come with me," Data Officer Tias commanded him.

Malo trudged behind him, one step at a time. The passages seemed darker than usual or was that his soul tainting his vision and perception of the environment around him.

He appeared stunned, but he couldn't reveal the voice roaring in agony within him. The void reared its head, almost consuming him without the light that had been ripped from him.

"I am attempting to trace the port. Did Lady Caro have anything on her we could use to trace her location?"

Malo shook his head. How arrogant had he been? How naïve? To think she was safe simply because she was with him? He should've secured her safety with an O.D.I. implant. Shouldn't have left her side, not for a second, not even to save Izzy. He drew in a shuddering breath.

"There have been no strange crafts, nothing to raise our suspicions. Which means one of the known ships was not to be trusted. We are scanning each and every signature, searching for human life forms, as well. We *will* find her, Operations Commander. Whoever took her is a fool. Of all the humans to steal, they chose yours."

"They will pay for this," Malo whispered when the roaring in his head lessened enough for him to formulate words.

"They hid themselves well, blending with the humans," Tias continued. "And despite the E.S.A's sec vids, additional security males, Garix and Ronin on guard, I found no clues except the second before Lady Caroline was ported." He tapped the display vid, and there, touching Caro's hand was a Yithian.

Red blurred Malo's vision. "I will destroy them."

"I agree. They have become troublesome. The issue is, Operations Commander, no Yithian ships were within porting range." Tias clenched his jaw, then sighed. "This is not as simple."

Malo gritted his teeth and flicked the images on the display vid. He paused on Izzy cheering from beside Garix. Ronin was a few feet to the side as per protocol, but between them were hooded figures. One clasped the edge of its hood and revealed yellow fingers. He frowned. A Maloid? As per the archives, Maloidians weren't known to humans. He slumped. Tias was correct. This wasn't a simple puzzle to solve. And that Maloidians and Yithians worked together was something Malo needed to share with King Xeus.

A Yithian circled Izzy then grabbed her from behind. She didn't struggle until she noticed the silver arm wrapped around her. Then she dropped, using her weight to unbalance her abductor.

"Izzy is secure but understandably distraught. Garix has remained with her and will be delivering her to the Valiant. Sub-Commander Vorn will ensure her safety, as well." Ronin settled beside Malo.

Malo nodded. Keeping Izzy safe would matter to Caro.

"We have set course for Yithia, regardless of knowing who the true culprit is," Tias said.

Malo spared Tias a pointed glance.

"Trav has sent out discreet feelers. If any of our allies know anything, we will discover it," Ronin said.

Malo sighed and met their gazes, their determination precious. His chest echoed with the same emotion. Along with the need for Caro that battered at him like an unyielding storm.

"Good," he rasped, his voice having been ripped from him. "Send me any information the moment you receive it. I am calling in favors."

"That would help." Tias tapped the console, the vid before him flickering with dialogue, scan results, and miscellaneous data. "Someone must know something."

"She is alive, Malo." Ronin gripped Malo's shoulder while clasping his forearm. "We *will* find her."

"Yes." He strode off, his destination his quarters. The moment he stepped into his room, and the door closed affording him privacy, he leaned against the bulkhead and slid to the floor. "Caro," he murmured, unable to control the shudders, the trembling hands, the need to hold and scent her.

He had to be strong. She needed him now more than ever, his timid *thamani*. He glanced at his quarters and moaned. The scent of her and their union lingered. His mind flashed images of her laughing, teasing, now tormenting him with her unattainability.

Staggering to his feet, he stumbled to the cleansing room. He splashed water on his cheeks before staring at his dripping face in the small reflect above the bowl. His eyes looked haunted. He needed to hide that, to appear invincible, not desperate. Desperation would only have them attacking him with a frenzy that would not be helpful. He drew in deep breaths, calling forth his training, infamous focus, and legendary control. Instead, fury engulfed him and hardened his ice blue eyes. They glowed with the emotions overwhelming him. That wasn't good either.

He stood in front of his display vid and commed the first on his list. Today, his name would drip from everyone's lips. He didn't care, not if it returned his life force to him. Nothing mattered but Caro.

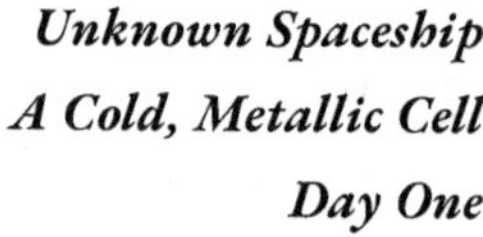

Unknown Spaceship
A Cold, Metallic Cell
Day One

THE LIGHTS FLICKERED TO white, and the massive door opened without a sound. Caro raised her head, expecting a silver alien to step through the door. The creature that did was beautiful. Caro's breath caught when she—and it *was* a female—glided across the floor.

She was tall, lithe with a pale-yellow skin. The black markings on her face were mesmerizing, and her tentacled hair swayed like willow branches in a gentle breeze, strangely calming Caro's simmering anxiety. Her garment was unusual, a mixture between a kimono and an evening gown, showing way too much cleavage. She smiled at Caro, but the solid black of her eyes showed no warmth. Caro had experienced way too much insincerity not to be able to spot it now. Not that she knew for certain whether this alien had expressive eyes. The black of her irises was startling against her pale-yellow skin and as menacing as the silver shark-headed aliens, who hovered in the background.

"She has been injured. I need you to attend to this, Bezu. This will not work with my plans for her."

The silver alien hissed something.

The yellow female faced him. A battle of wills and words ensued, all hisses and lisps. Eventually the silver alien called Bezu marched into the cell to rip Caro's shirt from her body.

Her cowering would gain her nothing, yet she hadn't expected him to do that. She shrieked and renewed agony set her shoulder on fire. She'd kept the pain at bay by being as immobile as possible. Fresh blood now oozed down her upper arm as pain pulsed anew. She shivered when her last remnant of warmth fell in jagged ribbons to the floor. He withdrew a patch of some sort from his military pants and slapped it on her, making her wince at his rough manhandling. The pain eased to a dull ache. She glared at the yellow female, looking for a distraction and hoping to at least get a few answers.

"Why are you doing this? Why not just let me die rather than heal me?"

"I do not want you dead, female." She curled her small mouth into what Caro had to assume was a smirk. "I, Imarri of House Zennr, want revenge. You will give me this or pay with your blood."

"I'm already paying," Caro snapped, despite her shoulders slumping. This female hated Etterians. Caro was but a pawn. "What revenge?"

"I will not reveal my plans to you, Earthian," Imarri spat. "You need not know them to bring me satisfaction."

Caro snorted. "You can't force me to be complicit in your revenge."

The yellow alien smirked again. "I can if you wish to eat."

"I have enough stored." Caro gestured to her wide backside.

"The journey is a maximum of two weeks. Will your stores be sufficient?" Imarri chuckled.

Caro scowled, deciding on the spot to despise this female, whatever she was.

"I thought not. We will start your training tomorrow. You will need to be more skilled than your pathetic self to survive your destination. Only the toughest can endure the first three days there." She turned to leave before glancing over her shoulder. "Every comfort must be earned. Tomorrow, you will fight for warmth."

Despite her best efforts, Caro shivered at the prospect of being warm.

"What does he see in you." The yellow bitch shrugged and left, taking her shark servants with her.

She'd said 'he.' Was this about Malo? Caro curled in on herself as the lighting returned to that sickly yellow after the door sealed shut.

Yellow had become her least favorite color.

Of all the aliens she'd met, there was only one species she liked and their skin was bronze.

Day Two

CARO WAS AN ICE cube. Even her goose bumps were frozen. At some point, her shivering had reached maximum vibrations. She'd moaned at being warm, at last. Which meant she was hypothermic. She wasn't sure though. So she'd pulled herself up and paced until the shivering began again. Then she knew she'd live. She hadn't been able to sleep for fear she wouldn't wake up. Nor could she get comfortable, not on the cold metallic floor, not under the nauseating yellow lighting, and not with the dull ache in her shoulder. It was better, but she still resented the healing they'd given her. Something told her she might have to pay for it with her soul.

To say she was miserable would be an understatement. Exhausted and wounded with anger and hate festering in her soul? Her stomach gurgled. She would soon add starving to the list. Not to mention, she had a desperate need to relieve herself but had no idea where she was supposed to do it.

The real torture wasn't the pain, the cold, or the actual kidnapping. It was the humiliation she would endure having to go in the corner of her cell, like an animal in a cage.

Then the bitch had dangled warmth at Caro, like a doggy treat. She hated getting angry, losing control, or that her actions fell to her untried instincts. Once her fury was spent, she'd surface to find herself on a ledge, teetering on the edge of darkness. It seemed like today was the day she would own that ledge or die trying.

At least Malo had cherished her for a few hours, truly valued her. For that alone, she missed him. The intense emotions he invoked in such a short time hinted at a long-forgotten legend...love at first sight. She snorted but the possibility lingered in her mind, ringing with truth. It sounded crazy but felt amazing.

He was searching for her. She couldn't see him abandoning her now even though finding her would be impossible. How could he track her without some sort of electronic device? And he couldn't know who'd taken her. She stifled a sob then staggered to the corner of the cell to relieve herself. Doing so made her spirits descend further. She swiped a tear off her cheek while tugging her skirt down with one hand.

She glanced at her pale skin tinged a sickly blue. Despite sleep clamoring at her, she couldn't allow herself to succumb. She'd die for sure.

As she paced her cell, she winced when she neared her 'latrine.' The acrid stench of urine was discernible. She whimpered at what had to be the most demeaning experience of her life.

"Get a grip, Caroline," she muttered. "Who knows what else you'll have to do to survive."

Gritting her teeth against her fate and the cold, she did something she swore she'd never do again, in her life, as in ever.

She did squats until her thighs and calves burned.

On wobbly knees, she leaned against the metallic panels and shivered when her bare skin touched the ice-cold wall. She lifted her head to stare at the ceiling, wondering what to do now. If there was one thing she hated, it was boredom, and she foresaw quite a bit in her future. She chuckled, imagining asking the yellow witch if she had a sudoku tablet on hand. Perhaps a tiny stylus? That would be great, thanks.

As the goose bumps spread, she limped to the center of the cell to sway her hips. Squats were out for now so perhaps a little dancing might keep the cold at bay. There was no music, but she had an imagination, and it was just last night she'd revealed her inner porn star to Malo. She remembered how she hadn't been able to shake the feeling he watched her avidly. All attempts to convince herself otherwise were irrefutably thwarted by a heart that had laid claim to an unattainable man. It was surreal that she'd been allowed to kiss and make love to him.

Recalling the beat of the one song she'd danced to, she let the 'music' flow through her. She lost herself to the moment. Hell, she might as well put it on repeat and go to town. There was no one to see her here, and she could be herself with no judgment forthcoming.

"What are you doing?"

Caro squeaked and froze with mortification, her cheeks heating for other reasons not linked to her recent spastic gyrations. "Dancing to keep warm." She faced Imarri. "I'm glad you came," she said, hiding a smirk when the witch's unibrow twitched. "Is there a place I can go?"

"Go where?"

"Go, as in to use the toilet, latrine, water closet, long drop, privy, outhouse?" Imarri's blank expression didn't promise any comprehension, so Caro tried again. "To relieve my bladder, to urinate?"

Imarri's brow twitched again. But at last, she sashayed to the back of the cell and pressed a panel. A compact toilet-like structure slid out.

Caro bounced on her toes. "Thank you. You touch the wall here for it to appear and disappear?"

Imarri demonstrated by stroking ridges in the panel, vanishing the toilet into the wall. "Ignorant Earthian. By the stench, you did it where you sleep." Her lips curled in disdain.

Caro gritted against her rising anger and the burn of embarrassment. How was she supposed to know there was a hidden toilet? Arrogant alien. The problem was in the word 'hidden.' Not that anything this yellow bitch said mattered to her, but since it echoed her opinion, it hit too close to home.

"You are stupid, lacking the knowledge all other species have. What Malo sees in a creature so beneath him..." Imarri sighed. "Regardless of what, that you snagged his attention is something I can use." She paused in the middle of the cell. "Now to discover what you are truly made of, Earthian. Let us begin your training." With impatience barely restrained, she gestured to the silver alien behind her to step into the cell. He did with the door hitting his backside. "Come closer, Earthian."

Caro hesitated, not liking the idea of this creature using her to mete out revenge. She studied the female then glanced at the silver alien who'd raised his black block-like gun. She hastily stepped forward, not wanting to get shot again. And the yellow light on the gun promised pain. She wondered about its significance. The pain that arched through her skull made her cry out. She tested the laceration inside her cheek with her tongue and tasted her blood, grimacing at the metallic flavor and the sting of the cut.

She glared at Imarri. "What was that for?" Her cheek throbbed and promised further complaints later. If Imarri tried that again, Caro would slap the bitch back. Pain was a two-way street in her world. Well, she would try.

"Prompt obedience is required," the alien snapped.

"Then get a pet," Caro spat.

Imarri swung her hand again, but Caro ducked, scowling at the same time.

"You have a sharp wit. This will not do well where you are headed, tewaa."

Oh? So the slap was to help her? Caro seethed. "Fuck you. I'll survive anyway I damn well choose."

The witch's laughter was husky and seductive. Caro almost snorted. She suspected everything this alien did was meant to seduce or beguile.

Still wearing a smile, Imarri met Caro's gaze. "There is hope for you yet."

Caro didn't see the punch coming, having never been in such a situation before. It doubled her over, firing agony through her belly. Air escaped her lungs in an audible ejection. While sucking in needed breaths, she glared at the alien's torso. She bluffed a forward stumble, but instead, swung an upper cut at Imarri, sending her flying backwards. Caro shot a glance at the shark servant, anticipating a blast from his gun. He hadn't budged, but she caught a glimpse of his upper lip curling, as if he was enjoying Imarri injured. Okay, so no love lost there.

Caro returned her attention to the yellow bitch. She didn't delude herself that she was this awesome fighter. The contact with the female's jaw had been a lucky shot. Yes, she had some moves, two to be precise. Years ago, E.S.A. had scheduled self-defense classes due to the riots terrorizing their campus. They wanted to ensure their staff could defend themselves. Caro had attended, but she'd believed she'd never need to use any of the techniques she'd learned.

"Good," the alien said as green blood dribbled from the corner of her mouth. "Get me the katac," she commanded the silver observer.

He hissed, and she spat something fierce, promising retaliation if he didn't obey. He grunted, stomped out of the cell and entered again a minute later. In the time he'd taken to do as commanded, Caro had stared at Imarri, not glancing away in a show of timidity. To survive her time with this witch, she would need to be bolder and stronger. If

Malo was searching for her, she'd ensure she was alive when he found her.

Imarri accepted the long shaft from the shark and faced Caro. "Step back," she commanded.

Caro pinned herself to the back wall. Imarri swung the stick, twirling it with a fluidity and speed that was breathtaking. Music emanated from the shaft, indicating that it was hollow. It also warbled with certain jerky movements, absorbing the force. Imarri's foot placements mimicked that of ancient Chinese calming techniques Caro had seen images of. She tossed the pole to Caro who caught it, sort of, whacking herself on the top of her head as a reward for her clumsiness. She winced but didn't pause to search for a lump.

"Now, swing it and practice placing your feet as I have demonstrated. It balances you."

Caro did as told, slowly and without grace. Every time she dropped it, Imarri slapped her, on the arm, face, or back...the closest part of her anatomy at the time. She stung all over and dodged automatically when the stick slipped from her weak grip.

"Continue. I will return in a few hours." Imarri exited, taking the menacing silver alien with her.

He shot Caro a glance, but she couldn't be sure what his expression portrayed. The door shut. She didn't move, just stood there staring at the stick in her hand. It was light, resembling a bamboo pole. In the center of the cell, she twirled, using both hands, relishing its mournful tune. The speed at which it spun made her stumble forward. The top end tilted to the floor. She spread her legs like she'd seen the witch do and swung again. This time the whistling was melodic, and the pole whirled quicker. She tentatively lowered one hand and kept on swinging. It went better without an audience.

Able to do this much felt good, flooding her with a sense of accomplishment. She changed directions in quick succession, finding her feet naturally balancing to compensate the abrupt changes. Her arms burned from overuse. Her shoulder had begun to throb as sweat coated her skin. She was warm, for the first time in hours.

When her arms could no longer lift the katac, she leaned against the refreshingly cool metallic wall and smiled. Even though she worked the damn stick like a two-year old, it didn't matter. She'd considered using the thing on Imarri but knew instinctively that she'd rip the stick out of Caro's clumsy fingers. Definitely slap her around a bit more too.

And besides, if Caro managed to escape the cell, then what? She didn't know what awaited her outside the door. More aliens? And being on a spaceship implied they were traveling fast to somewhere so far away it required *two weeks* to get there. She'd have to battle countless silver or yellow aliens to seize control of a spaceship she had no idea how to fly. They were also armed with those black guns flickering yellow freaking lights. She wouldn't stand a chance. Pushing off the wall, she picked up the katac.

Hopefully, over the next thirteen days, Imarri would give Caro different weapons. She needed something to hold back the boredom, and weapons training promised to do just that. And since she'd decided Malo would find her, she couldn't allow herself to ponder what-if-he-didn't. Therein lay despair and heartache, weakening her. To survive this, she needed to be strong or at least pretend to be. Even if she was deceiving herself.

Chapter Fourteen

Etterian scimitar Kevol

Officer's quarters

Malo awoke with a start. Alodon's hell. He rubbed his gritty eyes. Everything ached, from his shoulders to his legs, but sleep was elusive when his mind plagued him with every possible scenario—the worst ones. Was his Caro being tortured? Raped? Was she dead already? His heart lurched at the thought. She was still alive. Her death would trigger the Ethera's crippling agony as well as expand the void. The Ethera current displeasure was bad enough. Throwing his feet over the side of the disheveled bed, he rested his elbows on his knees and rubbed his face.

They'd received many responses to their enquiries. Ronin had sifted through them with only a few promising to be more helpful. More helpful? Malo wanted to punch something. They had nothing. They raced toward Yithia without knowing for sure if their destination was accurate. She might still be on Earth. He could be traveling away from her, and he hated the helplessness that paralyzed him.

Maker.

Pain lanced through his chest on a constant basis. He craved her smile, her witty conversation, just holding her hand, and needed to find her with a growing urgency. The Ethera compelled him, but there was also an intense fire in the region of his hearts he couldn't explain. It drove him more than the Ethera ever could. He knew not the name of this emotion. When she was with him, it burned as well but with light and not this debilitating darkness.

"Operations Commander." Tias's voice cut through the silence.

Malo frowned at his O.D.I and wondered if this had disturbed his slumber. "Yes, Tias."

"I may have found her."

Malo burst into a run, sans footwear or tunic. He didn't care that he looked like his mind had embraced the void. Any information on his Caro mattered more to him than portraying professionalism or following his cursed code. He burst into Tias's office and strode to where the male punched keys on his multi-lit console.

"Scans have shown the presence of a human female on one vessel. It's an Etterian scimitar."

Malo stilled. His mind reeled. This made no sense. "Etterian? Why? Why target Caro?" His anger rose.

"If I may continue, Operations Commander?"

Malo scowled at Tias but grunted, giving his permission while conveying his apologies.

"Scans also show the presence of a Maloidian female. I thought this unusual, so I traced the ship's flight path. The Etterian vessel hovered over Argaxx for approximately one hour. After which, it traveled to Earth with no dockings made en route."

"Not Yithia then," Malo whispered, his thoughts racing. Who had he angered that originated from Argaxx? The last dealing he had with a Maloidian was Imarri... That cesu. Alodon's balls, she wouldn't dare. "The scimitar's signature?" He pinched his lips, knowing the answer but asking anyway.

"*Iqiniso's*. It seems Ambassador Barro did not bother to change it to Maloidian."

"He is a proud male and her uncle. The truth is revealed." Malo paced, trying to push aside his fury to get to the heart of this. "Imarri? Why would she...do something like this?" He ran a hand over his face, cold stinging the edges of his mind. "We are allies. I did not sense any animosity on her part."

"It explains who took Lady Caro, who the Maloidian female is in the scans."

Malo grunted. All valid points. When he found Caro, he'd take Imarri to task, perhaps solve the mystery. Had he offended her by not escorting her to Argaxx himself? Her sensitivity to her ranking was notorious. Or was this more personal? Had his pseudo-seduction hit a nerve?

"Comm Alllero," he commanded Tias.

The male punched keys, making the communication request on Malo's behalf, which was accepted within minutes. The elderly queen's crystal clear image appeared. Her black markings had almost disappeared, but Malo believed it made her eyes bolder, more intimidating. He smiled with fondness at her.

"Malo, my favorite Etterian male, what seems to be the need for this comm?"

Thanks to the Ethera, warmth filled his chest, something he'd never experienced toward her. "My dearest Queen Alllero, you are as breathtaking as usual."

She giggled. "A sweet talking Etterian? Maszaks, this must be important." Her black gaze traveled his exposed chest then she grinned. "Not that I will complain if you comm me dressed as you are."

"Conversations with Citus inform me that I am not your only favorite. I am deeply disappointed."

She dismissed his comment with a wave of her delicate hand. "What is the matter, Malo?"

"My Dar Eth has been taken, my queen." He inched closer to the display vid so she could see his eyes.

She leaned forward as well, studied his face for a few moments, then beamed, jiggling her hands palms forward in applause. "But...this is wonderful. Xeus must be ecstatic."

Malo rubbed the back of his neck, trying to keep the exhaustion at bay. "He has also been blessed, my queen."

"Truly?" she gasped then giggled like a youngin. "I will comm him later to congratulate him. I assume it happened recently? Especially since my Serratu Kayarra have not informed me of such."

The Serratu Kayarra or Silent Sirens were infamous among all operatives. The Maloidian females were trained in all manner of seductions and promised to make anyone's erotic dreams pale in comparison. Imarri headed up this band of skilled females. Malo smothered a snort. She could learn a lesson or two from Caro.

"Yes, we found a compatible species that sparks the Ethera."

Alllero pursed her lips. "And she is the reason you look like death?"

"I suspect a Kayarra stole her."

Alllero's unibrow arched before anger darkened her markings.

He continued. "Our investigation indicates the vessel carrying my Caro last docked at Argaxx with ties linked to Barro."

Alllero tapped her chin. "Mm. I trust your sources, Malo. What you need from me will be granted. You truly are my favorite."

"Thank you, my queen, I...need her," he answered with all honesty, expecting to surprise the queen but not caring. He violated no code if he shared how he suffered.

Alllero stared at him for a few minutes, her face inscrutable. She glanced down, then his arm buzzed, receiving a message. "Those are my codes to the Serratu Kayarra's data cubes. Agent Imarri is not aware I have these, and I would like to keep it so."

"Thank you again." He thumped his chest, pinning his fist there as a sign of deep respect.

"She has softened you, Malo. It weakens *and* strengthens you."

He winced. "I am aware of this. Once I have her in my arms, I will take every precaution."

"And bring her to meet me when you find her."

"I will do so, my queen."

She gave him a curt nod and ended the communication.

"Operations Commander, I received a message from the *Iqiniso*. The source is unknown. The message has merit though." Tias tapped the console.

"Truth?" A message from within the ship? A traitor on board or his Caro reaching out to him? Excitement burst through his exhausted body, and he bounced on his toes.

"Imarri has her. That's all it says." Tias displayed the message on vid. "A confirmation, Operations Commander."

Malo clenched his fists, his vision red. "Comm Imarri."

"Operations Commander Malo, what a surprise." Her voice reached through the blank display vid. "I apologize, we are experiencing technical malfunctions. Perhaps comm me at a later stage when I can see your image?"

He gritted his teeth, unable to demand he return his Dar Eth. Doing so might jeopardize Caro's safety. *Maker.* He'd have to play nice. "Scans reveal you are near this worthless mid-grade planet called Earth. I was hoping you would join me for dinner... An apology of sorts for my impolite behavior."

"Dinner?" She sounded intrigued. "I must decline. An urgent request from Queen Alllero has me returning to Argaxx. Perhaps next time?"

Urgent? He scowled. "I am deeply disappointed."

Tias waved at Malo, then pointed at the display vids. There, in a cell, was his Caro. She slept on the floor, one hand to the side exposing a delicate wrist. The Ethera's demanding cries for her quietened, easing the pounding headache behind his eyes. He stroked the display vid, trailing along Caro's cheek. She was well and alive. He released a breath and gripped Tias's shoulder in thanks.

Hope fluttered in Malo's chest like trapped omeika.

He sighed at his strange comparison. Omeika were indigenous carnivorous fish that reproduced at such a rate that they stained Etteria's seas red. They were exported in great quantities since the flavor of them mimicked the consumer's favorite dish. They fluttered when out of the water, an image the sensation in his chest emulated.

"I will comm you on my return to Etteria," he said to Imarri.

"Please do, Malo." She ended the comm, that alone told him she thought herself superior.

"Accepting the comm granted a stronger access to the scimitar's system." Tias flicked his fingers and sent the images to Malo's O.D.I. reminding him of Queen Alllero's message.

What it contained tore a war cry from him, one he hadn't used since Gikaet. He leaned over to show Tias the code, not prepared to forward it lest it be traced. When Tias punched the code into the system, images flashed on the various display vids.

"They have quite an in-depth file on you, Operations Commander," Tias said.

Malo focused on the display vids and scowled.

"Various wagers have been set and never met. The largest odds are on bedding you."

"Not a word more, Tias," he threatened though he didn't mind the humor crinkling the corners of Tias's eyes. "Investigate each Etterian male they have on file. And create notifications for anything unusual. When they alert you, comm me immediately."

Malo paused at the door, glancing over his shoulder at Tias. "Good work," he muttered then sauntered to his quarters. Intoxicated by their progress, he notified Pilot Afax to set course for Argaxx.

Be patient, my Caro. I am coming for you.

Unknown Spaceship
Cold, Metallic Cell
Day Five

CARO RESTED AGAINST THE wall. She was thinking of naming her stick 'Vinnie,' for 'vindictive.' She'd developed an affection for the inanimate object and hoped she got to keep it. When the door swished open for the second time that day, she scrambled to her feet. She palmed her katac when it was just Bezu who'd stepped into the cell. He held no bowls or water packets, and his three-fingered hands twitched.

"Bezu?" Caro winced at her squeaky voice. Only thing she should fear was Malo never finding her.

"I heard *her*...Imarri mention Operations Commander Malo. Is this true? You are his?"

"Yes," Caro said, not hesitating. She *was* Malo's, if and when he saved her. Where the hell was he? What was taking so long? For someone with his authority, he sure was struggling to find her. The male had a battleship at his beck and call, for tart's sake.

"He's the most feared operative," Bezu said. "Many owe him favors."

She blinked. Operative? Feared? So, not an engineer as she'd suspected. She grinned.

Bezu ran his black gaze over her. "If you are his, as you say, then you are his Dar Eth."

"Dar Eth?" Caro echoed, trying to look like she had no clue what he was talking about.

"I understand why you must hide this from *her*, but it is pointless to pretend with me. We are aware the Etterians are finding their mates among your people. This does not concern me, Caro." He sank down the wall to sit on the floor. He'd come to talk. "I do not want Malo killing my spawn or me for my involvement in this stupidity." He rubbed the left side of his shark head, like a bald man stroking his non-existent hair. This close, tiny silver jagged markings ran along his thick neck to where it met his upper arms. "I sent a message to your Malo, revealing who took you. I cannot do more lest I anger the Maloidian. She is vindictive, a trait I admire, but..."

"Your spawn." Caro nodded while smothering an inner squeal. Malo knowing where she was...made all the difference to her. Hope blossomed anew, saturating the bleeding darkness that had stained her heart of late.

"I can make your stay comfortable, although, she must not suspect."

"Would...would you mind talking to me? I need the company," Caro said, desperate to converse with someone other than herself.

Bezu jerked away. "You wish to...talk to me? In what regard?"

"About you, any subject will do." She folded her arms across her chest and bounced on her toes. Standing still only made her colder. "What's your world like? Your spawn? How'd you end up indentured to *her*? You could read an instructional manual if it means I don't have to listen to myself think."

His lips curled upward in what appeared to be a grimace, but when he hiss-laughed, she realized he'd found what she said amusing.

"Very well, Caro. I shall stay after each meal. You are shivering. I find this temperature perfect. As a Maloidian, Imarri does too. I was not aware your species cannot tolerate temperature fluctuations. Come with me." He rose and approached the door. Pressing a tiny camouflaged panel to the right, he gestured to her to draw closer. He took her hand, his touch gentle, and held it palm down on a screen. A white light scanned her, then a symbol flashed in green. "Now the cell will modify the temperature to your core."

The urge to hug him came over her, but she wasn't sure how he'd react. So, she settled on giving him the biggest grin she could form. "Thank you, Bezu. I was so cold I was scared if I fell asleep I wouldn't wake up."

"That is possible?" He gaped, revealing massive sabreteeth.

She rubbed her arms and sighed, relishing the warm air circulating the room. "Yes. We become hypothermic then our bodily functions just cease."

"I never considered that other species could be this..."

"Squishy?" she teased.

"Vulnerable," he said, and his lips curled again.

"That too," she chuckled.

"To reveal all your teeth is to imply an interest in me, Caro. I do not find you..." He scanned her again. "Attractive."

She squeaked and stepped back, creating distance between them. "It does? I'm sorry. We smile when we're happy."

"This is good to know. I shall not take your invitation seriously."

She studied him for a moment, learning his subtle tells, the ones that revealed his humor, worry, fear, or horror. "What do you do when you're not stealing Earthian females?"

He susurrated while flicking his knee. "I must serve my remaining months, then I am free to farm."

"Are you serving time as a punishment?" Caro asked as gently as she could.

She couldn't ask him outright if he was a criminal or a slave. It might offend him, and from where she was standing, he was the only one willing to talk to her. She slid down the wall next to him, though not too close.

"Each Yithian must serve our king and Yithia. Every five solar rotations or years, I abandon my spawn and mate for the cold confines of a slave ship. This is preferable to mining the black rock in the deserts surrounding Mascroba."

She scowled. What a choice—slave labor or military service. "Mascroba?"

"The royal seat of King Urio, our great and illustrious ruler. Though, there has been talk of a rebellion."

"There's always talk, even in peaceful times," Caro said.

"You speak truth, Caro."

"So, what do you farm?" She couldn't picture sharklike males as farmers.

"Ah, in the depths of our oceans, areemi grow wild. Their orange and purple leaves are sweet and tender. When I farm, my estuuba—your word is family—will eat well."

"That's a noble goal, Bezu. Can I let you in on a little secret?" She raised her hand to touch the side of his head like he'd done earlier. His skin was cold, clammy, like how she imagined a fish's scales would feel. It was pretty though, the way the yellow light played along his shimmering skin. "On Earth, many centuries ago, there were sea creatures, fierce, powerful, and feared by Earthians. These creatures were called sharks, but we persevered and annihilated them all. The Great White reminds me of your species, of Yithians."

"The Great White...shark?" He activated his O.D.I. "I see the resemblance." He hiss-laughed and tilted his arm to share the holographic footage with her.

"They say, millions of years ago, there was a Megalodon, a massive shark."

He tapped the cuneiform and an image of a Megalodon appeared. "Our royalty reach that size after many years of rulership. It is why they are chosen to rule. None dare challenge them."

"What? Your King Urio is that size?" She bounced on her backside, her eyes widening. "Under the circumstances, I don't want to meet him but...a real honest-to-goodness Megalodon?"

"I too shall share something you may not know, Caro. An operative gifted the king with an Earthian female. Footage was sent to all Yithians. The operative claimed she was a half-breed, part Etterian with her black hair and short name. The king sold her to the Maloidian Ambassador Barro, none the wiser."

Caro gasped. *Monkey's bananas.* How dare these...aliens sell humans like cattle. The owner could do anything to this woman and no one would say anything, right?

"Is she...alive?"

"Yes, Barro sold her to Etteria's Prince Citus. This is why Imarri has an Etterian scimitar since Barro is her estuuba."

So the plot thickens. Caro grinned. In Etteria's clutches, she might be able to ask Malo to get this woman freed. "The purchase price was this ship?" Holy noodles, how much did one of these cost? "How rich is this prince?"

"The Etterians are beyond wealthy, but this matters not to them. Nothing is as important as a Dar Eth, Caro."

She patted his forearm. "I will make sure Malo doesn't harm your estuuba, Bezu."

"Thank you. We will land on Argaxx before your Eth reaches us. His influence is great... It is this I fear."

"If Imarri or your commanding officer find out about your message, will you promise to sneak off the ship and hide in Argaxx?"

"To what end?" Bezu shook his head. "If I do not complete my service, my estuuba suffer."

"I hate that I can't help you, Bezu." She squeezed his three-fingered hands.

"It is kind of you to offer, Caro. Just ensuring they survive is enough for me."

"Oh, I'll do that without you asking." She stared at his long fingernails sharpened to a point. "No estuuba should be collateral damage."

"Your species is demonstrative and kinder than expected." He studied their clasped hands.

She released him. "Yes, well, there are good and bad in all species," she blurted.

"It is a weakness Yithians will take advantage of." Bezu shifted to face her. "You must hide this, and it is best you show fearlessness toward Maloidians and Yithians." He squeezed her hand like she had done. "You have done well so far, Caro. This is almost over."

Chapter Fifteen

CARO HAD EARNED HERSELF a new uniform in dark green. Regardless, it was warm. And she received something edible once a day. All of it had cost her, though. Her muscles had muscles that ached—the pain a constant reminder not to become complacent. Her hands were raw with fresh blisters from gripping and swinging Vinnie, and she longed for a shower. New clothes didn't hide her limp hair or the foul smell that emanated off her.

Imarri, the witch, had suggested cutting Caro's hair. In reaction, Caro had swung her stick and swept the alien's feet from under her. Malo loved her hair. She wasn't about to cut it for anyone, especially not for her abductor. Of course, this action had garnered another slap. She had bruises all over her body and a split lip from her wonderful time with the yellow bitch. Many souvenirs to remember her by. One star. Wouldn't recommend.

What would today bring? They were about halfway through the journey. Caro dreaded and welcomed their arrival. The cell's metallic gray walls were driving her a little crazy with each day she remained here. Humans weren't designed to survive without the sun's rays, even if it was imitation. The body needed it, thrived on it to be productive.

No sunlight meant her soul suffered.

With a sigh, she pushed away from the wall and picked up Vinnie. Above a thin line in the flooring, she took up a position and swung the katac, trying to remember the daily techniques Imarri had shown her. If Caro 'performed' to the witch's satisfaction today, she might get to 'cleanse.' Blasted aliens and their overcomplications. It was a shower, for tart's sake. Water came from above and rained on her head.

The cleanser was in the cleansing unit in the cleansing room.

She far preferred human words. The damn shower was in the bathroom.

Regardless, she twirled Vinnie with smooth strokes, sonic vibrations rippling up her arms. Her shoulder had healed and didn't pain her as much as she'd expected. Five days to heal a bullet wound? That was incredible. Earth could use that technology, and she'd mention it to Reyes if she saw him again. Thinking of him shoved Izzy's image to the fore. Caro winced. She'd tried not to think of her dearest friend. She was fine, well, no doubt protected by Garix or Ronin. Or had the Yithians taken her too? Caro would ask Bezu.

By the time the door slid open, her breathing was ragged and sweat coated her skin. Despite her burning muscles, the sense of accomplishment was unparalleled. She lowered Vinnie but kept him close before facing her *guests*.

"Welcome. Please do come in," she said, sweeping her arm out. "Would you like a beverage?"

"Tewaa, I see your fire has not diminished." Imarri's lips curled in a semblance of a smile when she sauntered into the cell.

Caro straightened, tightening her grip on Vinnie. The friendliness always put her on guard. The yellow alien never did anything without a purpose. When she showed Caro any kindness, the person paying for that was Caro herself.

Two silver aliens stomped into the cell, coming to stand behind Imarri. She stiffened, raising the katac as if it could shield her.

"Ayetz will insert a device in your wrist. If you fight him, Naal will ensure you feel my displeasure." The shine in Imarri's black eyes revealed her eagerness, as if Caro's disobedience and subsequent pain delighted her.

Caro widened her eyes. No, first weapons and trained how to use it. Then an O.D.I. from where she could contact Malo? She almost shook her head. How stupid was Imarri? "Like an O.D.I?"

A slight squaring of Imarri's shoulders revealed her surprise.

Joy blossomed in Caro's heart at such a small victory. "Malo explained it to me."

Imarri's lips pinched at the mention of Malo, sparking Caro's curiosity. She'd plenty of time to analyze all scenarios as to the reasons behind her abduction. No matter from which angle she approached the enigma, she ended with jealousy as the catalyst. She studied the beautiful alien female and wondered why Malo had rejected her.

And of course, the next thought would have her asking why he'd chosen Caro, an overweight human woman. Even more amazing than this, was that he believed her beautiful. He'd said so many times, with large enough doses of sincerity that she'd begun to believe him.

"It seems he has been forthcoming with you. I find that...odd."

"Odd?" Caro dodged Ayetz's attempts to grab her left wrist. Naal raised his gun, but by then, she'd offered Ayetz her right wrist. "I'm left-handed," she mumbled. "I suppose he's not forthcoming with you?" Caro twisted the metaphorical dagger, hoping her words caused Imarri some level of pain or discomfort.

She shifted her gaze away from the sharp tool Ayetz pressed to her skin, hissing as agony seared her skin. Her instinctive urge was to snatch her hand back, but if she did that, he might do more damage. She bit her lip, freezing the scream that vibrated up her throat. Her gaze flew to her wrist, her blood dribbling onto the metallic floor. When Ayetz slid a piece of metal—the size of her pinkie-nail—under her skin, she whimpered. It scrapped tissue, blood bubbling around it. By now, her wrist was firmly held in his three-fingered grip. He tilted the same device, scanned her wrist, and the incision sealed. He rudely slapped her skin twice, activating the holographic buttons. At least the pain had ceased, with the forgotten red drops beading the floor and the perspiration dewing on her upper lip the only evidence of her ordeal remaining.

"He is Head of Operations and is only forthcoming if it serves a purpose." Imarri's bored tone didn't ring true.

Well, well, head of operations didn't sound like engineering. But she couldn't ask Imarri about it when Malo was so forthcoming. Caro tapped random holographic buttons an inch above her skin. Imarri squeezed Caro's wrist, digging her nails in. She punched the letters until they morphed into the English alphabet.

"Do not believe you can contact anyone from this device. Your O.D.I. has been restricted. The bulkheads also seal in any unauthorized communications."

"Like a Faraday cage?" Caro lowered her wrist to meet Imarri's gaze. So, have a connector device but limit it? Mm, maybe Bezu could help Caro unlock it.

"If that means all signals have been blocked, then yes."

"Why implant it at all?" Caro studied her unscarred but blood-stained wrist, wondering if the device could be programmed to explode, monitor her vital signs, or serve as a location beacon? The latter would be wonderful, guiding Malo straight to this ship.

Imarri ignored her before gesturing to the soldiers. They left the cell before her. "Come, Caro, if you wish to cleanse."

Exiting the cell as smoothly as she entered had Caro rushing after Imarri. Her focus flitted over the new surroundings, feeling surreal at the sight of something other than her walls. She followed down a passage that had matching doors leading into, what she assumed, were other cells. Who or what else had been captured? It had better not be Izzy. The grated flooring was harsh on her bare feet, and the air was noticeably crisper and cleaner. She rubbed the goose bumps forming on her arms despite the additional covering her new clothing provided.

"Is that her?" a silver alien whispered.

Caro's head shot up at a shark deigning to speak English.

"I do not see what all this trouble is about," his companion hissed before tightening something inside a yellow-lit hatch.

"I activated the Yithian Language Protocol, and of course, Maloidian. It's good to speak in a civilized tongue," Imarri said, turning a corner and continuing along another dimly-lit, cramped passage.

"They're not speaking English?" Caro stared at the hissing sharks, before stumbling after Imarri. "The O.D.I.'s a translator?"

"I'm speaking Maloidian now. Your English was...cumbersome." Imarri paused outside a door, activated the console with her palm, and entered the room.

Colors bombarded Caro's eyes, bright in their rarity. There were no furniture items, just beautiful carpets with strewn cushions on the floor. Nothing looked like Malo's quarters, well, except for the replicator and rehydrator in the corner. The cleansing room was also not in the same place. She prayed she got to use an en-suite and not shared ablutions, shuddering at the thought of showering with...Yithians.

"Malo's quarters are stark," she volunteered while she stroked a tapestry hanging on a wall. It was hand-crafted, the colors bold and fearless.

"He is Etterian. They care not for such décor. As long as it serves its purpose, then it is more than adequate." Imarri touched a door, and it slid open. "Cleanse."

Caro didn't need to be asked twice. She rushed in and turned to ensure the door closed behind her. No locking mechanism was visible and when she approached it to investigate, it slithered open. Imarri raised her gaze from where she leaned over a replicator. Caro hastily stepped back and let the door close. Despite being confined to four walls again, these came with some privacy. She had to trust Imarri not to intrude. And even if the witch did, it was a freaking shower Caro was being offered. Seconds later, she was naked and standing under the warm spray. The water cascaded over her body at the perfect temperature and like lover's hands. She swallowed the moan that traveled up her throat. If Maloidians had sensitive hearing, Imarri would realize that showering gave Caro pleasure and might withhold it on purpose.

Various jars in an embedded alcove implied the water didn't carry everything she needed, as Malo explained. She hesitated, needing to wash but not wanting to smell like Imarri. Gritting her teeth, she went with the water, hoping there was something in the water like soap, shampoo, toothpaste. Allowing herself a few more minutes under the spray, she stepped out and pressed the blue button to dry. Well, at least that was the same. Once the air shut off, she donned her green uniform and grabbed Vinnie.

Pausing at the door, she considered that this could be her last shower. Like a prisoner's final request before the execution. Now to the real reason behind this kindness. What the hell did Imarri want this time?

But sensing Caro's presence, the door opened again. An enticing aroma greeted her, triggering an answering stomach growl. It was rich, creamy...chicken. Uncaring that this could be her last meal, she snatched the bowl and cup of water Imarri held out to her.

"I am not familiar with your Earthian food, so I chose something called *chicken*. Have the Yithians been feeding you any of this?"

Caro scowled. That Imarri didn't even know what her accomplices were feeding her captive... Caro leaned Vinnie against a tapestry-covered wall, drew the bowl to her nose, and inhaled. Her eyes fluttered closed with her mouth-watering in anticipation.

"It's some sort of pasta dish. I'm not complaining though. Food is food."

"I want your stay with me to be pleasant," she was saying.

Caro blinked, doubting her hearing. Her fingers twinged with the urge to drop the spork and smack her. Instead, she tightened her grip around the handle and lowered herself onto the closest cushion, not waiting for permission. Spooning pasta into her mouth prevented her from commenting on that bit of stupidity.

"I am pleased with your progress, tewaa." Imarri gracefully sprawled on a cushion.

Images flashed in Caro's mind, drawing a muffled yelp. Of pink-yellowish trees glowing and growing downwards from cave ceilings. Their branches swayed, reaching out, seeking sustenance from the particles in the air. If they were bothered, they slapped the irritation before returning to their swaying. Their movements were similar to Imarri's undulating tentacles. Caro didn't know how she felt about being likened to a tree. Not that it mattered in the greater scheme of things.

"The next step in your training is seduction. The Serratu Kayarra pride ourselves on our ability to seduce any male, no matter their species." *Silent Sirens*, the O.D.I. translated, female Maloidian spies.

Caro said nothing, simply continued to spork chicken into her mouth. She'd let Imarri fill the silence, maybe reveal a little more of her motives. Though the pleasant tone of her voice was making Caro nervous. She gripped the spork tight again, trying to hide her trembling fingers.

"I have seen you do this *dancing*; you can teach my students this?"

Caro chuckled, then laughed, unable to contain the mirth bubbling from deep within her. The audacity of this alien. This explained her 'kindness.' She wanted something from Caro.

"Malo doesn't want me dancing for anyone other than him...," she grumbled, not wanting to share anything with the yellow alien. Seconds ticked by as Imarri struggled to control her features.

"What will it cost me to learn?" she whispered.

"Return me to Malo," Caro said, her breath catching on the blossoming hope in her chest. So sweet and bright, it was almost blinding.

"I...cannot, Caro." Imarri ran a finger over the rim of a paper-thin glass holding thick blue liquid. "You are but a plaything. Stealing you from him proved he does not know everything and is not as invincible as he thinks." She smirked. "Etterians are too arrogant, never once considering that we could be better than them with their silly honor."

So, this went deeper than revenge? Caro shook her head. "Why take me to Argaxx? Surely you've made your point." Her heart skipped a beat. She could be home in a few days. There was still time to turn the ship around, right?

"Unlike Etterians, I do not judge your species as lesser. You showed strength, stubbornness, and perseverance. These I admire." Imarri sipped from the glass and hummed in appreciation. "Training you as a Kayarra makes sense when I truly believe you mean nothing to him."

Caro blinked at the female, hating her situation, the vulnerability numbing her tongue, and the helplessness paralyzing her. She wanted to scream that Imarri had been betrayed from within, that Malo was indeed on his way. But until he was holding Caro, until his heart beat against her cheek, there was still the possibility he wouldn't find her.

"*I believe* he's coming for me, Imarri. To lose hope is to admit defeat and play the role of a victim. This...I can't do." Caro met her gaze. "Return me to him, and I'll teach you."

"Show me or suffer, tewaa. I may be Maloidian and love a good bargain, but on this, I will not budge."

Caro grimaced. "Suffer it is."

The markings on Imarri's temple darkened. "You would choose torture?"

"I choose freedom, something you don't realize matters to humans."

Imarri's shoulders twitched. "Perhaps another bargain? Your dancing for the seduction techniques of the Kayarra. It will be my pleasure to rid you of your innocence."

Caro frowned. Why would she need to learn the art of seduction? "I'm not a virgin and haven't been for a long time."

At her revelation, a smirk curled Imarri's lips. She was delighted to hear this, though why it mattered, Caro didn't know. Even if she'd been an innocent, that one afternoon with Malo would've 'cured' her of it.

"Does Malo know this?"

"We never discussed it to be honest." Caro forced a shrug. She relived Malo carrying her to his bed, blessing her with sweet ecstasy...many times over. She dipped her chin to hide her flushed cheeks, then ran a finger along the inside of the bowl for a last lick like that had been her intention all along.

When she raised her head, Imarri studied her, assessing the truth in her words and voice. As if Caro was lying, which she was. She had a reason to. She didn't want to share any of Malo with this witch. He was hers alone.

"How long have you known him?" Imarri tried to appear casual in her inquiry, twirling the blue liquid in the glass, but her focus was fixed on Caro's face.

"Two days." Caro couldn't lie in case it was a test. She didn't know how long Imarri had hidden in the shadows, stalking Malo. Imarri stopped swirling for a second before resuming. Well, well, Caro had surprised the female again.

"I have never seen him so open, so...affectionate. Tell me, what did you do?" Imarri unfolded her limbs to face forward, cradling the glass in her hands.

"Do?" Caro smiled. According to him, she'd sung, danced, wore sexy shoes, and a dress.

"To catch the attention of one of the most sought after operatives. He's lethal." Imarri's breathlessness revealed that she found Malo's deadliness attractive. To be fair, Caro hadn't seen that side of him.

"I don't know him as deadly,...but he *is* incredibly sexy." She hummed when she recalled their first kiss. "May I ask you a question?" Imarri waved a hand. Caro took that as a yes. "If he's so deadly then why risk taking me?"

Imarri barked out an almost vulgar laugh. "Your belief astounds me. That you still expect he will chase you across the galaxy."

Caro bristled. "He's an honorable Etterian. I have no doubt, he *will* come for me."

"He will not find you, tewaa," Imarri spat, her lips curling in an unattractive smug smile. "It is futile to hope. You must release yourself from hope's clutches."

"You're the deceived one, Imarri. If you fear his skills, his lethality, you'd know his determination's unparallel." Caro's heart palpitated at her words. Yes, Malo had pursued her with a focus that had snatched her breath and will. She'd been helpless to resist his advances.

"Maszaks, your arrogance is unappealing," Imarri spat.

Caro shrugged. "Confidence. You took me when his fascination with me had yet to run its course. You've increased the enjoyment for him. Human men like to hunt their women, and if Malo is anything like them...then yes, he's coming for me." It wasn't a complete lie. Malo was coming for his Dar Eth, as simple as that.

"We reach Maloid and sanctuary in six days," Imarri said with enough smugness to irritate Caro.

She jumped up, leaving her half-drunk cup on the floor. Her skin tingled like a thousand needles prickled along it. The urge to smack this alien witch grew with every minute she spent with her. She'd prefer the cold lifeless confines of her cell to Imarri's opulent quarters if it meant she didn't need to endure anymore of her ill-concealed jealousy.

"If you say so," Caro mumbled. Desperation to leave drove her hard. She barely held her tongue, a familiar anger burning deep within her belly. She needed this 'adventure' to end and soon. How was she going to survive six more days?

"I have not dismissed you." Imarri's voice was as sharp as ice picks.

And...the bitch was back. Caro fought an eye roll. What kind of childhood must this female have had to turn her into this vindictive creature? She didn't want to dwell on it, fearing it would strip away her anger. To feel compassion for her abductor wouldn't be wise.

"You are to instruct me on this 'dancing.'"

"For freedom." Caro folded her arms across her shirt.

Imarri rose to her feet, her stance menacing. "You will remain here until you have instructed me."

Caro stared at the now mustard-yellow features of the alien, her tentacles swaying serenely despite the tension emanating off her taut body. Caro smothered a giggle. Studying her abductor, she realized the poor thing hadn't known what she was getting herself into by kidnapping a human.

"Ah, so you want to keep me here until I cave?" Caro grinned and broke into song, "Nobody knows the trouble I've seen. Nobody knows my sorrow."

Imarri's eyes twitched. "What...what are you doing?"

"Singing," Caro said, then 'wailed' on like a drunk pelican. "Nobody knows the trouble I've seen. Glory. Hallelujah." She met Imarri's pained gaze. "I can do this for as long as I'm here."

"I will give you time to rethink my offer, tewaa." Imarri tapped her O.D.I. and the door opened to Ayetz. "Deliver this...female to her cell."

Grabbing Vinnie, Caro didn't dare hesitate to follow evil Ayetz, in case Imarri changed her mind. As soon as she stepped into the passage, she took a deep breath of frigid air. She wasn't naïve to believe this matter settled. A grimace twisted her lips. Torture was in her future, but she couldn't dwell on it when it might not happen.

Obedient for now, she trailed Ayetz, staring at his shoulders while tightening her grip on Vinnie. If this shark attacked her, she'd be ready.

Chapter Sixteen

ANGER BURST THROUGH CARO when she entered a cell she didn't recognize. They'd fitted a bed and mattress to a bulkhead, her blanket folded at the foot end. A mini-cleansing room sat in the corner. She wasn't delighted at this supposed boon. It was a slap in the face, a bribery of sorts.

How dare she? Caro curled her fingers into fists, fighting to calm the fire blazing through her mind and veins. She glanced past Ayetz to Bezu. "Get me Imarri."

"I do not obey you, Caro, and to summon Imarri will cost me much." His black eyes pleaded with her to understand. "I thought these would please you." He gestured to the cell. "They do not?"

Relief skirted her senses, but she hesitated to let go of her anger. "Is this your doing, or did Imarri order it?" If Bezu had risked his life for these luxuries, she'd thank him for his kindness.

"She ordered it." He lowered his gaze. "I shall take your request to my superior."

The door closed.

Caro paced, ranting to herself about the bitch's audacity. The shower had been incredible. The stickiness of her unwashed limbs and dank hair had eroded her humanity. But at what cost? What would Imarri demand in return?

The door opened to Naal with his lip curling in derision, exposing a sabretooth. He lived to inflict pain on others.

Caro trembled with anger winning over self-preservation. "Get me Imarri, or I'll kill myself."

Naal scanned her body and hiss-laughed, sounding like a broken bandsaw. "With what? You have no weapon."

She stared at him with morbid fascination. His mouth widened, revealing both fangs pressing on his bottom lip, and with his eyes tilting upwards, he appeared demonic.

She snapped out of the daze and forced a laugh. "You fool. You don't know Earthian physiology. I can cut off air and suffocate to death." She kept her voice even, fighting the urge to roll her eyes at her stupidity.

Naal's laughter dwindled. "You can do this?" He spun on a heel, the door closing behind him.

She didn't know whether he'd taken her threat to heart. Although, how she'd make herself hyperventilate was beyond her. A glance at the bed renewed her anger and determination. However she needed to faint, she'd do it.

'I want your stay to be pleasant' that yellow-skinned witch had said.

"Pleasant?" Caro spat the word. The bed had to go, the damned mattress, as well. She was being unreasonable, but to succumb to this was to forgive Imarri for the abduction, the bullet wound, and the entire debacle. Caro wasn't ready to do that. She was spiting herself by sacrificing niceties, but it was the principle of it. A blanket was courtesy, food and water, a necessity if the death of the prisoner wasn't the intention.

Why didn't Imarri just move her into an officer's quarters? She might as well give her free reign on the ship. Hell, how about introducing her to all the sharks on board. They could hold tea parties and braid each other's tentacles.

By the time the door swished open, Caro had riled herself into a frenzy with regular sightings of her bed spurring her on. Black circled her vision, more to do with the air she sucked in and spewed out in great gulps.

"What nonsense is this? Death by suffocation without a weapon?" Imarri leaned a shoulder on the door frame.

"You don't know Earthian physiology?" Caro arched a brow, mocking her. Go big or go home, right? "That." She pointed at the bed, her fingers trembling. "I am your prisoner, not your damn friend." She swung a forefinger at Imarri. "You took me from Malo. Nothing you can do or say will change what you've done, will save you from his retribution." Her breathing came in ragged gasps, tearing from her throat and discordant with her heaving bosom. At this rate, she just might faint.

Imarri sighed. "Ayetz."

The Yithian raised his blaster. Pain of another sort shot through Caro, stiffening her limbs, and ripping a scream from her.

She collapsed to the floor, her head bouncing off the metal panel as black circled her vision again. "I hate you," she whispered before the darkness claimed her.

Caro awoke in a puddle of drool and frozen limbs. She ached, having been in the same position for who knew how long. Strapped to the bed, she couldn't move, and of course, her nose itched.

When she tried to scratch it on her shoulder, a pinging headache reared to life. Pain originated from the spot that had connected with the floor. She whimpered.

Hate Imarri? Caro loathed her. She cleared her throat, her tongue swollen. If she could get her hands on Ayetz, she'd neuter him. If he had balls, that is. Small dick syndrome wasn't reserved for humans. Skirting sanity, she swallowed a giggle.

The familiar stench of urine wrinkled her nose. The stun must have done that, and her cell remained the same, bed, mattress, and cleansing unit. Her display of anger had been for nothing.

Tears welled and slipped down her cheeks, adding to the pain squeezing her heart and an unhappy refilled bladder. The moment she realized she might have to wet the bed had her sobbing, sending shudders through her aching body. There wasn't a light at the end of this tunnel. Malo wouldn't find her. She'd die under Imarri's thumb. Caro might as well suffocate herself now and have done with this.

Her giggles turned into wails, and she succumbed to a pity-party, wanting to wallow in her helplessness for a bit. When her tears subsided, she huffed, now a blubbering, snot-infested mess lying in a puddle of her doing.

The door swished open, and Bezu's face appeared above her. Concern furrowed his silver forehead, and his three-fingered hand hovered. He wanted to help her but didn't know where to touch her.

"Are you well, Caro?" He unstrapped one hand, then another before sliding his arm across her shoulders to help her sit.

She groaned, pain lancing through her, ricocheting in her brain at the abuse her body had endured. A tremble swept over her. Not from the cold because the cell's temperature was fine, dewing his forehead.

"Thank you," she rasped. "Tell me, Bezu, are there other humans on board?"

"Only you, Caro."

The warmth of relief flooded her, that Izzy wasn't in the same situation. Now all she had to do was endure, to survive this. She pinched her lips, refusing to speak another word.

Only Bezu would hear her voice during their chats. The rest of the aliens on this ship could go fuck themselves.

SINCE THE STUN INCIDENT, Caro had maintained her silence, sleeping on the floor with her blanket like a good little pet, practicing with

Vinnie, and enduring whatever Imarri threw at her. Each 'morning' loomed, that this would be the day she'd demand dancing lessons.

Training continued with the witch adding intricate techniques, inflicting more pain, but no matter what she said or did, Caro bit her tongue. Imarri attempted to garner a reaction from her with a few slaps given by her or Ayetz. Stunned again, beaten, or tortured only solidified Caro's silence.

Running her fingers over her inner arm, she winced at the cuts in her skin made during one of those sessions. Naal and Ayetz had taken turns crisscrossing a blade along her arms, threatening to mar her cheeks. Blood had dripped onto the metal flooring. She had managed to remain firm, with but a few whimpers escaping her gritted teeth. Ayetz had scanned her, healing her in an instant, only to repeat the process. They had yet to heal her after the last incident.

They starved her and denied her the use of a cleansing unit. They spiked or dropped the temperature of her cell. None of that mattered. She was a prisoner, and she demanded they treat her as such. No more nice-Caro with her eagerness to earn privileges vanishing, especially when she understood how she sold pieces of her soul.

To accept any kindness was to forgive, and she struggled with that. When Malo's arms engulfed her in a hug, maybe then.

Bezu was her saving grace. His regular chats brought laughter into her life. His twitching sharknose had her using the shower despite her best intentions. And when she'd yelled that she was clean, he'd showed her the laundry closet, where she could place her uniform and wake up to it dry-cleaned. He anchored her determination when he mentioned he'd snuck a message out days ago, that Malo would find her soon.

Caro could've kissed the poor Yithian.

Time slowed. Days blurred. And just that 'morning,' Bezu had revealed that they approached Argaxx.

She wasn't afforded the opportunity to watch the spaceship descend as it broke through Maloid's atmosphere with the barest of shuddering. Bezu escorted her from the confines of her cell to the shuttle then strapped her to a chair. The cockpit had side-to-side screens through which she caught glimpses of lilac lightning bouncing off the planet's rocky surface. The shuttle's shields absorbed a few strikes powerful enough to rattle the craft.

They plummeted with too much speed, blurring the scenery. Just as a scream bubbled up her throat, they jerked to a crawl while falling through a crevice. Swallowing past her heart in her throat, she gripped the armrests, so grateful to be strapped to the side of a death-trap.

Orange, blue, and red fungi grew on the crevice walls. A few Maloidians hung down the sides, farming the plants, scooping yellow jelly into hovering carts or barrows.

The shuttle touched down with the door sliding open. Bezu unclipped her, and she rose on unsteady legs, taking a moment to study the blue-black rock while the ramp lowered. The air pouring into the shuttle's compartment was rich with organic life, but the heat of it hit her, coating her skin like a wet blanket. Her lungs constricted. Unable to breathe through the damp warmth, she gasped for air.

She scanned the crevice—the height of a mega building. The walls shimmered. Lilac flashed against the black sky, too high to be a threat.

Imarri faced Naal. "I consider your debt paid."

"As expected. A transport is on its way." Naal gestured to his males.

Bezu hesitated, handed Caro her katac, then with a slow curl of his upper lip, trailed his superior.

"This way." Imarri disappeared down a tunnel.

Caro hesitated. Off the jagged edges of the platform was a molten silver river, tumbling and gurgling. A glance up showed no escape either. She settled on the cave entrance through which Imarri had disappeared and hurried to follow. The organic smell intensified. Caro brushed her hand along the walls, her fingers coming away wet. Rubbing the tips together revealed it to be water.

Where the tunnels merged, a tree hung upside down from the cave's ceiling. It swayed and arched its fronds.

"A tewaa." Imarri stroked the bark, and it slumped, its movements calming.

She strode past it. Caro circled the tree, keeping close to the walls. Why would her nickname be that of a tree? Since she'd taken a vow of silence, she couldn't ask.

It was cooler in a large cavern they entered. To the left was a rock-hewn dais. More tunnels led off the room. The stone floor was smoother than expected with one section set aside for sparring where females in red uniforms worked through familiar techniques. Matching red sashes hid their faces, and a few raised yellow faces from where they sat at tables to the left, bowls of yellow goop before them.

"They are Kayarra in training." Imarri gestured. "Like you."

Caro met her black gaze. She. Was. Not. In. Training. And in no way a Kayarra.

"This day, we will see how you handle a katac with a blade." She sighed at Caro's continued silence. She marched down a tunnel with many doors cut into the stone. A glimpse inside when she passed showed beds carved out of stone and niches in the rock as shelves.

"Your room."

The air in her room was cooler but stale. Against one wall was a small rehydrator and replicator.

"Cleansing is at the end of the tunnel with heated rock pools." Imarri hesitated, pinching her lips. "All Kayarra receive such a room, and we adhere to a strict training schedule." She smirked. "You will remain here."

Caro snapped at the silly alien then croaked, "Until Malo arrives."

"Fool." Imarri huffed. "Very well. Until he arrives, you will train and consider yourself a member of the Kayarra. I will not tolerate any more trouble from you."

"Why don't you just lock me in another cell? Why bother to train me at all?" Despite her raspy voice, Caro glared at her and sucked in calming breaths. "Why this false civility?"

"Malo *is not* coming for you, Caro. None of my sources know of his whereabouts." The expression on Imarri's face was smug.

Caro grinned, her faith in Malo unwavering, especially after what Bezu had shared with her. "He's *that* good."

Granny's nipples, she missed him. She ached to have his arms around her. Some nights, she'd jerk awake with the phantom sensation of his body beside her, his fingers feathering along her skin.

Imarri led her down the tunnel into the cavern. "Regardless, you *will* train."

"Fine." Caro twirled Vinnie with confidence. "As long as I can keep this katac."

"Silly, Earthian." Imarri muttered something under her breath. "Dessa."

A Maloidian female broke away from those at the tables. She pressed clasped hands to her chest in greeting.

"This is Caro. See that she learns the life of a Kayarra." Without another word, Imarri sauntered off.

Caro watched her leave. Justice was hovering, on the cusp, at the edge. Soon, Malo would storm this cavern, her knight in black armor.

Chapter Seventeen

"Operations Commander, I have tracked Imarri's ship." Data Officer Tias loomed.

Malo stiffened, having not heard the male approach. Staring at a half-drunk coffee, the way Caro liked it, he was lost in memories of her shy smile, her featherlight touch, her sweet purr, and the spicy taste of her lingering on the tip of his tongue. Enough to tease him but not to satisfy.

Tias waited until Malo met his gaze. "She arrived at Argaxx twenty-one hours ago."

Relief flooded Malo's body with warmth. He allowed his shoulders to sag and a smile to form. "Good, we are close."

"Engineering has indicated they can relay a few non-essential power banks to increase our speed by twelve per cent. I have instructed them to do so." Tias hesitated. Something else needed Malo's attention.

"Speak your mind." Malo shoved the coffee aside. He pinched the bridge of his nose, trying to ease the burning in his nostrils.

"Perhaps a cleanse and a few hours of sleep will prepare you. Lady Caro needs you at your best, and nothing requires your immediate attention." Tias ran his gaze over Malo, who scowled at him for his insolence.

He looked like hell. Felt like it too. His limbs barely obeyed him, his skin itched, his nostrils burned, and his eyes stung. The Ethera wouldn't let him rest. His craving to scent her drove him mad—to feel her against him, to taste her, to bury himself deep within her softness. The memories of his time with her haunted him, parts of him beginning to disbelieve her existence.

"I will cleanse, Tias, but I *will not* rest." He brooked no argument. That he couldn't recall when last he'd slept was something he wouldn't share.

In his quarters, he disrobed on reflex. He stepped into the cleanser, unclipped his hair, and stood there for the required time, fighting to keep his mind clear of thoughts lest it triggered the emotions roiling within him. He ignored his agitated hair and his body's demand to attend to the daily chore. None of that mattered. In twenty-one hours, he'd hold her.

He shuddered with his skin prickling in anticipation and his arousal bobbing in eagerness. He stepped out of the cleanser and bypassed the air-dryer to pace his quarters. With nothing touching his skin, the Ethera was almost...bearable.

Maker. He needed to fight, to battle, but no warrior was willing to spar with him, not when he was in this state. It wasn't honorable to command them to either.

His door chimed, and he permitted it to open, grateful for the intrusion.

Medic Brynr entered, his strides purposeful. "Operations Commander, I have scoured the annals and discovered a sedative that will grant you a few hours of rest. I cannot guarantee more than that." He raised the device, blue liquid in the vial. "It's documented as being effective during the Ethera when an Eth is without his Dar Eth for whatever reason."

Malo grimaced. "I do not..."

"Commander, look at your scans." Brynr shoved his O.D.I. at Malo. "If you were another warrior, what would you advise?"

Malo frowned while he browsed through his medical results. His hormonal levels fluctuated which explained his unstable moods and pent-up energy. His heart rate and blood pressure spiked. He paused to listen to his galloping hearts and scowled.

"Very well, Medic Brynr, administer the sedative, but wake me two hours before we arrive."

"As you command, Operations Commander." Brynr pressed the device to Malo's neck. The slight pinch was negligible. Brynr left without another word.

Malo stared at the closed door, analyzing his body, the calming of his heartbeats, the sagging of his muscles. He could breathe without pain crushing his chest. Treatment implied he was a weak male. He gritted his teeth. As the operations commander, he'd trained his body to process most toxins, to anticipate all scenarios. Yet here he stood, brought low by his life force bond, forced to rely on his warriors and unable to endure on his own strength.

Exhaustion slumped him over, and he hurried to reach his bed, stumbling once which only highlighted his situation. How he made it, he didn't know. The moment he fell across the bed sideways, sleep consumed him.

Planet Maloid

A cold, damp, rock cell

Date? Unknown. October-something.

CARO COULDN'T SLEEP. THE excitement that skittered along her nerves wouldn't let her rest. It was late or early in the morning, and silence consumed the Kayarra barracks. Fungi glowed on the walls, lighting her way as she ambled down the tunnels leading off the main room. Trainees slept in their little caves, uncaring that she prowled.

Dessa hadn't shown much kindness, but Caro didn't care about petty agendas. The silly female had thought Caro was here to stay. She snorted.

The deeper into the tunnels she went, the cooler the temperatures. Sighing with relief, she pressed a palm to the moist wall. She paused. Something had shuffled, grunted...something biological. She was a fool to wander the caverns on an alien planet. Who knew what lay hidden in the shadows?

She jerked back, planning on rushing pell-mell down the passage to relative safety. Pale light from a room snagged her attention. She peered inside to where a lump lay on the floor. Covered with nothing but a thin blanket, long limbs and familiar bumps indicated whatever it was as humanoid.

"Hello." Her husky voice broke the silence, and she stepped in when the person stilled. "Are you all right? Can I get you anything?" She almost rolled her eyes at her offer. No Kayarra would come if she called.

His head popped out from under the blanket.

She gasped, stumbling back to bounce off the wall. When she fell to the floor, landing on her knees, she winced but didn't remove her gaze from the face of an Etterian man.

"You're an..." She swallowed, crawling forward to stretch out a hand. Realizing the audacity of her actions, she lowered her arm and sat back on her heels. "Why would Imarri imprison an Etterian?"

"What are you, female?" He spoke in Maloidian, as did she. Rising to a sitting position, his blanket pooled on his lap exposing his expansive bare chest marred by puncture wounds. His cheeks were sunken with his coloring darker around his deep blue eyes. He was just skin and bone, as if starved. A collar circled his throat, an ominous red light beeping.

"I'm a human from the planet Earth. How long have you been here?" She tilted her head, assessing him. He was a young man, not as broad in the shoulders as Malo.

"Time has no meaning here." He lay down again, dragging the blanket over his shoulders but not soon enough to hide his trembling nor the chain attached to his wrist.

"Hungry?" She gestured to the rehydrator and leaped up, rushing toward it. "A blanket? Food?" She worried her bottom lip. "Can it make a key for the chain, undo the collar?"

"You wish to free me?" He sat up again, eagerness bright in his face before he shook his head. "Escape is futile. Where will I go?"

She touched the rehydrator's screen, scanning names of meals she didn't know. Her stomach wrenched into a tight knot, reminding her that she hadn't eaten either. Sliding over to the replicator, she read through the Maloidian cuneiform, choosing a blanket. As soon as it appeared on the surface, she snatched it up, offering it to him. "With Malo."

"As in Operations Commander Malo?" The man arched a brow, his disbelief warring with humor.

"My Eth." She flicked out the blanket. When he didn't take it from her, she draped it over him, tucking the edges under his bare feet.

He barked out a hoarse laugh. "You have courage, little one, to make such a claim."

"Why? Do you think him too old to find love?" She huffed. "His eyes changed color, turned ice blue. He said it was the mark of the Ethera."

The male stilled, gaping for a moment. "He *will* come for you."

"I know. I didn't tell Imarri that I'm Malo's Dar Eth." Caro sat on the cool floor, crossing her legs. "He will save you too, when he comes."

"No." The man was loud in the small cave. "Do not tell him about me. Let me die here in shame."

She frowned. They had such a precise view on honor, maybe he thought he wasn't worthy of a rescue? "There's no shame in being a prisoner, and to survive the ordeal is honorable."

He stared at her for a while, then gave a slight nod. "I could not fight my way out, nor could I bargain. They took me en route to Gikaet where I was to begin my training." He tugged on his collar. "Maloidian steel. Unbreakable." He grimaced and dropped his hand into his lap. "I am Veor et Goor."

"Caro…. What is Malo's last name?" She shrugged. "In my culture, the Dar Eth assumes her Eth's name."

Veor grinned. "He is Malo et Dalo but you are Caro of Malo which would mean Caro et Malo."

"…Et Malo." She rolled it over her tongue, testing out the sound of it. She liked being of Malo. "If we have children?" Like Malodóttir or Maloson?

"*Damu?*" Veor shuffled on his backside until he rested against the wall. "Your son would be et Malo."

"My daughter will have the same?"

"Daughters?" Veor shook his head. "They are rare, but should you be so blessed, then she would take on your name, et Caro."

Or et Caroline? Malo had mentioned the scarcity of their females, but that felt like months ago when they'd first met. So much had happened since then. She drew in a shuddering breath while picking at the hem of her tunic. "Can I unlock your collar or chain? Are you hungry?"

"Your concern is genuine, little one, and I appreciate the offer. The keys are alongside the doorway." He nudged his chin at the objects in a carved niche. "Freeing me too soon might tighten their guard. Perhaps leave me as I am until Malo arrives."

"If I steal a dagger for you?" She scanned the small room. "You can defend this, can't you?"

"I must sleep at some point." Veor rubbed a puncture wound on his forearm, wincing as if it pained him.

Caro gritted her teeth. Those bitches hadn't healed him. Even Ayetz had done so, albeit to re-inflict pain. She hesitated. Drawing in a deep breath, she blurted, "What did they do to you?"

"They took blood samples and injected toxins into me." He grimaced, shifting on his backside before dropping his hand between his thighs, as if to protect his sex. "Once a day, they perform my daily chore, stealing my seed."

She gasped. Ice drenched her spine, and she shuddered. She bolted out of the room, scampering down the tunnels as silent as possible. In the cavern, she studied the weapons wall, choosing a dagger and a blaster before returning to Veor.

She placed the weapons in front of him then snatched the keys off the shelf. "You can guard yourself for a day or two?" She shoved the keys at him, not knowing how to undo either locks. "Free yourself, and pretend to be a prisoner when they visit you. Clothe yourself where possible, and eat something. You might need your strength."

Veor took the offered keys, then stared at them. His lips curled into a smile, color and energy returning to his face. Within minutes, he had the collar off and the chain undone. He rose to his feet and ordered food from the rehydrator then ate standing up, tearing meat with his teeth.

"How long?" he asked around mouthfuls.

"I don't know. It could be tomorrow or three or seven days?" Pain twinged through her. *Please, Lord, let it be soon.*

Veor gripped the plate in one hand and returned the keys to the niche. "I must suffer a little longer. I am an Etterian male. I can endure much."

She squared her shoulders. "I'll continue as if Malo isn't coming, and you don't exist."

His grin was eager and wicked. "But if they try to take my seed again, I'll kill."

"Fair enough."

She meandered to her room to sprawl on the cool stone bed. Sleep was out of the question, her mind reeling with what they must have put the male through. Why would the Kayarra experiment on an Etterian male? Why force him to donate his sperm? What was Imarri up to?

Caro tossed, unable to find comfort on the hard slab, nor ease the hope burning through her. Malo would save her *and* Veor. Monkey's bananas, he better hurry because she wouldn't put it past Imarri to shoot Veor if he killed one of her trainees.

Chapter Eighteen

Caro hunched over a bowl of jelly-like orange goop. The aroma was a mixture of sickly-sweet vanilla and almonds. She tried not to breathe through her nose. Kayarra chatted, whispering when they glanced at her. Their exposed faces revealed their opinion and distrust of her. *Well, the feeling's mutual.*

"Do not let them bother you." Dessa sank on the bench beside her. "To fear the unknown shortens one's career, does it not?" She raised her voice, glaring at the audience.

Silence reigned for a moment, then the chatter resumed.

"I apologize for my mistreatment."

Caro sliced a glance at Dessa, distrusting her. "What has changed? Yesterday, you were meaner than a skunk caught in a trap."

Dessa frowned. "I do not know this 'skunk.'" She spooned in the goop, licking her lips like it was honey. "Yes, I was...rude to you. I knew not the details of your...situation." She dipped her head to whisper, "Is it true Imarri stole you from Operations Commander Malo et Dalo?"

Ah, there it is. Caro straightened her spine. Dessa was being nice, hoping to milk information. *Oldest trick in the universe.*

"What did Imarri reveal?" Caro shoved her uneaten meal aside, craving a coffee or pancakes, something from home and with substance.

"Imarri has not explained your presence, nor must she. Still, to steal you from Malo, race to Maloid, train and feed you..." Dessa hovered her spoon halfway to her mouth. "It is odd, even for one such as her."

"Then ask her yourself." No way was Caro spilling the beans.

Dessa's cheeks darkened to mustard. "Doing so will require too much Jucot wine." She smiled, leaning back to rub her belly like goop was filling. "Should there be truth to the rumors, then Imarri may have jeopardized the Serratu Kayarra. Etterians do not take kindly to anyone stealing what is theirs." She slid off the bench. "Come, Caro, I am to train you on the use of the katac-isi."

Caro sighed. With a katac, smacking someone left a bruise or a broken bone. Adding a blade to the mix could be fatal. She was dreading this because someone was about to get hurt, and she prayed it wasn't her.

Screaming pierced the din. She stiffened, glancing at the tunnel leading to Veor. Had he done something? She closed her eyes and sent up a quick prayer. Giggling Kayarra chased each other into the cavern. Caro slumped, releasing a slow exhale. Her heart pounded in her ears. A day had passed since she met Veor, and already her nerves were strung so tight she just might snap.

She leaped to her feet and trailed Dessa to the training floor. Spears, swords, and bows shoved in barrels lined the walls. Dessa withdrew a spear and tossed it at Caro. She caught and twirled it, testing the balance. Something weighted the butt of the shaft to compensate for the blade. Going through the techniques required minor adjustments—how far she spread her legs, how much tighter her grip, with more force to her swings.

"Mm, I can see why she kept you, Caro. You have a natural grace…" Dessa smiled.

Caro snorted. "All lies, Dessa. I'm as clumsy as an ox."

"Ox, I do not know. Grace, I do." She withdrew a spear.

Without warning, she thrust it at Caro, who deflected it with a flick of the katac-isi. Vibrations at the contact rippled up her arms. She gritted her teeth and raised the shaft in front of her like a shield. Lunge, parry, deflect and repeat while dodging sweeping strikes with the shaft left her dripping sweat. Her breathing grew ragged, her arms weak.

"Despite your grace, Caro, you lack stamina." Dessa huffed. "And I thought I saw what is special about you." Holding the shaft like an ax, she brought it down, smacking Caro's fingers.

She cried out but didn't release the spear. Doing so would get her stabbed for sure. She pushed through the fiery agony and lunged, thrusting the spear at Dessa.

The female's eyes widened, and she stumbled back, but it was too late. The blade sank into her shoulder. With a whimper, she collapsed, gripping her wound as green blood trickled between her yellow fingers.

"Enough." Imarri strode onto the floor and kneeled beside a sprawled Dessa.

Fighting for air, Caro lowered the spear. Her lungs constricted, and lack of food spun her vision. She leaned on the shaft, clinging to it, then winced, her finger twinging. Kayarra gathered to watch the scene play out.

Sure, she'd injured one of them, but she had no guilt. *Don't give a weapon to someone not skilled enough to use it. Accidents happen. Duh.* She smothered a giggle. Laughing would get her killed.

She slumped, missing Izzy and her cheerfulness. But thinking about her saddened Caro, summoning tears she hastily blinked away. If she thought laughing was bad, crying would be worse.

Kayarra hurried to help Dessa to her feet, the bloodstained tunic the only evidence Caro had hurt her.

Imarri faced the room and gestured to Caro. "Put away the katac-isi, and let me heal your hand."

Heal? The witch held one of those black boxes Ayetz had used. Spinning the spear, Caro shoved it into the barrel butt first, then offered her hand to Imarri.

"Perhaps training with the katac-isi is too soon." She smirked. "This bloodthirsty side of you is a surprise, tewaa."

Caro huffed. "I didn't stab her on purpose."

Imarri pocketed the box then gestured to the multi-colored padded walls. "For that, you have earned punishment."

"What?" Caro squeaked. Was she supposed to have killed Dessa?

"All wounds must be deliberate. This is how we learn to control our strikes and survive any attack, Caro." Imarri paused in front of a blue pad. "Punch this five hundred per side." Before the brown pad, she swung a roundhouse kick. "Do this a thousand times per leg." She smirked when she glanced at Caro. "And if you're still standing," she gestured to the red pad, "knee this for two thousand each."

"What?" Caro scowled. "Why?"

"After which, we will test your skill with the katac-isi again. Perhaps this time, you will fight for your life." She sauntered off.

Caro stared after her, everything within her burning, furious, and tingling. If she had her way, she'd stomp out of this warren and find Malo. But she had Veor to think about. She weaved around the staring Kayarra and stopped by the blue pad.

She swung a punch. One, she didn't know the tunnels well enough to navigate them. Two, nor did she know what dangers lay in wait. Three, making it to the shuttle platform would gain her what? An okayish view of the night sky and freedom just out of reach? And four, who knew how long Malo would take to get here. She could be out there for days.

Punch after punch reverberated through her arms, the satisfying whack of flesh meeting pad merged with the Kayarra in various exercises, grunting, huffing, or cursing. Caro couldn't make it past a hundred when she drooped. Imarri hadn't said all at once, had she? Taking a chance no one was paying her any attention, she faced the brown pad and kicked. At least this gave her arms a chance to rest.

The bell tolled for lunchtime. She lurched to the nearest bench and collapsed on it. Her uniform stuck to her; her body was on fire, and her breathing came in gasps. Her vision spun. She slipped to the floor, lying there, uncaring that Kayarra had to step over her.

A cold hand cupped her cheek. "Drink."

She obeyed, downing the sweetest water she'd ever tasted. Opening her eyes, she blinked at Dessa. "Why...?" she croaked, licking her lips to moisten them. "Why help me?"

"I was not always a Kayarra. I do remember my broodmother's teaching on kindness having its own rewards."

Broodmother? Caro rolled over onto her knees and staggered to her feet. "Thank you, Dessa."

"Now, eat something and finish. Not doing so will bring on harsher punishment."

Caro pursed her lips. "What's harsher than this?"

"Thirst or hunger, no healing, denied sleep?"

True. Caro glanced at the pads. "It will take all day." She studied her palms and bleeding knuckles. "I can't," she whined.

Dessa placed a bowl of goop on the table and guided Caro onto the bench. "Do it in manageable sessions. Ten punches, kicks, then knees."

Gritting her teeth, Caro spooned in the 'food,' forcing herself to swallow before her tongue could test the slimy texture. "I can do this. Ten on each side," she whispered until it took up a litany in her mind.

On the fourth spoonful, her stomach cramped. She ignored it, assumed it was due to the alien or actual food. But when the ache tightened until the goop lodged in her throat and a wave of nausea rose, she knew.

She dropped the spoon and faced a beaming Dessa. "Why? I'm no threat to you. I'm not your enemy."

"You wounded me, zseera," Dessa spat.

Bitch? Caro glared at her. "What?" She smothered a groan as a spasm threatened to bend her over. "Little me hurt oh-so-skilled Dessa? Is that it?" She pushed off, using the table for leverage. "I was going to spare you *when* Malo arrives, but now you can go fuck yourself."

Limping off with her head held high took all her strength. By the time she reached her cave, the agony blazed, crippling and folding her spine, affecting her ability to walk. She collapsed onto the bed with a heartfelt sigh. *Fuck them all.* She didn't care if Imarri punished her for not finishing. She was done with this horrid adventure.

The tears fell. From the pain, her circumstances, missing Malo, she couldn't say. Her skin prickled, icy then hot, taking turns to churn her stomach. She had nothing to purge, and for that, her muscles spasmed, the pain so sharp it stole her breath.

Hours passed. She slipped in and out of consciousness. Her mind played tricks on her, that Imarri visited her cave, but when the pain remained, Caro dismissed it as a dream.

It was a hot hand on her temple that woke her.

Veor leaned over her.

"Veor?" She tried to sit up.

He held her down. "No, little one, lie still." He ran a box over her, the cramps easing immediately.

She sighed and melted against the stone bed. "Thank you," she rasped.

He pocketed the box then offered her a cup of water. "Drink, *ensa.*"

She did, trusting him more than she should have Dessa. The cool liquid slid down her throat. She sat up and downed the water, uncaring that some dribbled off her chin. The full magnitude of the risk he'd taken settled on her. She sliced glances at the doorway, half-expecting Imarri to storm in.

"You should go. I don't want you punished because of me, Veor." She dipped her chin. "I couldn't bear that."

"They rest without a care, like *damu.*" He grinned. "I heard what Dessa did to you. It was...dishonorable." He rubbed a wound on his upper forearm. It wouldn't surprise Caro if Dessa had inflicted it.

"I'm so tired, Veor. What's taking Malo so long?" She snapped her mouth shut, wishing she hadn't revealed her greatest fear.

Veor captured her chin and forced her to meet his gaze. "He will die without you, Caro. For this alone, he will arrive soon."

She released a breath in a whoosh. Shame enflamed her cheeks, that she'd lost faith, doubted Malo cared. "I know he will. Maybe tomorrow."

She lay down, resting her head on a folded arm. The box had taken away the cramps, the persistent dizziness, along with the pain in her muscles, but it couldn't heal a tired soul. Veor drew a blanket over her, then snuck out. She listened, sharpening her ears for sounds that would put him in danger.

Nothing but deafening silence reached her. Only then did she let her eyes close.

Chapter Nineteen

__Planet Maloid__

__The Caverns of Dooirin__

The roughly hewn rock walls did nothing to cool the air. This far down, in the bowels of Maloid, the air was fecund and stale. He adjusted his sense of smell, lowering its sensitivity. The purifiers didn't penetrate this level, which meant not much foot traffic disturbed the workings of the sorority of assassins. Their renowned skills had never tempted Malo when the cost of a single night would be far-reaching. Not to mention, the standing wager. He'd known about it. His king expected him to know every secret.

Malo strode along the passages carved through the rock, ignoring the dripping walls and thick heat. He had one goal and could barely catch his breath as excitement coursed through him. All his information had led him here, Argaxx, the imperial city of Maloid, home to Queen Alllero. Sometimes they could port down, depending on the severity of the planet's continual storms. Today wasn't one of those times. The kuta's slow descent had been unbearable. All worth it if Caro was near.

He strolled into the vast cavern and onto the stepped terrace, halting alongside Imarri who observed her students with a keen eye.

"You are training them better, I see," he said, though the urge to grab her by the throat and pin her to the wall barraged him.

She glanced at him but said nothing at his unexpected presence, at his intrusion on her most-hallowed ground. In silence, they observed two students battle with katacs. They wore the uniforms of recruits—loose pants, tunics, and headscarves in greens and browns.

"Law of escalation. We must keep ahead of other species."

"That one has grace *and* efficiency. It is hard to learn one without sacrificing the other," Malo said as if he had a right to. When her brow twitched, he grinned. He was too jubilant to care. Caro was near. That was all that mattered to him.

"She is a new recruit. I have trained her for a few weeks. Although, she forced me to return her to staves yesterday. She injured another when she tested blades. I fear she may have a bloodthirsty streak. Her adaptability has surprised me. I do not wish to see her leave." There was true sorrow in Imarri's voice.

He grunted. It wasn't unheard of for a teacher to become attached to a recruit. Yet only after a weeks? Absurd. Imarri must be softening. "She is leaving? Are you releasing her with the training incomplete?"

"I must. You have come to collect her, have you not?" At Imarri's smirk, Malo's head spun to study the female in question.

Caro? Nothing of this female seemed familiar with her face and body hidden. Her movements weren't of his timid *thamani* either.

He scowled. "You mock me, Imarri. Please do not encourage my need for retribution. You will not like the results." His tone had lowered, now lethal and dripping with menace. He didn't appreciate her toying with him, not after what she'd put him through.

"Caro," Imarri called out.

His gaze settled on the sparring pair. A female finished off her opponent with a sweep of the stave, before tossing it to the floor. Her head lifted, and she stilled. Ripping off her headscarf to reveal her joy amid falling tears, Caro bolted toward him.

He wasn't aware he'd moved, that he met her halfway until she filled his arms.

"You found me," she whispered, her breath fanning his neck, her arms tightening around him. She pinned him to her, her strength improved. Beneath the loose clothing of the Kayarra, she was thinner too but as soft as he remembered. And she scented the same. He sucked her scent in, filling his lungs to their maximum capacity.

"Caro," he ground out, unable to form other words. Her light imbued his soul, vanquishing the darkness, and easing the overpowering Ethera. Leaning back and with trembling fingers, he brushed hair from her face.

He kissed her. Sipped at the nectar of her lips. Reverence, longing, joy, he revealed in his gentle touch. He crushed her against his body, drinking, drowning in her taste, relearning the crevices of her mouth he'd doubted the memory of.

"I am pleased to have found you, *thamani*. I have died these past weeks. Are you well? How is your wound? Maker, I have missed you." He finished with another hug, not wanting her to leave his embrace.

"This is a little overdramatic, do you not think?" Imarri snapped, drawing the attention of the other recruits.

He glanced at her, his grip tightening around Caro's waist, not letting her stray too far from him. "Is Caro a Kayarra?" He despised Imarri's smug expression.

Imarri stiffened and peered at him, her brow furrowing. "Yes."

"Good, then give her the reward." He feathered his lips across Caro's temple, longing to do more than hold her.

"What do you mean?" Imarri scowled.

"I've joined with her." He grinned when Imarri jerked back, her eyes widening. Few things caught her by surprise, he was certain.

She studied him, then Caro. "I do not believe you."

"Etterians do not lie. Many times have I joined with my Caro and with more to come." He rested his gaze on Caro's upturned face. "As I expect with my Dar Eth."

"Your what?" Imarri squeaked. She gaped, then clamped her mouth shut. Her pale-yellow skin darkened as she peered into his eyes. "I...I apologize, Malo. I did not know."

Her regret meant nothing. The female was dishonorable, and for that alone, he had no mercy. "And had you known?"

"I would not have taken her. I know how your males seek their life force." She pressed her palm to his forearm, silently pleading with him to forgive her. "I have always respected you, but when you declined my offer, I became angry. I planned to inconvenience you by taking your toy. I did not—"

"It shouldn't matter if I'm his Dar Eth," Caro ground out. Her anger rippled through her tense body and vibrated along the arm he'd wrapped around her waist. He pulled her closer. "You don't go around kidnapping people. It's rude and arrogant and...and selfish."

"My Caro is correct. I should claim your life for this. Instead, I went to a higher power. Alllero would like to see you, and do not delay, she is not a patient female."

"You commed my queen?" Imarri's skin darkened to umber. He didn't care. Her fury meant nothing to him.

"Of course. The moment you took my life force, I sacrificed every ally I had. I commed you, Imarri, granting you one chance to save yourself." He shook his head. "I kept Queen Alllero abreast of the situation. She is most displeased with you. Should you not be aware of this, your uncle is off-world and cannot assist you."

Imarri raised a hand to cup his cheek, hesitated, then lowered it. "Malo..."

He flicked a wrist, silencing her. "Pay my Dar Eth, Imarri. I wish to leave this sodden hell hole."

When she snatched Caro's wrist, he growled. She gentled her touch and swiped her forearm over Caro's wrist. Flickering holographic letters confirmed the transfer.

He smiled. His Caro having an O.D.I. saved him from insisting she have one implanted. With a muffled sigh, he rubbed that familiar ache in his chest.

But Imarri didn't release Caro, instead, she laced her fingers with hers. "If you ever need anything, tewaa, I will be there for you."

Caro arched a brow, one he longed to trace with a fingertip. "I need you to release Veor."

Imarri frowned. "How did you—?"

"Release him." Caro stiffened her shoulders.

"Caro?" Malo tilted her head to caress her jawline. "Who is Veor?"

She spun into his arms, layering her body along the front of his. Heat exploded outward. "She has an Etterian male trapped down here, Malo, and they take turns...hurting him."

It took a moment for Malo to understand. Blinding fury blazed through him. He curled his fingers into fists then relaxed, not wanting to harm his Dar Eth even by accident.

"Imarri," he roared, facing the Maloidian. She trembled under his glower. "Bring him now, or I will end you where you stand."

She gestured to her females to do so. Two scurried off, returning a few minutes later with an emaciated Etterian male. Malo hadn't wanted to believe it possible. That she would dare to imprison one of his own... He back-handed Imarri, his fury demanding he do more. Uncaring that she lay sprawled on the rock floor, green blood dribbling down her chin, he punched on his O.D.I. and called for his males.

"I found him the night I arrived." Caro smiled at the male.

"As I said, Caro, your Eth will come for you." Veor thumped his chest. "Operations Commander."

"Answers must wait," Malo grunted.

His males burst in. He tasked them to search the tunnels and to bring what they found. Within minutes, a small gathering of prisoners crowded the center. Kayarra shuffled toward the rear of the cavern, fear darkening their yellow faces. A single prisoner stood out—a pale-faced Maloidian female.

"Veor?" She took a hesitant step, then halted, flicking a gaze at the Kayarra then Imarri.

"I am well, Teela. Come." Veor gestured, and she hurried across to him.

"Teela." Imarri clambered to her feet, holding out a hand as if to halt the young female

She paused, ran her gaze over Imarri, then settled beside Veor. The way he gathered her close revealed far more.

Curious but aware now wasn't the time, Malo faced his males. "Gather them all. The prisoners are to be returned to their homes. And should the Kayarra resist, kill them."

His well-trained males acknowledged his command with a chest thump. The capture was swift with a few females wounded in the process, those too stubborn to realize they'd brought this upon themselves.

Ronin appeared at Imarri's side and nudged his chin at the passage.

"What do you intend to do, Malo?" Gone was her smirk.

"Fuyra," he answered out of respect for what she'd once been. Her Kayarra gasped, and scuffles broke out again, subdued by his males with ease. "I will comm Alllero when we return to my battleship. Perhaps she would prefer to mete out justice."

"Fuyra?" Caro gazed at him.

"A small moon where we mine rock." He brushed a curl off her cheek. "Is there anyone you wish to spare?" He swept out his arm to the Kayarra.

When she scanned them, her eyes narrowed on a single female. "No."

"Tewaa?" Imarri stretched out a hand then lowered it. She gave Caro a stiff nod and marched down the passage. Ronin trailed her.

Malo had one kuta, but they'd need many more. His hungry gaze traveled over Caro's face and braided hair to linger on her exposed neck. "Are you ready to leave, *thamani*?"

She scanned the cavern, slid her hand free, and hurried to collect the katac she'd thrown down. While she returned to him, she called out, "Mine."

With her hand in his, he pulled her behind him, taking the passages he had but within the hour navigated. He meandered along them like he'd been born there, having memorized the routes to ensure they'd escape unharmed. When they reached the platform, he commanded Afax to power up and take them to Alllero.

He took his time strapping his Dar Eth into her seat. Doing so brought him a peace he couldn't describe, as if such a task conveyed the depth of his emotions. Ronin guarded a somewhat subdued Imarri. Veor whispered soothing words to Teela as he too secured her to a seat.

Malo traced a finger along Caro's cheek. "We must spend a few moments with Queen Alllero."

Caro smiled and caught his hand to kiss his knuckles. "Protocol."

He flipped his fingers and caught hers, pinning their clasped hands to his thigh when he settled beside her.

The shuttle shot up, passed foragers, broke into the lightning-intense sky, and across rocky caverns.

"It's pretty." Caro leaned around him to stare at the forevids.

So close to him, he caught the delicate fragrance of her skin, the pale perske hue in her cheeks, the flutter of her dark eyelashes. He wanted to spew that she was far prettier than a planet but bit his tongue. They were not alone, and any compliment he gave her should be for her ears alone.

"We will not tarry," he said.

She met his gaze, and her eyes darkened. "Good."

Plummeting down another crevice, this one as wide as it was deep, saved Malo from doing something stupid, like kissing her again. His chest constricted. His hearts thumped, in and out of synchronicity.

When the shuttle touched down and the door opened, royal guards lined the perimeter. "My queen will see you now." An emissary in a silk tunic reaching his knees, tight leggings, and useless slippers gestured to a well-lit tunnel lined with artifacts, artwork, and strange objects.

Caro gasped as Malo ushered her along the straight yet long tunnel to a small cavern. Sitting areas in a kaleidoscope of colors peppered the space. The rich aromas of various foods greeted him. To the side was a common room with overladen tables and auto-servos bearing trays.

Silence descended. Groups of familiar and unknown species watched as he followed the emissary to the massive gilded doors. They opened as they neared. Ferusi-green marble floor met pillars reaching levels high to a ceiling mimicking the star-filled skies over Argaxx. Warmth glowed from wall-mounted lights. A five-feet diameter chandelier hung over Alllero's throne, no doubt made from gold. Cushions softened the three-seater stone throne. And in the middle sat Alllero, frail and petite.

On the display vid, she'd appeared as vibrant as he remembered.

"My queen," he thumped his chest while refusing to release Caro's hand.

She dipped into a half-bow. Princess Oriana had done the same. Malo considered it an odd gesture when meeting royalty.

Alllero pushed off her seat and waddled over to clasp Caro's hand. Glancing at Malo, she smiled. "This is Caro? She is beautiful. What species are you?"

"Human, your majesty, from the planet Earth."

"Majesty?" Alllero giggled. "I do like that. Deeezo, my address will be so."

"As you wish, your majesty." The emissary tapped his O.D.I.

"I cannot reveal how Imarri has angered me." Alllero grimaced. "I am to maintain my calm due to...health reasons. What do you wish to do, Malo?"

"Stealing my Dar Eth and an Etterian male is grounds for war." Malo sighed. "King Xeus has fought so hard for peace. This cannot be the trigger. I refuse to allow Imarri to be successful if that was her agenda."

"I watched it unfold, Malo. I am most displeased." Alllero rubbed her temple. "Fuyra?"

He gathered Caro closer. "Yes to Fuyra. Imarri's length of stay is for you to decide."

"I shall comm Xeus." Alllero turned to her throne but wavered. Malo lunged for her but halted when Deeezo caught her by the elbow. "Thank you for bringing your Dar Eth to meet me, Malo. As per usual, Etterians remain honorable."

Dismissed, he trailed another emissary to the shuttle, climbed in, and strapped Caro in again.

"She's ill?" Caro captured his hand when he sat beside her.

"Older than we know, I suspect." He offered a smile. "Now we go home."

He tapped commands on his O.D.I. while the shuttle headed for the *Kevol*. Ronin was to take a few older warriors and escort the Kayarra to Fuyra. Then Malo leaned back, draped an arm around Caro, and counted down the seconds until he could have her alone.

As soon as they broke through Maloid's atmosphere, Afax ported them to Malo's quarters. For that, he would earn another commendation.

Malo glided the katac out of Caro's hand and leaned it against the bulkhead. Then he spun and pinned her to the same bulkhead, claiming her mouth with a desperation that couldn't be silenced. He ravaged her, attempting to meld with her, unite their souls, to cease the endless torment. Emotions swelled and engulfed him. He needed her with him, near him, touching him. He ached to hear her voice, inhale her scent, have her bless him with smiles.

He broke the kiss to rest his temple on hers. "Do not leave me again, Caro. I cannot survive it."

"It wasn't by choice, Malo," she muttered then moaned when he cupped her breast through her garments.

"Within weeks, you have decimated my foundation, my understanding of who I am as an Etterian warrior. With my skillsets, I could not prevent you from being harmed."

Her shoulders slumped. "I'm sorry."

"No, *ensa*, you misunderstand. I am not angry with you. There was nothing you could do, there was nothing I could do, but yet you were hurt under my protection."

"But you found me, Malo. I knew you would." She stroked his cheek. "I missed you," she whispered.

He groaned and ripped her uniform off, tossing the fragments to the floor for the auto-servos to clear away. "What has she done to you?" He studied Caro's body, running his hands over familiar and unfamiliar curves. Her soft stomach had definition, along with her thighs. Her hips were still there, and he grabbed those, like long-lost blood-bonds.

"Nothing pizza and chocolate ice-cream can't fix," Caro said, a smile teasing her lips.

"Are you hungry, *thamani*?" His need to care for her overwrote the urge to be buried in her. If he was patient, he could do both, appeasing the Ethera and his sense of honor.

"Hungry for you." She tapped his chest, releasing his armor.

Shrugging it off, he let it fall to the floor. He shuddered when she touched him, traced the ridges and dips, and brushed over his taut nipples in the process. She fluttered her fingers up his chest, caressing his neck, to slip in his hair behind his ears.

"How about you take me fast then slow?" She raised her heated gaze to his.

Maker, I adore her.

"Caro." With one destination in mind, he swung her over his shoulder and placed a caressing hand on her bare backside.

Chapter Twenty

Etterian scimitar Kevol
Malo's Temporary Quarters

CARO REFUSED TO BLINK. She was home, Malo had come for her, and Imarri along with her ilk were on their way to a mine. Veor was safe too. She gazed at Malo in all his naked glory, trying to hold back the tears. Now was the time for celebration.

He layered his body over hers. The weight of him brought on a sigh. She wiggled beneath him, luxuriating in the velvety texture of his skin against hers. Half-expecting him to plunge right in, when he stroked an eyebrow, cupped a cheek, rubbed his thumb along her jaw, then brushed curls off her face, her heart fluttered. What was this? He peered into her eyes, his crystal blue and so beautiful.

Without a word, he placed a kiss on the tip of her nose before doing the same on her chin, cheeks, forehead, eyelids, and lips. His breathing turned ragged, but he didn't change his pace. He dragged his fingertips down her throat, across her collarbone to cup a breast.

She quivered, a thousand nerve endings sparking to life. The darkness within her soul faded under his caresses. While he flicked her nipple, he kissed her throat, shoulder, peppered pecks along her jaw to her ear where he dipped his tongue in.

Heat coiled and released, tightened and melted until she squirmed beneath his seeking fingers. Her hips jerked, as if to beg him to touch her where she ached the most. He took his time, trailing the new ridges in her belly and squeezing her hips.

"Caro," he whispered, meeting her gaze for a moment. Blue flames burned in his. He stroked her seam, slow, dedicated, and determined.

She whimpered.

He smiled and slipped a finger between her lips, rubbing across her nub.

She cried out, spreading her thighs without hesitation.

"You *have* missed me," he teased.

She nodded, unable to speak past the ecstasy barreling toward her with each flick of his finger.

He pulled back, drawing forth her mewl.

"I do not wish for fast, *thamani*, now that you are here." He shook his head. "I hurt for you, but I can bare a little longer." He rested his forehead on her stomach, a shudder jarring his shoulders. "You are home, *ensa ra ensa*, with me."

He ventured lower, trailing hot kisses to her sex. She clawed his upper arms, urging him on, silently begging him not to stop.

With a swipe of his tongue, she arched off the bed, panting his name. He didn't stop, digging his fingers into her ass to hold her still for his onslaught. It had been weeks since her last orgasm, but with the way her body trembled, wept for him, it might as well have been never.

She splintered into a million mirrors filled with her love for him. Each shard of sheer bliss carried an image of his beloved face. Not that he let her descend from her orgasmic high. He settled between her thighs and rubbed the head of his cock along her entrance.

She twitched, curled her legs around his hips, and tried to force him to fuck her sooner.

He chuckled, clasped her hips, and slid into her an excruciating inch at a time.

Everything stilled—her breathing, heartbeat, and time. She cupped his face, running her thumb across his plump bottom lip. "Kiss me, please."

He obliged, capturing her mouth and plunging to the hilt. Nothing had felt this good...ever. She threw her arms around his neck and clung to him, kissing him with her heart in her throat. His sunbaked scent, his heated muscles beneath her fingers, all had her believing she had died and gone to heaven.

Breaking the kiss, he kept himself pressed to her, holding his weight off her on his elbows. But he buried his hands in her hair, their gazes locked. With a slow withdrawal, he thrust into her hard, snatching her breath. Sensations, like sparks of pure joy, ricocheted inside her. Again, he withdrew, slow as grass growing before slamming into her, hitting her G-spot each time.

She moaned his name, pleading with him to hurry. He didn't, not once glancing away from her. When he pistoned in and out, pleasure swept through her. Her eyelids fluttered.

"Do not look away, *thamani*. I want to watch you find your fulfilment. This moment will be cherished for an eternity."

Her heart melted like a ball of hot toffee. She sighed and met his gaze, just as he thrust into her again. It was too much. He was too... She shattered, arching and writhing beneath him but not once breaking eye contact.

His cheeks darkened, his eyes aglow. "You are beautiful, Caro."

And she believed him.

Lingering ecstasy scattered through her when he increased his pace. With a roar, he orgasmed. His eyes widened then narrowed, but he didn't stop pounding into her, didn't glance away. He groaned her name, his body shuddering when another orgasm slammed into her. It was so unexpected, she dug her nails into his arms and exploded, uncaring that he watched her at her most vulnerable.

"Maker, when you do that..." he rasped, collapsed on top of her, gathered her close then rolled them over.

With her face pressed to his chest above his heart, she snuggled against him, content to doze off to the erratic rhythm of his heartbeat.

CARO MOANED, SNUGGLING DEEPER into the warm embrace of Malo's phantom arms. She didn't want to wake up, to face whatever hell Imarri had dreamed up. Malo would fetch her soon, she knew this, yet the waiting was draining her soul.

A hand slid over her hip and tugged her against a broad chest, pressing her cheek to a heated pec.

She froze, fear skittered down her spine, and ice raised the hair at the nape of her neck. *Where am I?*

On a softer bed not made of stone. The male holding her smelled Etterian and had a bronze skin tone.

Veor?

She racked her brain, trying to remember if she'd returned to Veor when she couldn't sleep? No, breakfast was the usual weird-ass food, orange goop tasting like slimy spinach. She'd kill for coffee.

Sitting up in one fluid motion, she gaped at the male sprawled beside her. Emotions boiled to the surface, that she was free, that he had come, that she loved him, mixing with relief, gratitude, and awe. She sobbed, allowing the tears to flow except for when they blurred her vision of him. With dismissive swipes of her fingers and sucking in great gulps of air, she fought for calm despite wanting to squeal and bounce on the bed like a teenager.

He was too beautiful to be real.

"Caro?" He sat up to pull her against him, as if to shield her.

"You came for me," she gasped, squeezing the words past her trembling lips.

"My Dar Eth, you are my world. No one will take you from me again." He kissed her temple, lingering there while he tangled his fingers in her hair. "I am sorry. All that you have suffered is my fault. I did not protect you as I should have." He dipped to meet her gaze. "It pleases me that you have an O.D.I."

She winced, Ayetz's face coming to mind. Part of her wanted to yell, to blame Malo, but she knew better, that this was on Imarri. Tilting back, she cupped his smooth cheeks to brush a kiss across his mouth. His grip tightened, and a gasp escaped his parted lips.

"I don't blame you, Malo. How could you have known she planned this?" Caro chuckled. "Just hold me and often until you become my normal."

He crushed her against him with a grunt. "I will hold you as much as possible, *ensa ra ensa*."

He ran his hands up and down her back as if to soothe her. His O .D.I. beeped, but he ignored it, huffing when the intrusion persisted.

"Operations Commander, I cannot ignore our king," Afax grumbled. "I have delayed him for two hours."

She giggled, slipping out of Malo's arms. "Duty calls, my Eth." She climbed off the bed despite his glower declaring he hated her leaving him. "I'll shower and eat."

As she headed for the bathroom, tears of joy streamed down. A moment of privacy, a shower, new clothing, and human food? As soon as the door shut, she punched the air and did a jig, wiggling her ass. She allowed laughter to bubble up, to split her cheeks. An incredible sense of freedom and happiness followed her into the cubicle.

Never would she take things for granted. What Imarri had done was prove to Caro that she was more than capable of surviving the wide universe and handling bullies. Imarri had taught her how, the stupid witch. "I have kidnapped you, but hey, here's how to use a weapon." Caro mimicked Imarri's voice then giggled at her silliness. "Granny's nipples, what an idiot."

Bolstered by her husband and the might behind him, Caro had a right to be victorious. Stepping out of the spray, she activated the air-dryer and waited. Something in their water softened her hair which had been like straw for so long.

With a robe wrapping itself around her, she padded to the rehydrator and encountered a dilemma. Pancakes, waffles, bacon, eggs, sausages... She started with a coffee, dropping into a comfy to savor each sip. Holy noodle, did it taste divine.

"I'm in love, you nectar of the gods." She kissed the cup before taking another sip.

The rumble of Malo's voice in the bedroom had contentment soaking into every pour, and she snuggled deeper into the comfy. He'd made love to her too many times to count, fueling her wildest fantasies. Even though her body ached from his loving, she could go another round. She'd dreamt of him doing that, which might explain why she'd thought last night was yet another illusion.

Hell, when had she developed into such a nympho?

"Have you eaten?"

She raised her gaze to rest it on Malo wearing nothing but his low-riding yoga pants. As casual as fuck, he leaned against the door frame, bulging his pecs. Monkey's bananas, could anyone blame her? Muscles rippled from his molded chest to his pants, his waist dipped in, and his Adonis belt peeked out, tempting her to run a tongue along every indent.

She sucked in a breath and shook her head, remembering he'd asked her something. Food? Yes, the wrenching of her stomach lining said she should eat.

"Caro." His tone admonished her, but she didn't care, not when he strolled toward her like a digi-mag model, his long braid swaying behind him.

"Coffee first, Malo." She gestured to the rehydrator. "I can't decide."

He sighed, took the empty cup from her, laced his fingers through hers, and ushered her to the rehydrator. "Choose."

"So bossy." She tapped without thinking, relying on instinct, or else she'd never eat. "Let's start with bacon, pancakes, maple syrup, and another coffee. Would you like anything?"

She faced him, but he crowded her, his taut stomach warming her hip. He grabbed her, yanking her against him. She yelped, raising her hands to his chest as if to hold him back.

"I would like more of you, *thamani*." He snatched little kisses then with a groan, deepened one to plunder her mouth.

She clung to him, her knees trembling. Lord above, this male devastated her senses.

He pulled away, anger twisting his features. "My apologies, Caro. I should not distract you, but that you thought of me after all you have endured... I adore that about you."

Adore? Heat bloomed on her cheeks. They had yet to talk about feelings, and she had yet to tell him she loved him. "Kreso?" Okay, her voice came out in a squeak, but with her heart beating a parsec a minute, acting normal was out of the question.

A slow smile curled his lips, and her heartbeat went supernova. "Please. I will sit and observe my Dar Eth. Alodon's balls, Caro, I have missed you."

She used the task of ordering to hide her face. Tears threatened to fall, the burn in her throat and nostrils implied a good cry was on the horizon. He'd said so yesterday, that he'd missed her. Joy bubbled inside her like champagne, fizzing, spiraling until her fingers trembled, and she couldn't breathe.

Why am I so emotional?

"Giyua juice?" She tapped in his order when he answered her but kept her back to him, unable to face him as ice tingled along her shoulders. Her monthly was late. No biggie, the trauma and stress she'd endured could explain that.

Fresh heat bloomed on her cheeks when she realized she'd need a doctor. Discussing menstruation cycles with men was a minefield. Explaining it to an Etterian male doctor might be entertaining. Or not.

She carried their plates to the table before choosing the comfy beside him. While she nibbled on the bacon, the salty-explosive flavor a little intense, she wondered how she felt about being pregnant. If she was, that is.

If she wasn't?

Disappointment stuck true with bitter darts of sadness. She sighed. There was her answer.

Chapter Twenty-One

"Operations Commander Malo said you asked for an examination, milady?" Medic Brynr hovered in the door, not entering unless she invited him in.

Caro grabbed his wrist and tugged him into the quarters, drawing a grunt from him.

"Brynr, call me Caro. I want a full assessment, just to make sure there're no ill effects from my…adventure." She gestured to her leggings and baggy T-shirt. "Want me to undress?"

He shook his head, fear and horror in his wide eyes and gaping mouth. "That will not be necessary, milady." He tapped on his O.D.I. with trembling fingers.

"Caro." She raised her arms at her sides and let him scan her.

He did so from numerous angles, silence thickening the air. When he had finished, he stepped back, his cheeks a darker hue.

"And?" She lowered her arms, her fingers twitching while she waited for the verdict.

"You are well if not a little malnourished, but rest and frequent meals will repair that." He tapped on his O.D.I. "I have added nutrients to the cleanser."

Disappointment teased at her heart. She gritted her teeth, fighting the urge to smack him even though not falling pregnant wasn't his fault. "And?"

"What concerns you, milady?" He lowered his arm and met her gaze.

"Caro." She gestured to her lower abdomen. "My...cycle is late, Brynr."

"Of course it is." He nodded like a sage old man, as if nothing fazed him. "As per Medic Aldur's findings, your menstrual cycle pauses when you are with *damu*."

She punched him on the arm.

He yelped, leaping away but not before glaring at her.

"Start with that. Tell me I'm pregnant first, Brynr. What? Am I supposed to guess?"

"My apologies, mil...Caro." He tapped his O.D.I. but kept his distance. "Have you had other symptoms? Nausea, swollen breasts, lethargy?"

"None of those. A little emotional, but I've only known Malo two and a half weeks. Isn't it too soon to be pregnant?" She snorted, rolling her eyes. Look who she was asking.

Brynr stared at her, hesitant to speak. "Let me know if you need me."

"Wait, what about a due date?" Dizziness struck. Frowning, she flopped into the nearest comfy. *I'm pregnant with Malo's child.* They hadn't had a chance to be a couple, to flesh out their marriage. Did he want children?

A memory surfaced the day of their first kiss. Yes, he wanted many with her. She sniffed and rubbed her flat stomach. This news would make him happy. A slow smile formed, and she raised her gaze to meet Brynr's worried dark blue eyes.

"I'm pregnant." A sob escaped her lips, and she laughed, letting the tears flow unchecked.

The poor male bolted, leaving her alone in her blubbering state. There was no one except Malo to tell. Vorn protected Izzy was all Malo had said when Caro had asked about her this morning.

She'd also put in a request that he help Bezu somehow, explaining how a Yithian male had befriended her and sent Malo her location despite the danger it had put him in. He'd been there for her when Imarri had her tortured. That had led to a fuming Malo contacting everyone he knew. In the end, he'd promised he'd ensure Bezu and his estuuba would be safe.

Veor was somewhere on board, receiving the best care.

The door slid open. Malo burst into the room, snatching Caro out of the comfy for a crushing hug. "You are with *damu*." He kissed her, stealing her breath despite her pounding his chest.

She wasn't about to succumb to his delicious mouth and his wonderous tongue when she was fuming. "This was *my* news to share. How dare he tell you." She shoved Malo back, aware he allowed her to do so. "Patient-doctor confidentiality?"

She threw her hands in the air, pacing to burn off the anger coursing through her. It was her first pregnancy. She should have been the one to tell Malo, to reveal the change in his role. Not...this. The ass didn't show remorse either, instead, he wore the biggest, brightest grin. She sighed, torn between her heart and the injustice of it all.

"He was concerned for you, *thamani*. You are his first human female and now, his first pregnant one." Malo chuckled, gathering her within his arms. "Then you cried. The male did not know what to do."

She sucked in a long calming breath, pressing her temple to Malo's uniformed chest. "I frightened him?"

"He entered the comm room, stuttering about crying, offers to undress, and ended it with the news." Malo leaned back to tip her chin up with a delicate touch. "Is it true? You carry my *damu*?"

Faced with his handsome features and the ice blue of his eyes, she couldn't deny the truth. She was going to be a mom.

She gasped. "Oh, no, Izzy will make the worst aunt."

He frowned. "We will keep her away from our *damu*."

Caro laughed. "No, I mean she'll spoil him with gifts and affection."

"Males are not shown affection." He jerked back as if he couldn't understand the idea of it.

"Male?" Her heart twisted. She'd have liked a daughter. "Did Brynr's scans reveal the gender?"

"No, most *damu* are male, *ensa*." He hugged her gently like he feared to harm her.

"Yes, I remember. A boy." She looped her arms around his neck and feathered kisses along his jaw. "Need to hurry back, or can you spare the mother of your *damu* a little of your body?"

"A little?" He smirked, a dimple forming.

She rose onto her toes to dip the tip of her tongue in the indent. "I want fast, Malo."

He stilled before bending to kiss her on the lips, small sips, humming when he did so. "No more fast, only slow, careful." A growl rumbled from his chest and up his throat. "Thorough."

He plundered her mouth, ravaging her senses, stealing her will to breathe, but he kept his eyes open, his expression intense. He broke the kiss, sucking in ragged breaths. "I do not deserve you, *ensa*, but I will never cease to cherish you."

She grinned, loving this softer side to him. "You're an engineer-operative-whatever, not a murderer, Malo."

He arched an eyebrow, a smile twisting his sensual lips. "There is a difference?"

"To me there is, especially when you saved me." She wiggled closer, drawing a moan from him.

"You could have saved yourself, Caro. Your technique was...impressive." He slid his hands down to grip her hips while dropping a kiss onto the tip of her nose.

"It sounds like you want a demonstration." She stepped back, studying his face. Vinnie was stowed in the corner of their bedroom.

"Please." He darted around her to sit in the comfy.

She tossed him a lust-filled look. He shifted in the comfy. A glance revealed a large bulge she was fond of. "Let me grab my katac."

In the room, she stripped out of her leggings and shirt, tossing them and her underwear onto the bed before grabbing Vinnie. Malo had his back to her when she marched to him. She spun the katac to warm her muscles. When she paused in front of him, he stilled. His heated gaze trailed from the tips of her toes to her breasts.

He groaned, leaning back in the comfy to spread his thighs. "Caro, this is madness."

She twirled the katac, moving through every stance with deliberate slowness. With each lunge, spin, and thrust, his breathing shuddered. By the time she rested Vinnie on the floor, the demonstration complete, a fine sheen of sweat dewed Malo's forehead. He gripped the comfy's arms with white knuckles.

"Still think it's madness?" She pouted, running an appraisal along his taut body.

"Maker, you drive me to incredible, sinful insanity." He bolted out of the chair to place a kiss on her pebbled nipple. With an arm around her, he tugged her closer, granting him access to her breasts, which he lavished his attention on.

"You didn't like my demonstration?" She battered her eyelashes at him, trying to appear innocent or unaffected when desire had her throbbing and panting. "I'll go shower. I'll see you later after your shift?"

"Alodon's balls, *thamani*, I am not leaving these quarters, not until you have screamed my name and eased my longing for you." He cupped her cheeks, keeping her in place for his intense gaze. Something promising swirled in their beautiful depths. "I ache for you, Caro. When I am with you or not, it makes no difference."

He desired her, nothing more. She lowered her gaze, hiding the sting of tears. "I'm your wife, your Dar Eth, Malo. I'm yours as you're mine."

Pain gripped her chest, but she shoved it aside. What had she expected? They'd known each other for less than a week, Imarri's adventure notwithstanding. Caro had to remember they were in the honeymoon stage where sex was on the agenda and not the state of her heart.

Pasting on a smile, she clasped his hand, trying to lead him to their bedroom. She would love him, and perhaps, one day, he would return it. If his species couldn't love, she'd find consolation in his warm regard and the joys of being a mother.

Yet, despite those brave thoughts, her heart wrenched, having longed for the rainbow tower in the clouds with the happy-ever-after. Granny's nipples, her love for him trapped her. Etterians couldn't divorce, and if they could, she wouldn't leave him. Fool that she was.

Chapter Twenty-Two

Malo studied the female asleep beside him. His heart expanded like it would explode with the warmth of adoration and gratitude she invoked. He cupped her belly, stroking his thumb across it. There lay his *damu*, his son.

Maker. What had he done to deserve such blessings? Wiping the tear running down his cheek, he slipped out of bed. He had tasks to perform, those he had discarded in the pursuit of his precious Caro.

She didn't understand how much he needed her, how she'd changed him, his life. Sorrow lingered in her eyes, and nothing he said erased it. Yet it had been something he'd said to place it there.

No matter how he replayed their conversations, he couldn't find the words that had brought her such pain. Had she longed for a daughter? He'd told her they were scarce, which she must have forgotten. No, he recalled her saying the gender didn't matter.

He pulled on his armor, his movements silent. Brynr had warned of mood swings, exhaustion as his *damu* grew, and to be tolerant with her. If she asked for a moon, Malo would find her the brightest, most beautiful moon. If she asked for a gem, nothing would stand in his way while he hunted for the perfect one. Couldn't she see that?

Yet she asked for nothing.

He drew the blanket over her then tucked a stray curl behind her ear. Leaving her summoned a deep ache in his core. He had to scent her all the time, to relive her gentle touch. That was the madness he referred to earlier when she had gone through the katac techniques with grace, agility, and the most sensual movements any Kayarra would be proud of.

His groin had caught alight, burning need through him. How he remained in the comfy for the demonstration, had to be due to his training... to resist temptation or torture. Each lunge and thrust had sparked something primitive within him. Never before had lust driven away all thoughts and stripped him of his control.

When he'd buried himself in her, her channel still spasming from her fulfillment, his had followed in quick succession. The too exquisite sensations were almost painful. He would repeat the experience without hesitation, for as agony met pleasure, it was also addictive. He understood the line between them, one he'd crossed on numerous occasions for the good of Etteria.

Never had he expected his Dar Eth to inspire such ecstasy. When he'd pondered the suitable characteristics of a female, he'd thought of her like a battle-bond, certainly not this obsession.

He scooped Caro's panties off the floor and shoved them into his pocket. If he had to complete his tasks, he needed to focus, and he couldn't do it without her scent. The great Operations Commander Malo et Dalo weakened by a human? By his Dar Eth? Satiation thrummed through him, energizing him. Yes, he would succumb to her, not caring what others thought, of how it impacted his reputation.

His forearm buzzed. He hurried out of their quarters, not wanting to awaken her. They had found fulfillment twice, and a third time teased at the edges of his senses. The annals mentioned such an intense period in their relationship as the Ethera completed their union. With her carrying his *damu*, he had to be careful not to tire her.

The O.D.I. vibrated along his arm again. He answered once he stepped into the passage outside their quarters. "What is it?"

"Earth has announced your impending return. They have their warriors ready to arrest you for kidnapping, Operations Commander."

"And?" He arched a brow, not that Afax could see it. Stomping his way to the comm room, he waited for the male to elaborate.

"Director Reyes would like to speak with you when you have a moment. Also, I have Joshua Guardian on standby to discuss underwater crafts." Afax's voice held skepticism.

Malo grunted, bursting into the comm room. He gestured to Afax to connect the comm to Director Reyes while he assumed a position in front of the large vids.

"Director Reyes," he said by way of greeting, folding his arms behind his back.

"Did you find her?" The human had aged, with dark circles under his eyes.

Malo allowed a wide smile to form. "Yes, and she is well."

The male slumped in his chair. His head fell back, and he closed his eyes. "Good, and the culprits?"

"A vindictive Maloidian operative."

"Maloidian?" The human male scowled. "I'm aware there are new species living and working at our stations on the outskirts of space, but none, other than the algri, have officially introduced themselves."

"We will share what we have on known species." Malo flicked a glance at Afax. The male punched on his keys. "I have shipped the Maloidian and her accomplices to our Fuyra mines." He unfolded his arms and gripped the console, leaning in. "Still, I need to know how Yithians made it past your security, Director Reyes. Find out who granted them access. Someone in E.S.A. might not want Etterians on your Earth."

Director Reyes gasped, sitting up in his chair to rest his elbows on the table. "I'll put my best men on this. I must warn you, Malo, my superiors are intent on arresting you for Caro's disappearance. I've explained the situation, but our media has blown this out of proportion. The arrest is just a formality, and I would consider it a personal favor if you don't resist. You will, of course, be released."

Malo pinched his lips, debating whether he should reveal that imprisonment wasn't new to him, nor did he fear it. "As much as I would enjoy the time spent in your custody, I am suffering from the Ethera. I cannot be away from Caro for long." He scowled. "My Dar Eth would need to be detained with me, Director Reyes, and this I will not allow."

"Oh, dear." Director Reyes frowned. "I'll bring this to their attention and revert soonest. Send Caro my love."

The vid went blank on Malo's scowl. He held a higher rank than Director Reyes, and how dare the man ask him to send...love. What did that even mean?

"Joshua Guardian." He stared at the display vid, expecting Afax to make the connection. A male with brown hair and pale-green eyes appeared. In a uniform hugging his torso and his bearing erect, he showed neither impatience nor anger that Malo had kept him waiting.

"Joshua Guardian, I am Operations Commander Malo."

He grinned. "It's Joshua Bennett or Josh, Operations Commander." His light brown hair was shaven.

Malo twitched, finding it hard to accept that for humans, short hair didn't mean dishonor. "Josh, Director Reyes informs me that you are the Earth's liaison and expert in submarines."

"I wouldn't say expert." His shrug contradicted his prideful blush. These humans were too easy to read. "I've spoken to Quin and can confirm the submarine chosen will suit your interests but not your physiology. We don't have submarines large enough to cater for the average height of an Etterian. It is why I agreed to join the shipment, to help Etteria in building your own."

Malo nodded. "You have my gratitude."

"I have been in contact with Ambassador Brenin." Josh's lips curled, revealing his opinion of the male. "Lucas and I will be traveling with him."

"Are you saying my mission on Earth is complete?" Malo held his breath then released it on a silent sigh. At the thought of taking Caro home to Etteria, he couldn't stop the exploding emotions warming his chest.

"I can't confirm or deny this, Operations Commander, since I'm not aware of your mission parameters."

Malo grunted at having asked the human the question. He would contact King Xeus and Sub-Commander Vorn. Perhaps there were one or two tasks he had to attend to, and of course, his impending imprisonment.

"Thank you for taking the time, Joshua Bennett."

The male tapped his temple with two fingers before the screen switched to black, this time at Afax's instruction. Malo dropped into his chair and rested a fingertip on his data tab. He dragged the device across the metal table, tapped it on, and grimaced at the endless communications awaiting his attention.

Time waits for no male, even one in the throes of the Ethera.

Speaking into his O.D.I., he summoned Data Officer Tias and started the arduous task of sifting through his comms.

"Operations Commander," Tias greeted when he entered the comm room.

"I need you to sort through in and outgoing comms at E.S.A., specifically from the day we arrived. Someone there endangered my Dar Eth, and this will not be tolerated." Malo pushed his data tab away and buried his fingers in his pocket, cherishing the silkiness of Caro's undergarment. "Share your findings with Director Reyes. I do not want to anger the only ally we have."

"Yes, Operations Commander."

Dismissing Tias, Malo gestured to Afax. "Comm Sub-Commander Vorn." He drummed his fingers on his data tab, waiting. "Vorn, status report," he said the moment the sub-commander's image appeared on the large display vids.

The male winced. "Not good, Operations Commander. The humans are circling the *Gladio*."

"They think I kidnapped my Dar Eth. Do not fire upon them, and keep the peace as best as possible." Malo pinched his brow. "How is Izzy?" He had to ask. Caro was desperate for news.

Vorn hesitated. "I tasked Supreme Commander Oyaz to rescue Lady Simone, Lady Izzy's sister. An incident occurred. Elite Warrior Danic was injured but is healing. Supreme Commander Oyaz and Lady Izzy are missing."

"Missing?" Malo straightened, ice sliding down his spine. "For how long, and where did this occur?"

"A week ago." Vorn stiffened.

"What?" Malo burst to his feet. "What steps have you taken, sub-commander?"

"It took a day to realize they had not returned from their excursion." Vorn raised his chin, accepting the full blame on his shoulders. "My apologies, Operations Commander. I assumed the newly mated pair sought privacy."

Malo grinned. "Oyaz and Izzy?"

"Yes, Operations Commander. Supreme Commander Oyaz's O.D.I. is inactive. I have sent teams to Lady Simone's house, found traces of an ambush, blood from a Yithian, and a cold trail leading into the forest to the east. They camped the night, then Izzy contacted Elite Warrior Garix. After this, we lost them completely. I have scoured the land surrounding the area and analyzed all escape routes."

Malo grimaced, unable to share this news with Caro, not in her current condition. He growled into his O.D.I. and waited for Tias to arrive. "Tias, assist Sub-Commander Vorn in locating Supreme Commander Oyaz and Lady Izzy. Vorn, forward what you know to Tias. We are a week out. I can fully assist then. This is not good news, and the fault rests on my shoulders. I incapacitated you by taking the *Gladio's* data officer with me."

"My thanks, Operations Commander. The *Valiant* awaits its data officer since Supreme Commander Oyaz is newly appointed. Supreme Commander Nerx is en route, as is Adviser Cales and Prince Citus."

Malo gestured to Afax, who ended the comm. "To vanish for a week, maybe longer? My instincts say this is not the Yithians."

"I agree, Operations Commander." Tias glanced up from his O. D.I. "I will attend to both tasks with the utmost urgency."

Malo dismissed him and focused on the display vids. He didn't want to comm the king after the morning he'd had. "Send all this to Advisers Cales and Kanzo. Let them decide what the king should see. I am heading home to my Dar Eth."

Lunch with Caro and a fast mating might refuel his flagging spirits.

Chapter Twenty-Three

"Director Reyes sends his...*love*." Malo sat on the edge of their bed and rubbed his Dar Eth's bare hip. He had spent just two hours in the comm room. Gritting his teeth, he pinched the bridge of his nose before flopping down alongside her.

"Thanks." Caro stretched, arching her back and thrusting out her breasts.

"Do not tempt me, female." He grinned, for it was too late. Just scenting her when he approached their room was enough to rouse his interest.

Her smile was slow and sensual, implying she knew how she affected him. His chest expanded with that earlier warmth into something more intense, crushing his ability to breathe.

"You're back so soon, my Eth." She rolled over and rubbed his chest. Sighing, she stroked his neck where his armor ended. "New rule, no armor in the bedroom. Leave it at the door."

He chuckled. "You want me naked."

"Damn straight." She thumped the release mechanism, and his armor loosened. "I love the feel of your skin." Sliding her fingers under his armor proved her words.

He sucked in his breath when she tweaked a nipple.

"I was hoping for a meal." He sat up in a single motion to whip off his armor before cradling her in his arms. "*Thamani*, perhaps fast then slow is in order?" Meeting her gaze, he tried to read her expressions, whether she was as eager as he was, or whether their *damu* made her unwell.

"A quickie?" She kissed his chin, then dragged her hot mouth along his throat.

He groaned, unable to nor did he want to stop the ripple of shivers she summoned across his body. His O.D.I. flickered his eyelids, and he grunted. "I like the sound of a quickie."

"Strip." She bounced off the bed. "I want you before the nausea realizes I'm awake."

He rose to remove his pants, but when he faced her, she leaned against the bulkhead, cupping her stomach. "Too late." She paled and ran, streaming her dark hair behind her.

"Operations Commander Malo." Afax's voice cut through the sexual tension strumming Malo's body, leaving only concern.

"Not now, Afax." Malo barreled after Caro, kneeling beside her while she purged into the waste receptacle. After gathering her hair into one hand, he rubbed her back with the other.

She moaned, slumping. "That feels so good, Malo."

"My apologies, Caro. I am selfish to assume you will ease the Ethera and carry my *damu*."

She wiped her mouth on the back of her hand and leaned into him. He dropped her hair and lifted her onto his lap.

"I shall have my males move the bulkheads, bringing the cleansing room closer to our bedroom."

Her smile was weak, and the way she curled into him strengthened his resolve to be a better Eth.

"That would be wonderful." She cupped his cheek when he urged her to her feet.

He rubbed her lower back while she brushed her teeth—a uniquely human thing to do. Not that he liked how the toothpaste dominated the taste of her. He complained to her about it daily.

Patting her mouth dry, she stretched to kiss his chin. "I changed it to something herbal. Better?"

Frowning, he rubbed his mouth across hers and caught a hint of something sharp then her, all Caro, his Dar Eth. He grumbled and grabbed her ass, lifting her off the floor for his descending kiss. Thrusting his tongue between her lips, he delved into her, unable to satiate this need to know all of her. No matter how many times he kissed her, it didn't soothe this desperation within him.

"Operations Commander Malo, I cannot keep the king waiting."

Sighing, he ended the kiss and held his temple to hers.

She chuckled, feathering kisses along his nose to his chin. "Speak to King Xeus. I will eat something to calm my stomach, shower, and await your attention in the bedroom." She trailed a finger down his throat to his nipple. "With my thighs spread wide."

He watched her bare ass sway when she headed to the rehydrator.

"And if you take too long, I'll play with myself."

His breath caught, and he didn't bother to stop the shudder and flow of memories her words incited.

"I am on my way, Afax." Malo snatched a hard kiss and bolted for the door.

"Um, Malo?" She covered her mouth, smothering a chuckle. "Clothes might be a good idea."

He grinned at his naked body before hurrying into their room. Striding out, he snatched her close for another quick, hard kiss, then abandoned her. Staying meant offending King Xeus, and he needed the male to release him from this mission, post finding Izzy, of course.

When he entered the comm room, the display vids flickered.

"My apologies for keeping you waiting, Adviser Kanzo."

Kanzo smiled. "As an Eth myself, Operations Commander, I assumed there might be a delay. You are on time to speak to the king. He has had an unusual morning."

Kanzo stepped aside for King Xeus, who bounded from behind his desk. The male looked happy. The tension the void had added to his face had eased. "Malo, congratulations on finding your Dar Eth."

"Thank you, my king. The humans believe I kidnapped her and are intent on imprisoning me for said crime."

Xeus's jaw tightened. "I cannot allow that."

"It is but a diplomatic issue, King Xeus. My bigger concerns lie with my Dar Eth carrying my *damu*, and the impact—"

"She does? This is splendid news, Malo." Xeus's smile split his cheeks wide. "I have tasked Supreme Commander Nerx and Medic Aldur to secure a human *and* female obstetrician."

Malo's eyelids fluttered at the strange word. The knowledge of such a skillset eased a little of his concern. "A wise decision."

"Attend to the final items on your task list and return to Etteria as soon as possible."

Relief flooded Malo. To go home, to ensure Caro was safe and cared for, and with the permission of his king, it was more than he could've asked for.

"Let us discuss this unsavory Kayarra issue. I spoke to Queen Allero within the hour. For her crimes and those of her operatives, Imarri ag Zennr will while away her time on Fuyra as you decreed. I need a selection of your finest males. The queen would like to test the Kayarra's skills."

"Oh?" Malo hadn't expected such a solution.

"Should the Maloidian females manage an escape, we are to consider all offenses forgotten."

Malo pinched his lips. Not much shocked him, but this had.

"Including a permanent discount on future Maloidian steel imports. With the construction of submarines and an impending war with Yithia, this is a stupendous gain."

"Well done, King Xeus." Diplomacy was at play, and his king thought long term. Still, Malo's father would not have spared Imarri's life. "I will send additional males to assist those already escorting the Kayarra to Fuyra."

King Xeus glanced to the side, and something or someone snagged his undivided attention.

Malo grinned, assuming Queen Macera had entered the king's office. "Will that be all, my king?"

"Yes, Operations Commander." Kanzo dominated the display vid's image when the king strode past him, followed by a feminine squeal of delight.

The comm ended, and Malo bolted, running pell-mell to his Dar Eth, who'd promised to start without him should he delay.

"Caro, *ensa?*"

A soft moan, a gasp, a sigh drove him to their bedroom. He shuddered, and his malehood pulsed, burning his nerves and setting his insides ablaze. Yet, in the doorway, he froze.

She wasn't on the bed with her legs spread. No, she stood before him wearing an outfit he would forever remember. Transparent black fabric, serving no other purpose but to mold to her curves, and thrust her breasts up, her nipples visible and hard. Something wrapped her hips, and strips clung to her gauze-like leggings that ended mid-thigh. She wore no undergarments she called panties, and his gaze snagged there for an unmeasurable moment before settling on her eyes.

"What are you wearing, Caro?" His voice was hoarse and harsh enough to hurt when he spoke. Stumbling into the room, he stripped, tossing his armor without care.

"Lingerie. You like?" Her hair cascaded over a shoulder, and bold red lipstick on her lips made his breath hitch.

"It is unwise to tempt the Ethera, *thamani.* I can barely keep my control around you." He gripped her hips, drawing her closer.

With a shake of her head, she tapped him on the chest. "I want your promise, Malo."

He jerked back, his lips moments from grazing her skin. "Anything."

"No touching me until I say you can."

Growling, he dipped his head to meet her gaze. "Why not? Have I offended you, my Dar Eth?"

She smiled, tracing her fingers from his neck, along his shoulders to squeeze his upper arms. "No, never. I want to try something, to see if you'll like it."

"Not touch you?" He trembled. Was she insane? The Ethera demanded, and if the past weeks without Caro had taught him anything, he wasn't as strong as he believed he was.

"Surely the great Operations Commander Malo can resist touching little me?" She swirled her fingernail around his taut nipple.

He pinched his lips, wishing he could convey how the Ethera affected him, how being this close to her tossed his control to the corners of the known universe.

"Why?"

Her smile faded, and the tension in the air thickened. "It's about trust, Malo."

He closed his eyes. "For how long?"

She stroked his cheeks and kissed him, dodging his mouth when he made to deepen the kiss. "Give me five minutes. If you want me to stop, then I'll release you from the promise."

For such a short time, he could endure. "You have my vow."

"Lie down in the center of the bed."

He did so with his gaze fixed on her.

"Place your hands behind your head." She climbed onto the bed and crawled across it to loop a black sash around his eyes.

"Caro." He caught her wrist, careful not to bruise her.

"Trust me, Malo, please."

Grunting, he obeyed, cupping the back of his head in his palms after she blindfolded him. Without his sight, his sense of smell and hearing intensified. She moved from one side of the room to the other before the warmth of her brushed his right side.

Something incredibly soft glided from his collarbone to his malehood. He gritted his teeth to swallow a moan. That wasn't her hand. It felt like the furs of an Eiltur—a small sea creature once found on the protected shores of Durn.

"Another thing, Malo. Show me your reactions. Don't hold back, my Eth."

"If it pleases you, *thamani.*"

Something slapped across his thigh, drawing a gasp. Not a stranger to pain, he understood the fine line between that and pleasure, but when she ran the Eiltur over the unexpected sting, his breath caught. Heat spread from there to his throbbing arousal. He couldn't soothe it, couldn't bury it in her depths, not when he'd vowed five minutes.

She gripped his knees, spreading them wide before grazing her nails along his inner thighs, stopping before reaching his malehood. He burned for her to touch him, to run the Eiltur over his length.

She soothed the path her nails had scoured with her hot mouth, sucking and nipping.

Then her warmth was gone. He stilled, searching for her past the lust pounding his senses. A hot mouth on a nipple tore a groan from him. He was Fuyra hard, needing to end this, for her to free him from the vow.

She sucked hard, and like a blaster shot, fire scorched a path from his chest to his core, coiling and rousing something deep within him.

"Maker." A tremble lay claim to his limbs, and he struggled to keep his hands off her.

"What's this, Malo?" She touched the ridges running along the length of his arousal.

He growled, arching off the bed as shivers, fire, ice took turns spiraling outward. "My denit." He hissed when she continued to stroke it. "Sensitive."

"Remove your blindfold. You'll want to see this."

He whipped it off. She straddled his thigh and had undone her black lingerie so her breasts could squeeze through the deep V. He feasted on her beauty, the bright pink of her cheeks, her parted lips, and the rise and fall of her breasts.

A slow sensual smile curled across her red lips. "Not me, silly." She dipped and ran her tongue from his balls to the head of his arousal, across his denit.

He cried out, curled his hands into fists, and fought lunging for her. Alodon's balls, the graze of her tongue along the length of him was… He closed his eyes then blinked them open when she straddled a knee, rubbing her wet sex along his skin. She needed him as much.

But when she wrapped her mouth around the head of his malehood, sucking while rubbing his denit, the fulfillment he had barely been able to hold back rushed along his length.

"Caro," he roared, arching off the bed. "Stop. I cannot bear more."

A fine sheen coated his body, and he flexed his fingers, hoping to return blood to them.

"Spoilsport." She licked her lips as if he tasted divine, but at least she was no longer tormenting him with her mouth.

Sliding up him, she wiggled her hips until the heat of her drenched his tip. Then she impaled herself inch by excruciating inch.

She is killing me.

Her mouth parted, and her eyelids fluttered shut on a breathless moan. "So good, Malo." She angled her hips and rode him, back and forth, scraping her nails over his nipples, before dipping to kiss him. He tasted himself on her tongue, along with pure, intense lust.

He wasn't above begging. "Please, *ensa*, I need—"

She shook her head, sitting up to arch her back and ride him harder. Her breasts bounced with each move she made, and deep whimpers escaped her. She was mesmerizing, exquisite, his deepest fantasy brought to life. His fulfillment aligned with hers, heat gushing from her, from him, and he arched, gritting his teeth at the painful intensity slamming into him.

Stars, like an exploding supernova, burned his eyelids, as a mountain of breathtaking pleasure rolled over him.

She didn't stop riding him while she found her joy, one after the other, extending his fulfillment until he thought he would snap.

"I release you from the promise." Her whisper sliced through the tension twisting his body, seconds before she collapsed across his chest.

He didn't hesitate, bolting upright to roll her over and thrust into her again. She mewled, her eyes widening as another fulfilment crashed, drenching him in an exquisite fire he couldn't name.

"Maker, Caro." He didn't know how to describe the crescendo of emotion sweeping through him.

Her blue eyes warmed, conveying something his hearts recognized, responding with an answering heat that slowed his desperate thrusting. He kissed her, capturing her lips, teasing them, slipping his tongue between them to find solace in her taste, in the welcoming depths of her mouth.

"*Thamani*, sweet *ensa ra ensa*."

As his nerve endings caught alight once more, rubbing his arousal and denit along the walls of her channel, a sweeter, deeper fulfillment claimed him. That moment, that instance, was the purest joy he had ever experienced. He slumped beside her, content to allow the tiny ripples of her fading pleasure calm his own. She rolled onto her side, offered her back, snuggled against him, then tugged his arms across her belly.

Minutes passed while their breathing slowed, and in the silence, she tried to smother a sniff.

"Caro?" He was gentle when he tilted her onto her back, concern warring with the contentment thrumming in his veins.

Her smile was tremulous through her tears. "*Damu* hormones, Malo. Nothing to worry about."

He sensed a lie and frowned, not understanding the motive behind it.

She stroked a fingertip along his jaw and kissed him. "Just hold me, my Eth."

"As you wish, *thamani*." He gathered her against him and rubbed her lower back the way she liked.

She sighed and drifted to sleep in his arms.

Chapter Twenty-Four

MALO HAD JUST LEFT with yet another non-declaration of love. Caro was a fool to hope. He'd made such sweet love to her after she'd tortured him with the rabbit fur, and the way he'd looked at her had given her hope. She sniffed.

"Lady Caro, Lady Izzy is on the comm." Afax's voice cut through her misery.

Joy gripped her, and she whooped, wiggling her butt in the comfy, making it grow and shrink. She chuckled. That was mean of her.

Izzy. Caro sniffed again, missing her bestie so much. "Thanks, Afax, please put her through."

Caro leaped to her feet to stand in front of the display vid. Dark circles under Izzy's eyes and a little weight-loss said much. "Izzy? Where the monkey's bananas have you been?"

"You're one to talk after you've traveled the galaxy. I merely had an incident and just returned. When Garix said Malo found you, I had to call you. I need you, babe. The shit's hitting the fan, and I don't know how to handle it."

Caro folded her arms across her belly, needing someone to hug. "That doesn't sound like you. Your solutions are usually too creative for me." Izzy leveled a glare on her. Caro chuckled and held up her palms. "Okay, start from the beginning."

"When those bastards took you, I was so scared, but not once did I think it was me they were after. A second attempt to take me changed things. I was shafted from stick-up-his-ass Vorn to some other guy named Oyaz. I didn't care who as long as they rescued Simmy. Can you imagine her alone?" She shook her head. Alone in her house, Izabelle's blind sister Simone was capable, but against an intruder, she wouldn't stand a chance. "Regardless, after Oyaz brought her to the battleship, I met him." She beamed and bounced. "My Eth, Caro. At last." Sadness ripped across her petite face. "But on a mission to collect Simmy's art supplies, Yithians ambushed us and blasted Oyaz's O.D.I." She sobbed behind her cupped hands. "Oyaz awoke not knowing who I was, and while I tried to drag his huge ass into the forest to hide, his memory didn't return. I couldn't contact Garix or Reyes, stranding us."

Caro placed a hand on the vid, wishing Izzy was here with her. "Holy noodles, Izzy. Does he remember you now?"

Teats dripped off her chin. "I found my alien only to lose him." She paced across the screen, disappearing for seconds in each direction, her high-energy returning. "No other male has claimed me, so I assume it's Oyaz or no one." She raised her big eyes to Caro. "I don't want anyone else. What do I do?"

"Granny's nipples, I don't know what to tell you, Izzy. What did the medic say?"

"There's no medical reason for his memory not to return." She paced again. "Maybe he doesn't want a soulmate? Maybe he doesn't want me as his Dar Eth?"

"They can't choose, babe. It happens once in their lives. If he dropped to a knee for you, I'm afraid the poor bastard is stuck with you." Caro forced a chuckle, hoping to calm her friend. "Now, be patient. Yeah, I know it's a curse word for you, but let nature heal him. He'll kneel for you again."

"Patient? That's worse than a rash." Izzy pouted. "You look good though, Caro. Are you glowing?"

Caro drew in a shuddering breath. "As expected of a mom-to-be, Aunt Izzy."

Izzy gaped, and in all the time Caro had known her, she couldn't once recall her friend speechless.

"I'm an aunt?" Izzy squealed, threw her hands in the air, and danced. "Way to go, Malo. He has super swimmers, he does." She stilled and flipped her hair out of her eyes, a smile still lingering. "But how are you doing, babe? You seem off. Are you unhappy about the baby?"

"No, never that." Tears pricked behind Caro's eyes. "He doesn't love me, Izzy. I'm not even sure they know what love is." She let herself cry since it was becoming a favorite pastime. "The sex is amazing, and he's attentive, even affectionate."

"I can't believe that, babe. I mean, once they feel, they throw themselves in, boots and all. They have no idea how to hold back emotions. Maybe he doesn't know what he's feeling is love?"

Caro snorted. "Getting a human man to admit love exists is like pulling teeth. How the hell am I going to teach an Etterian how to recognize it, Izzy?" She slumped, the massive task too much for her. "It's impossible."

"Let me know if you figure out how. Once Oyaz returns to his senses, I might need that how-to-for-dummies."

Malo stormed into their quarters.

Caro gasped, spinning her back to him to wipe her cheeks. He worried when she cried.

He crushed her in his embrace, and like an addict, she burrowed deeper, needing his natural cologne, the strength of his arms, and the warmth of his body through his armor.

"Hi, Malo." Izzy waved.

"It is good to see you, female. Your disappearance would have delayed heading home. Now that you are well, I will show my Dar Eth my Etteria sooner."

"What?" Caro squeaked. "We're not going to Earth?"

"*Thamani*, I need to speak to you. Bid Izzy farewell for now."

She huffed, waved at Izzy, and ended the comm. "We decide things together, Malo. It's what *married* couples do. Explain this."

He didn't but reached around her to activate her O.D.I. She glared at him, not understanding why he had to fiddle with her O.D.I. now, of all times.

"Izzy is correct." He released Caro's forearm to cup her face, holding her still for his penetrating gaze. "Etterians can feel—"

"You eavesdropped on my conversation?" Ice slithered down her spine, and she tried to leave his embrace.

"Your safety above privacy, always, beloved."

She pummeled his chest, trying to get him to release her. "No, and no. It implies a lack of trust, as if I would lie to you."

"And if any of my enemies found a way to take you from me, heart?" He snagged her gaze again. "Caro, I need you."

She huffed. "No privacy, Malo. Can't you understand that sometimes I just need to be with Izzy as me. Not as your Dar Eth, not as a soon-to-be mother, just a human woman with a friend."

"And can you not understand that I am nothing without you, Caro." He gathered her close, tucking her face into the curve of his neck. "You are the universe to me, heart of my hearts."

Agony sliced across her chest at his words. Heart of his heart? Did he even know what that meant? "What's with the strange endearments? I like your Etterian ones better. Your language is beautiful, Malo."

He chuckled, his teeth bright against his bronze skin. She loved it when he laughed. "I did not realize your Etterian Language Protocol wasn't activated. I have attended to it."

Her mind was a fog, and she struggled to clear her thoughts. "So, I can speak Etterian like Yithian?"

"Yes, beloved." He chuckled, kissing her temple then the tip of her nose. "Now, you will hear my love for you."

She squeezed her eyes shut as something heavy, like a thick, down blanket wrapped around her chest. "What are you saying, Malo? It doesn't make sense. You've been calling me 'heart' since the beginning."

"Alodon's balls, Caro, you have had my hearts from the moment you tilted your face to your blue Earthian sky and gifted me with birdsong."

The day on the beach after too much ice cream? She swayed, her knees weak, and had he not been holding her, she would've slid down his body into an undignified mess.

"Beloved?" He lifted her into his arms.

"You love me?"

He laughed, then kissed her, snatching what breath she had found. "Always, heart of my hearts. Always."

EPILOGUE

MALO FEATHERED KISSES ALONG Caro's chin, careful not to disturb her sleep. Holding her brought him pleasure, contentment, still, he struggled to convey how much he cherished her. He twitched his lips, only now understanding what had bothered Caro so many days ago.

The fault lay with him. He had known she invoked intense emotions, knew right from their first meeting that she was the air to his lungs, his very breath, his salvation, yet he hadn't been able to name it until he'd listened in.

Her tearful, "He doesn't love me," had been the revelation he'd needed. Love? He wasn't an Etterian who didn't believe in such feelings, having seen much in his life. But when she had thought he couldn't love her, he'd identified his intense emotions with certainty.

Maker, I am a blessed male.

Not only had Oyaz and Izzy returned to the *Valiant* ending Malo's last task, but that Oyaz was Izzy's Eth meant Izzy would be well-cared for. This nonsense about him not remembering her was lunacy. Once Oyaz fully recovered, Malo had no doubt the male would succumb to the Ethera again.

His O.D.I. tingled along his arm, and he twisted to activate it, reading the message from Tias. He had found the leak at E.S.A. Extricating himself from Caro's embrace, he kissed her temple and pulled on his armor.

"Who is this human?" Malo strode into Tias's data room.

"An engineer at E.S.A. The comms between him and a xenophobic organization called No More Galaxy Whores began the day you arrived. It is this group that fired the ancient weapon, harming your Dar Eth. I suspect they were aiming for you, Operations Commander."

Malo gritted his teeth. "Then how did Imarri involve herself?"

Tias shook his head. "There were no comms between Peter Duncan and the Yithians or Maloidians. She must have trailed us to Earth. This does not please me, Operations Commander. The location of Earth is now shared across all Maloidian ships."

"Alodon's balls. Two separate attempts at the same time? And Yithians stealing humans for slaves? Now Maloid's involvement? Send this information to Adviser Kanzo, asking for reinforcements. With the Maloidian greed in play, who knows how they might exploit the planet." Malo gripped the console. "Show me this Duncan."

The male's image had him cursing and slamming his palm onto the console, denting it. He knew the face of the male who had treated Caro so poorly. A grin formed, surprising an arched brow from Tias.

"He is Caro's enemy." Malo never explained, yet Tias had worked hard and deserved to know. Malo tapped his O.D.I. "Afax, continue on course to Earth and increase speed."

"Should I send this information to Director Reyes?" Tias gestured to the display vids.

"No, this is for our use. I will appraise Director Reyes when I am in his office." What Malo wanted was to smash his fist into Duncan's face. Without including Reyes in his decision meant he jeopardized the tremulous peace. Malo pursed his lips. "On second thought, comm Director Reyes."

He folded his arms across his chest and waited for the connection.

"Yes?" Reyes rubbed the sleep from his eyes. "Operations Commander?"

"We have found the leak. I would like to pulverize the male, despite him being human and working for E.S.A. As an Eth, I deserve vengeance."

"Oh, dear." The male straightened, facing the vid.

"To do so would bring me great pleasure, Caro as well, yet the negotiations between Etteria and Earth still need to be finalized."

Reyes sighed. "Well, let's start with who the culprit is?"

"Chief Engineer Peter Duncan."

"Shit." Reyes pinched the bridge of his nose. "There will be an inquiry, a panel will review the findings, and a judgment made."

Malo grimaced. "Tias, forward what we know. How long will this inquiry take?"

Reyes rubbed his face and hair. "Weeks."

That was time Malo didn't have. "It goes against the core of me to leave this unresolved, Director Reyes, but I wish to remove my Dar Eth from danger."

"I'll need a recording from her with regards to your supposed kidnapping. In addition, a full medical report will ensure she wasn't coerced or drugged during the recording."

Easy enough. "Very well, Director Reyes, I will ensure both are sent through. Will this end this nonsense?"

"I explained the situation again, using the information Oriana provided. It made no difference to their accusations. Without being able to locate Izzy, the arrest warrant remained valid." Reyes grinned. "She submitted a formal statement earlier today. Along with Princess Oriana's retelling of her Ethera experience, they have agreed to drop the charges."

Malo nodded. Everything was falling into place, except for this Duncan issue, but he was a patient male. "This is good news, Director Reyes. I will inform Caro and have her comm you." Malo ended the comm.

He tapped the console, undecided. Deep within him, he knew what he would choose—an immediate change of direction for Etteria. He had blood-bonds now that were his highest priority.

"Tias, I need you to ensure justice by my standard is met. Contact the closest battleship heading for Earth and have them rendezvous with us. You have my authority to meet out my vengeance if E.S.A. fails to deliver an honorable judgment."

Tias stood, faced Malo, and thumped his chest with his fist. "Yes, Operations Commander."

Malo's thoughts reeled while he hurried to their quarters. Never had he imagined returning to his estates on the outskirts of Issneen would summon such joy and excitement. For the first time in decades, he was going home, and he wasn't alone.

Glossary

Etterians worship one God, one Maker, since the universes have only His fingerprint on all of it, a single golden thread through all of creation.

Tokens: intergalactic form of currency

Kliks: predetermined length of distance.

Hatimaye – To bring an end (Hutt-ee-my-ee)

Etterian

Alodon (A-low-donn): who accidentally shot his balls off with his own blaster.

Teacher: lima (lee-ma)

Great teacher: lima kuu: (lee-ma koo)

Directions: semit (semm-it)

Lemon: giyua (gee-you-a)

Young one: damu (daa-moo)

Heart: ensa (enn-sa)

Heart of my heart: ensa ra ensa (enn-sa raa enn-sa)

Beloved: thamani (ta-mar-nee)

Little joy: minus susa (mee-nas soo-sa)

Little cat: minus cesu (mee-nas sess-oo)

Large: magnus (mag-nis)

Orgasm: fulfillment/deite asteri (see stars) / released (day-ta ass-tare-ree)

Starfighter: asteri peju (ass-tare-ree pear-joo)

Collection of glass vials: virak (vee-ruck)

Scum of the galaxies: xemi (ze-mee)

Hair up: malia pa (Mar-lee-a par)

Hair down: malia pado (Mar-lee-a par-dow)

Lysaran

Visitor: kashi (Kaa-shee)

God: Kaiha (Kigh-haa)

King: Kuna (Koo-na)

Orange fleshy fruit: Lemte (Lem-ta)

White flowers: Myameru (My-a-me-roo)

Precious: Delica (Dell ee-ka)

Sweetheart: Sali (Saa-lee)

Arum Lily-type flower: D'nastu (D-nass-too)

Love Blossom: aroa loulu (A-row-a low-loo)

Maloidian

Title of respect: lommia (Lomm-ee-a)

Stubborn, lethal tree: tewaa (Tee-wah)

Tokauri/Kulai

Blade – Sulac (soo-lack)

Bone – Ukog (you-cog) - bone from some dumb animal, probably an ukog.

Braided – Gisul (gee-sool)

Father – Danno (dan-no)

Heart – Kassu (cass-soo)

Maker – Mugbu (Mug-boo)

Mother – Manno (man-no)

Sapphires – Buha (boo-ha)

Shit – Saho (sa-ho)

Star - stuon (stoo-on)

Stupid – Ungog (oon-gog)

Vessel/ship - sakay (sa-kay)

Pronunciations

Names

Aaro - Ah-row

Adda – Ay-dah

Aldur - Al-durr

Alllero - A-le-row

Balllio – Bah-leee-oh

Bos - Boss

Bry-dar - Brigh-darr

Brynr - Brin-ner

Cales - Cale-es

Cento - Sen-tow

Citus - Sigh-tuss

Coldar - Coal-daar

Cria - Kree-ah

Eriz - Sigh-low

Danic - Dan-eek

Deeezo – Dee-zoh

Der - Durr

Diso - Dee-sow

Diyo - Die-oh

Eira - Eye-raa

Enyl - E-neel

Eriz - E-rizz

Garix - Ga-ricks

Gayn - Gain

Iddan - Ee-dann

Idon - Eye-donn

Illan - Ee-lann

Jarg – Jar-g

Jokta - Jock-tar

Kanzo - Can-zow

Keelu – Key-loo

Keryr – Kerr-eer

Ksal - Ka-sell

Lazu – Lah-zoo

Lurz - Lurr-z

Malo - Mail-oh

Matir - Mat-teer

Myan - My-ann

Myn-ras - Min-russ

Naio – Nay-oh

Nerx - Nurcks

Nuos - New-oss

Oyaz - Oh-yaz

Prex - Precks

Ronin - Row-nin

Saan - Sarn

Sena - See-na

Sy'mar - Sigh-marr

Syna - Sigh-na

Tamra – Tum-rah

Taro - Tah-row

Tenu - Ten-oo

Trav - Trahv

Tinh - Tin

Vytus - Vie-tuss

Vodin - Vo-din

Ulriq - Yule-rick

Vorn - Vawn

Vyar - Vie-arr

Xan - Zan

Xeus – Zeus

Zaro - Zah-row

Ziot - Zye-ott

Places

Argaxx – Are-jax

Crustiiu – Criss-tee-oo

Dyuqa - Dee-you-ka

Etteria – E-tare-rea

Galaza – Gah-Lar-Zah

Gikaet – Gee-ka-ett

Iphara = Ee-far-ra

Kulai – koo-ligh

Lysara – Liss-saa-ra

Mascroba – Mus-crow-ba

Resia Cay – Ress-Ee-ahh Kay

Sarvis – Sarr-viss

Sosu – Sow-soo

Tokauri – Too-cow-ree

Yithia – Yith-ee-a

Battleships

Chikara – Chee-kar-a - Force

Gladio – Glad-ee-oh - Sword

Kushin – Cush-shin - To Pierce

Surata – Soo-ra-tah – Beginning

Usaha – Oo-saa-hah - Endeavor

Shuttles

Celeeri – See-lee-ree - swift

    Denessi – Denn-ess-ee - sodge

    Eshima – Ee-shee-ma - respect

    Kevol – Kev-oll - agony

    Kuta – Koo-tah - modular shuttle.

    Liri-ny – Lee-ree-nye – freedom

    Misaia – Miss-aye-a - memory

    Sasay – Sass-ay - whispers

    Yakin – Yuck-kin - belief

Creatures

Asnu – Ass-Noo – buffalo/donkey

    Eiltur – Ale-turr

    Gracc – Grrr-ack

    Ilag – Ee-Lug– leggy slugs that feast on sol.

    Kreso – Kreh-soo

    Omeika – Oh-may-ka

    Pagsu – Pug-Soo - cocksuckers

    Reshy – Resh-Ee - huge, like the size of a kuta shuttle, with massive jaws and rows of sharp teeth.

    Sogair – Sow-gare

    Wilanegy – Will-anna-jee

About the Author

Sevannah Storm is a fiction writer who immerses herself in fantastical worlds both magical and science fiction. She has a flair for the creative having studied art and interior architecture and spends her time drawing, oil painting, and writing. An avid reader from an early age, Sevannah finds her inspiration from various sources: games, novels, music, and the land of make-believe. The unique versus the practical has brought on numerous debates.

In her spare time, she does Krav Maga, CrossFit, and rereads novels that snatch her breath away. Having embraced the social media world, you can find her on most platforms.

Her home is a land south of Wakanda, where animals roam free. Born in Zimbabwe, she grew up in South Africa. The crisp blue skies with cotton-candy sunsets expand her heart and soul, encapsulating a sense of freedom.

Words she lives by: "Know your pothole and dodge it. Don't work in a pencil factory if you're a vampire."

Sevannah loves to hear from her readers. You can find and connect with her at the links below.

Website/Newsletter:

https://www.sevannahstorm.com/

Facebook:

https://www.facebook.com/sevannah.storm

Instagram:

https://www.instagram.com/sevannah.storm/

Twitter:

https://twitter.com/sevannah_storm

Thank you for taking the time to read Shadow Forged. If you enjoyed the story, please tell your friends and leave a review. Reviews support authors and ensure they continue to bring readers books to love and enjoy.

https://sevannahstorm.com

SOUL FORGED

Know-it-all Oriana agreed to travel with aliens who need women. But she didn't agree to abduction, life/death battles, and escaping with a bossy, arrogant man. She was sabotaged, attacked, and kidnapped, but she is far from beaten. Forced to participate in an alien battle arena with no promise of freedom, she has to forget the loss of her family and focus on surviving.

Enyl has given up hope. His people are dying due to a genetic modification gone awry. Darkness is consuming his warriors, and his world, as he knows it, will end. His father, the king, has rolled out a plan to save them all. But Enyl doubts a solution will be found in time.

And when a compatible female is found...and lost, he must rescue her, a human female capable of surviving despite all odds. However, freeing Oriana serves to anger the aliens holding her captive. Ensuring she is cared for—as per Etterian protocol—he is stunned by the strong connection between the two of them. Such a bond was only experienced between Etterian mates.

Is she his salvation or is that wishful thinking on his part?

Read it here:

https://books2read.com/u/mlAWr9

FATE FORGED

Jacqueline (Jack) Dunois struggles to find a man not intimidated by her career as a law enforcement instructor, especially in the small town she calls home. She would sacrifice a kidney to find someone who would make her ovaries clap and didn't live with his mother. Then she meets a supreme commander from another world who thinks the stars in the galaxies shine in her eyes... What's not to love about that?

Supreme Commander Ulriq doesn't believe in love, an archaic term for a volatile and untrustworthy emotion Etterians were no longer subjected to. Until he meets Jack who triggers the Ethera, the soulmate force that irrevocably changes a male when he finds his ideal female. At that moment, his world, his focus, his very loyalty shifts. But when she is taken from him, it is too much to bear. Under the influence of the Ethera, he launches a rescue. He'll start a war and kill anyone who dares stop him, just to have her back in his arms.

Read it here:

https://books2read.com/u/bMY09v

SUN FORGED

The Gifting Series #3

Meeting a drop-dead gorgeous man, who falls onto a knee the first time they meet, sounded too good to be true for Ava. Of course, with her luck, he had to be an alien. Thrust into an unknown alien world, meeting weird and scary creatures, and fearing for her life, Ava tries to survive as best as a hairstylist can.

Kanzo never expected to find a life mate, a Dar Eth. Since he was young, he was taught that pairings were rare with fewer females born. The statistics on finding his Dar Eth would be slim to none. Instead of dreaming and longing for companionship, he focused on being the best male possible, to end his life on a battlefield with honor. But when he experiences the Ethera—the life mate force, and is blessed with his female, he isn't prepared for the level of pain, pleasure, and need she invokes within him.

Unable to save her as she's teleported from him, the dark consuming pain in his chest drives him into a blinding rage. With no idea who stole her or where to begin the search, he will scour the known universe to find her, to hold the female he never wanted.

Read it here:

https://books2read.com/u/3n5vaB

WAR FORGED

The Gifting Series #4

Being kidnapped by aliens does not sit well with Quinlan. Not only would her seven guardians give her hell if she doesn't attempt some sort of escape, but she refuses to be at anybody's mercy. With her practiced military skills, the help of an underground lounge singer and a personal assistant, she takes over the alien slave ship. Not knowing how to fly the damn thing, she sends a distress signal. ...The rescue comes swiftly in the form of a bronzed man with exquisite ice-blue eyes. Leaving her to ask the true question: has she just given up her newfound freedom for a gorgeous man who seems determined to have her for eternity?

As Elite Supreme Commander of the Etterian Forces, Xan answers a distress call in Earth English. That is all he did. The female who captured the slave ship shows remarkable skill, making her a warrior in her own right. Said skills should be respected and honored. Except she is his Dar Eth, calling forth the Ethera—the soulmate bond. How can he protect his female when she can do so herself? What can she possibly need from him? What can he offer a female, not Etterian but human? Not that he can think clearly in her presence when she scents so good and makes him want to kiss all of her.

Maker help him.

Read it here:

https://books2read.com/u/bz1QGD

STAR FORGED

Macy is feeling a little left out, as usual. Who would have thought moving from one planet to another wouldn't change that loneliness? She is never alone these days since Etterians guard human women with an urgency she understands. But the lack of companionship is like a dark aching abyss inside her chest. On some days, it threatens to implode, and Macy Mitchell would cease to exist. Looming is her impending meeting with King Xeus of Etteria. How is she supposed to keep her shit together when presented to royalty? Not after she ran from the last king she met.

For Xeus, the void expands daily. Duty, honor, concern for his dying people, and endless loneliness fill his life. Having decided to search for pairings among other worlds, he is pleased his son found his soulmate among human women. It doesn't mean that Xeus's loneliness and longing haven't ended until he stumbles upon a crying female. Meaning only to soothe, he is spellbound when her presence brings him peace. Unable to resist, he forms an attachment to a female he can never have

Read it here:

https://books2read.com/u/3nXgp5

EARTH FORGED

The Gifting Series #7

Guilt hounds Izzy, who caused her sister's injury and subsequent blindness. But no matter how she cares for Simone or what she sacrifices, it doesn't ease the ache in her chest. With Simone and naive Caro, her best friend, Izzy's role as protector is fully realized. The cost? Hiding behind quirkiness, pseudo-joy, and giving up her hopes and dreams. What she needs is a knight in any armor. After all, beggars can't be fussy. She has no idea that armor, in her case, means black military and that a knight could come in any color, specifically bronze.

Oyaz wants to find his life force, his soulmate, and he'd like her to be human. Earth's females are soft, amusing, passionate, and their scents rival a garden of hahyt blossoms. His task is to guard their planet that promises so many salvations for his males. It's a duty he's pleased to perform, one he would die for. When Operations Commander Malo orders Oyaz to retrieve a human female, he's eager to oblige. That it would lead to his salvation is something he couldn't anticipate. What he hadn't planned for is an ambush that costs him more than his memory, the loss of his soulmate.

Now what? Nothing in their training prepared him for this.

And yet, despite not remembering kneeling for Izzy, he longs to claim her with every inch of his soul.

Read it here:

https://books2read.com/u/31V82D

LUST FORGED

The Gifting Series #8

Ex-socialite Leona wants nothing more than to enhance the mechanics within sex-cybs, not to mention improve their performances with their 'lovers.' It's a job where she's safe in an all-woman factory on Callisto, and far from her matchmaking mama. When the chief engineer is incapacitated, Leona's required to gift—her term would be pimp—sex-cyborgs to prospective clients. On an Etterian battleship, surrounded by gorgeous males, she tries not to think of sex when it's her work, especially with the Sub-Commander Aaro whose neon-blue eyes are the stuff of her erotic dreams.

As a diplomatic favor, Aaro must abandon his task to guard Earth, and perhaps find his Dar Eth or soulmate, all to protect cargo en route to many worlds, including the dangerous and unpredictable Yithia. Princess Oriana is most concerned for the two human female engineers determined to ensure the deliveries are successful. A simple enough mission until one human enters Aaro's cargo bay, dropping him to his knees.

But revealing to independent Leona that she's now trapped in a marriage isn't something Aaro can bring himself to do. He violates all he stands for, every ounce of honor by not telling her the truth. All in the hopes that she will choose to love him.

Read it here:

https://books2read.com/u/3LdA1w

www.ingramcontent.com/pod-product-compliance
Lightning Source LLC
Chambersburg PA
CBHW061014120726
47910CB00006B/1926